GUY

by JR Rockwell

Fred&Barrel

PUBLISHED BY FRED & BARREL: BALTIMORE

978-0-9794850-1-5 - PAPERBACK ISBN
978-0-9794850-2-2 - KINDLE ISBN
978-0-9794850-3-9 - EPUB ISBN

DEDICATION PAGE

In honor of the late **JAMIE C. HEARD**, my brother and fellow writer. You always were there for everyone, putting your health at stake to lighten the burden of others. May your legacy of living life to the fullest - confidently, truthfully, and honorably - live on forever.

In honor of the late **SID AHMED**. Decades of debilitating, excruciating pain would cause anyone to crumble. But you looked up to the strong, to boxers, and you kept living. When offered amenities, you selflessly would say, "No really, I'm fine," although it hurt to even speak. May your incredible force of character inspire all those in constant pain. You would have made an amazing boxer.

To the late **MRS. SHIRLEY HOWARD**, the selfless founder of the Children's Cancer Foundation. Your dedication, pluck, and strength inspired me to keep moving.

To my **MOTHER**, who keeps me humble by making fun of me every day. I owe all my successes to you. All the sacrifices you've made for me, all the prayers, and your kindness make any dedication inadequate.

& To my **FATHER**. That car ride in Ohio changed my life completely. It was just a conversation about "The Cask of Amontillado" and "My Last Duchess," but it spawned Guy's struggle. Thank you, Dad, for the conversations, the advice, the road trips, and for being my teacher.

FORWARD

Many people have asked me how to view this book. Is it supposed to be funny? Satirical? Serious? Well, quite plainly, this is my account. Take it as you will.

I am Guy, which rhymes with "free," not "fry." I am thirty-five years old. However, I wrote this book during my junior year of college. These events took place during a point in my life when most of the strong blue loom of energy I had lackadaisically woven was nearly completely consumed by scattered moths. I didn't go through the process of deleting sections and altering the narrator's parts because of a combination of weak discipline and even weaker fingers. The nerves in my fingers were so ultra-sensitive that even an innocuous square of cotton placed beneath them would feel as if it were both rapidly stretching and forcefully compressing my fingertips. Funny how when we're well we squander our time, but when we want to get down to business we become physically unable. My ailment was Raynaud's Disease. While it's "for life," I'm living proof that miracles can and do happen. It took fourteen years to put this together, and I am truly grateful to finally be able to share it with you.

I haven't written any poetic pieces since completing the Backward section. Instead, I have invested my time, complete concentration, and energy in my all-time favorite hobby—making paperclip sculptures. I wish! No, I work full-time, designing blueprints for stadiums, but I still make the time to twist paperclips into random objects. It's a lot of fun—I find paperclips all over the place, and after I sculpt one into a masterpiece, I return it to where I found it. The next day, it disappears. Apparently people like my work! Haha. Anyway, I love my job. I travel around the world, meeting with clients of many different nations. So, happily, I often use the language skills I developed during college.

Junior year, I was majoring in Architecture and Modern Language and Linguistics and practically lived in the Architecture Research Center (ARC) just off campus. I'd often rush back to my drafting table in the ARC between classes and meals in order to finish up my Studio II projects.

In order to get to the ARC, I walked from my apartment, down the hill, past the soft mist of laughter and genuine happiness that moistened the area around the day-care playground, past the new Rhody dorms, the dining hall, and the shady, overlooked physical plant. While I enjoyed this environment, it's right when I got off campus that I really started to breathe. See, the ARC is only visible from campus when the woods temporarily lose their luscious foliage. Just beyond my school's borders lies a creek surrounded by healthy, sprightful trees which serve as hearth for hundreds of friendly cardinals. Many scenes take place in this wild, natural oasis. The play starts as I'm walking through the trees alongside the timid, placid creek, half an hour before tennis practice.

Two notes: first, I am a habitual self-conversationalist. While I enjoy meeting people and engaging in discourse that increases my ken, it's more common for me to use my vocal chords to explain situations and options to the best listener I know. Naturally, I always listen attentively and heed my own advice, so I never regret getting to know myself verbally. Now the second thing: I have a problem with understanding who the omniscient "narrator" is in your typical play. How can a nameless outsider truly comprehend each person's hopes, motives, and feelings? The mysterious "narrator" is so powerful. While he or she should be neutral, this all-knowing storyteller is much like your everyday brainwashing news anchor who presents scraps of news in a certain bending way.

This newscaster has the platinum power to shape and then plaster the audience's brain putty. However, no human knows me better than the narrator of this book. Yes, I am the narrator and I wouldn't have it any other way. I recall being dropped off from the school bus at the top of the hill in fifth grade and a voice in my head would chronicle every detail: "As the wind ferociously blew, his bottom lip began to bleed. For the greenish chapped skin could maintain its faltering integrity no longer." No, more like, "The frigid air cut his lip as he carried on." I found this constant narration utterly annoying and bizarre. While I don't recall doing this continuously since then, I really got into it and was about to abandon this play altogether and write a novel in its place. However, vibrant dialogue is much more interesting than descriptions alone. Consequently, this book is a roman à clef play and the narrator is the voice within Guy's head.

One more note: as you read, you may be wondering, "What's wrong with this guy's English?" I'd like to inform you that while architecture classes took up most of my time, my Modern Language and Linguistics studies were just as important (if not more so). So yes, I know the rules, but I nevertheless chose to use "who" for animals. I see a bird as a "he" or "she" instead of an "it."

Lo! It is my pleasure to finally present to you *Guy*. Bon appétit!

ILLUMINATION

I

SMILE: Breathe through me and life tastes sweeter.

GUY: Stop.

SMILE: Wear me; they need you to, for the world is bereft of compassion.
As the trembling biceps flounder, the poignant message rises
Through the lives that make me.

GUY: No. The slimy scorpions swallow all the vitality I have left.

SMILE: But you must not let them win. They want you to be miserable—
To spread ignominy—To kill,
(points to his mouth)
All with those forty-three muscles.

GUY: So if I decimate them, other populations will grasp anyone that sees me.
I cannot help them.

SMILE: Commiseration is just a whisper of acceptance.
You must show the valley dwellers just how high the precipice can reach.

GUY: So that someone can push their ignorant, fallacious selves down?
Why pretend? The wrath of thorny indifference encompasses the entire universe.
Pluto would never risk sustaining even a microscopic abrasion to try to help Neptune.
What benefit would it bring her? The foul repugnance that kindness delivers
Serves to stab the dove in the back at some point.

Guy

Smile

SMILE: Yes. It takes a brave man to open his eyes
and see the world in all its hues.
However, a Hero would summon all his strength
to bring respite to people's lives.

GUY: I don't believe in respite. You contradicted
yourself.
How can a man be honest and want to make
people happy while tricking others into
feeling a fake, dwindling contentment?
Times are rough.

SMILE: The shining snake coils itself around the
muddy planet,
Squeezing the very essence of the violet
springs.
Do you watch then, or try to fight it?

GUY: How? I am powerless. It's draining me.

SMILE: But that's life—a challenge. Your thoughts are
a manifestation of possession.
You hold the urn of ink. Thrust your soul into
it. You've tasted its putrid flavor.
Now extract the ribbon caught underneath the
flanks, and share it.

GUY: You want me to illuminate their dim, hollow
minds?
Then I'd surely have to estrange myself from
you.

SMILE: No. You need me. I realize I am inappropriate
When you exchange solemn words,
But I elicit a spark of optimism which will help
gather the eclectic sounds.

GUY: Voices and cooperation from all corners?

SMILE: Yes. In time, all will finally reach the crescendo.

GUY: Smile.

SMILE: Yes. Don't desert your cause. Peace begins with you.

GUY: But I am not even at peace! It hurts. I still can't do it.

Smile grins and walks away.

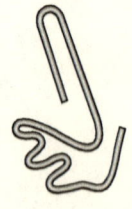

SOLILOGUY

II

GUY: Smile, he says; stroke the bright yellow flower,
        While drawing a crimson pistol at the
            possessed devotee.
        It tries to devour me. It attempts to blind me.
        It glistens in the sun with the puce, artificial
            dew
        That tastes sweet only to the poor wretched
            soul that cannot stay away from it.
        I am stronger than that.

        And yet,
        I am trampling the green springs that try to
            liven the goat.
        I am treading roughly on hope. The goat must
            eat the yellow flower.
        But who?
        Who can eliminate such an invincible foe?
        I do not want a single being to harm himself to
            save the people....

        But if I could have the flower wilt.... Perhaps
            neglect is the goat we need.
        Yes! The people will leave it be.
        Then and *only then* will we dissolve the
            impurities, the concentrated odors,
        The scarlet nourishment of death.

        Ha ha ha!

        Your destructive pollination ceases right now!

DEALING WITH A LEARNED JERK

III

Guy walks on towards the Student Union Building, his dark-green tennis bag bouncing against his back.

JERK: Hey Loser, I don't like fools on the same
             sidewalk as me.
           Get off. Go to the trash can where you belong.

GUY: Help wilt the Flower of Despicability!

JERK: Get **off** the sidewalk!

Guy sighs and pushes stiffly downward. He lets the strap of his tennis bag slide off his shoulder, onto the ground. He then smiles the biggest smile imaginable, showing his large teeth.

JERK: What the—

GUY: *(His body suddenly assumes a stern semblance*
           although he is smiling.)
           I will not hate. You need to love. *(pauses)*
           Peace.

JERK: Alright, you wanna **fight**?

GUY: *(continues smiling)* No, just wanna talk.

JERK: That's it. You've—

GUY: Listen! To the music! Don't interrupt it!
           (starts waving both his index fingers in the air
           like he is conducting an orchestra)

           Your fiery breath burns only the weak.
           The speckled thirst trapped within your timid
               soul
           Needs to be cleansed of the filth
           Which prevents it from revealing its shiny
               silver reflection of tranquility.

(Guy's face becomes angry.)
Quench it.
Let it overpower the misplaced hunger.

(Guy pauses; Jerk looks confused and annoyed.)
Quench it! Smile!
Show the nefarious wizards,
That their potent concoction fetters only the
    unwilling from pressing their heart
Firmly against the crackling twig that is merely
    brushing the breast.

*(Guy starts waving his index fingers more rigor-
ously and starts bobbing his head left and right;
Jerk becomes frightened.)*

(sings:) Quench iiiit!... Or eeeelse!

*Guy starts waving his hands towards Jerk's face and then
uses the tips of his index fingers to softly press the corners of
Jerk's mouth upward, forcing Jerk to smile.*

GUY: *(fingers still on Jerk's lips)*
    You're a misunderstood man.
    Once you peel the bright yellow crust,
    I know that you will be appreciated for your
        true glowing soul.
    (slowly removes his fingers from Jerk's face)

JERK: *(looks solemn)* You obviously are charbroiled—
    Your passion clinging to a gel motorcycle
    While flowers lean in to feel your presence.
    (sighs)
    Yeah. Soot riddles your parched, burgundy
        body,
    Allowing only the essential flavors to percolate

into your soul.

GUY: Never! I am a broken pillar amongst the hatched,
Ever-firm rooftops that lie heavily on my
      turbulent torso.

JERK: See? Never can true serenity be shared. You
      have allowed the twig to shatter your heart
      while trying to graft! And your thirst?
You are merely searching for a purpose.

Guy picks up his tennis bag and watches in disgust as Jerk coolly walks away.

GUY SCREAMS AT HIS ARCHENEMY
IV

GUY: Failure!

You are the plague I am oft-running from!
I thought I found a sturdy table under which to
      hide from your infectious agents.
But alas, you hid underneath the long dark-blue
      tablecloth with me.

I would have never imagined that you were
      with me all the while
Had you not thrown your white handkerchief
      out to that insolent man!
Poor man,
Picked it up and as soon as I saw his pallid,
      doomed semblance, I knew.

I knew.
I knew you didn't know you were infectious.
But having killed one, I must run.

So here I am, Duke of Ferrara!
I tried to keep the tablecloth from being lifted.
So many people tried to hide with me. I wrestled
      the desperate hands,
With unbreakable pluck.
Alas! You somehow opened your end to throw
      that white handkerchief.
Had you fought alongside me, the rude man
      would not have seen you
Nor been infected by you.

INSPIRED, BUT DEEMED FOOLISH AT THE STUDENT UNION

V

Guy walks towards the food court. He likes to sit in the busy dining center amongst people passing through to get to class, others hanging out, and yet others wrinkling their foreheads, struggling with some physics problems. He doesn't eat there. Nor does he read or write. He merely sits upright (his posture remarkable) and lets all the different people glide into the jetting boundary of his cognizance, as he has been wont to do since the first day he came to this college. *Guy sits down and rests his dark-green tennis bag on the floor against his left lower leg.*

GUY: There they go, busy as can be.
                Why can't everyone stop for a minute? It's
                    such a wonderful day outside!
                Let nature be your mentor;
                It's the only entity left that's unspoiled.
                Sure, others have ruined the environment (and
                    continue to do so),
                But the leaves of grass do not sacrifice their
                    vigorous spirit for anything.
                They stand as green as they can,
                As others step on them.
                They never harm themselves.
                It is we who squander the wealth of the
                    foliage.

Guy's COUSIN walks by and stands by his table.

COUSIN: Hey Mellow. I heard you lost your cool today.
                I didn't believe it, but several people said that
                    you were barely recognizable.
                Why the idiosyncrasy?

GUY: Hello Cus. *(Cousin sits down across from Guy.)*
                I usually avoid letting the syrup seep out,
                But, as sweet as it is, it cannot stay inside.

COUSIN: It has to stay inside. We have a Russian test
        Tuesday.
        What time do you want to study?

GUY: Hold on! It's my mind!
        It has to cut through the cage although the
        cage only wants what's best for it.
        What benefit can an idea bring, though, to a
        single soul?
        That single soul needs to free itself from
        estrangement.
        Although it may involve ripping my thoughts
        into purple and black shreds,
        If I can inspire a single person, it'll be worth it.

COUSIN: Inspire someone to do what?

GUY: To change!
        To feel what life is, the Creator's presence, the
        blessings,
        To abominate the hatred that trammels all
        souls in one way or another.
        To rid oneself of the poison that is pessimism.

        It bites the foot, sucking the blood,
        Forming a balloon that flies around the head
        of the sweet neighbor
        That has to hold it, has to touch it....

COUSIN: Guy, the world's not all that bad. Everyone
        knows that.
        I'm not sure why you're so glum.
        Even if what you say is true... so what if
        there's some floating balloon filled with the
        evil of this world?
        Let's go. We can study for the test in the—

GUY: No! The balloon!
        It pops, letting the blood trickle all over that
            neighbor's orange hair!
        She's finished.
        She must breathe the filthy air with contentment
            because it is now what she is.
        She will live her life accordingly. It gets
            absorbed,
        And is then part of her!

        The foot, meanwhile, has that venomous,
            expandable goo that can inflate, spread,
        And stay in one place all at once!
        It's so amazing; no wonder its texture binds
            people to it until they taste death.

COUSIN: *(sighs)*
        That's why I cannot agree with you.
        You are so caught up in things that don't
            matter.
        Death is the only real thing.
        'Course, it isn't real til it's happened,
        In which case it's too late.

GUY: What? How can it not be real
        When all those around us are experiencing it?

COUSIN: Well, a man is not his neighbor,
        So when his neighbor dies, he does not truly
            grasp what has occurred.
        He does not feel the claw, the tightening,
        The solemnity in the ruinous questioning
        Which brings to light what should have really
            mattered.

        No. The other man merely lives.

So he should live as if he were to expire when
    he sees the next cardinal.
Do all that he can between now and then while
    not avoiding going outside
Or looking out the window.
The bird will come in all its brilliance.
It can be beautiful if the mortal was good,
    helping mankind,
Cherishing and protecting the vulnerable
    beings
That are constantly praising Him.

GUY: So pessimism does not matter as long as I am
    a decent person?
I could walk around, crying. I could sit right
    here, frowning.
If I lived my life crying and frowning,
My, how I would spread depression!
How would that make me a good person,
Regardless of what I accomplish?

COUSIN: Then smile like an idiot all the time!
I don't care! *(Cousin gets up.)*

GUY: *(softly)* I am not mad.

COUSIN: Make sure you smile when you fail the Russian
    test!
Don't leave without a smile on your face,
Even if you're going to a funeral! Hey, why not
    laugh, too?

GUY: *(Guy speaks softly again.)* I am not mad.

COUSIN: You vex me like no other.
Don't you see? There is no moderation for you!

You have to be happy or frown and cry
continuously.
You are the very embodiment of Orange Puss!
You lie on the corner of the daffodil's leaf,
And obviously, you need to either leave or
change your hue!

GUY: *(continues to speak softly)*
You are insulting me, but I am not mad.
I have no reason to be.

COUSIN: *(raises his voice)*
So your classes are but figments of the
imagination, OP.
And you would have to be large and blue
To be able to encompass the hexagonal
university subjects
That sit firmly on the edge of the seesaw.

GUY: Your thoughts are jumbled up as you slight
my beliefs,
But I am not mad.

COUSIN: Yes!
The seesaw that will never let you on, because
you are so light, Puss!
You want to save the world by making
everything perfect,
But you are powerless!
Powerless to do well in school,
And even more powerless to stop the
Pessimistic Epidemic!

GUY: No.

The crescendo will begin with me.
Sorry.

COUSIN: What?

GUY: I am running late,
          You all can have the study group without me.

Guy leans over, picks up his tennis bag, and leaves the Student Union.

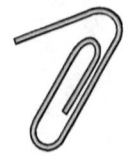

TENNIS PRACTICE

VI

Guy walks awkwardly towards the eight outdoor hard courts by the gym. As usual, he arrived five minutes early.

KEVIN: *(kneeling down, tying his shoes)* What's up Guy?

GUY: Nothing much.

Guy set his tennis bag on the bench and started jogging around the tennis courts with KEVIN, a Filipino student. Neither was racing. While they ran, Guy thought about displaying an old escalator in the museum he was designing for his Design Studio II class. Soon, the whole team was stretching.

KEVIN: *(His left arm holds up his right, which reaches across his neck.)* So you comin' tomorrow night?

GUY: Where? *(stretches his neck)*

KEVIN: *(switches arms)* Eric's Surprise Party!

GUY: I'll try.

Guy would usually be frank. "I'm not coming; my design project is due in two days and I'm so behind." But he had this optimistic impulse driving down his head that, by some stroke of genius, he would finish early that night and wouldn't need to be selfish.

GUY: *Well, there's another incentive to increase my efficiency today and tomorrow. I want to be there.*

Guy takes out his racket, BECKA, and walks over to the second court behind JORGE, a strong Mexican man who is Guy's height, six feet four inches. Jorge is an introverted Economics major who, ironically, talks to practically everyone on campus, although he has only three close friends—his tenista sister Samantha, Kevin, and Eric.

JORGE'S TENNIS RACKET: Pnk! *(Jorge seems sleepier than Guy.)*

BECKA: Pk! *(Guy focuses on the blurry ball.)*

JORGE'S TENNIS RACKET: Pthnk!

BECKA: Pnk!

The rancorous sun challenged each gallant athlete. While their sweaty faces exposed the golden star's strength, the bright green ball reigned supreme. The tennis ball captivated the players with its charm as it tried to tunnel through their rackets, sending an explosion vibrating down their tanned, resilient arms.

Guy welcomed the chance to hydrate himself. As he drank, he looked on towards the nearby woods which sheltered all the balls he had accidentally hit too high. He didn't think of the balls, though. Instead, he thought of his little sister and how he had missed her soccer game four days earlier.

His eyes returned to the court where he saw Coach Paul looking at him. He valued every word of advice from Paul, a patient, slender man from Zimbabwe, who could easily pinpoint Guy's every weakness during practice.

Guy walks sloppily towards COACH who is watching him.

COACH: Alright Guy.

Hit a forehand crosscourt, a backhand approach shot down the line, backhand volley crosscourt, and finish with an overhead.

Guy felt his attention attenuate. Luckily, his thirteen years of experience helped him register the sequence with ease.

BECKA: Thnk. Thnk! Pthnk!   Pfth—

The team continues to practice sequences.

Guy longed for a clay court where he could slide while destroying any opponent. His mind reverted to thoughts about a studio he was to design the following year in Design Studio III.

GUY: *Yeah! If I could get some special clay, the whole studio could be done in clay, and—No, that could damage the pens.... But the floor should definitely be backflip friendly. Acrobatic, sleep-deprived architects will love it.*

Finally, he was done practicing with his helpful, scrutinizing coach.

The graduating senior on the team, ERIC, motions to Guy to join him on the adjoining court. He then turns towards the water cooler.

ERIC: Yo Aldair! Come on!

ALDAIR is a freshman from Venezuela who is studying economics. Although he rarely walks (he always runs to and from class), he somehow has more energy than everyone else on campus. Kevin and Guy were ready as Aldair quickly finished his drink and took his post behind Eric. Aldair took out the furry lime from his right pocket, threw it up, and smashed it. It soared at 115 mph, almost directly over the crouching Eric.

Kevin answered with a forehand return that caused the evasive Eric to dash towards his left. The ball bounced at dangerous speeds. Guy read his opponents' every move. He and Kevin tried to be unpredictable, but their efforts were drowned in the net which, like a potent magnet, drew the ball and every racket towards it.

Serving

Eric and Aldair did an excellent job of moving together, as if to keep a rope taut between them. Kevin was annoyed that Aldair and Eric had become just as good as they often claimed to be.

TENNIS RACKETS: Thwak!   Pnk! Pnthnk!—
           Thwnk!   Pnk! Thnwk!

Everyone was tired, but pride and dignity were at stake. Each man did a wonderful job of concealing his fatigue as he tried to evade his opponents.

TENNIS RACKETS: Thwnk!   Pnk! Pnk!—
           (Kevin uses the alley and Eric dives backwards while Aldair stays in front, in anticipation.)
           Pthnk! Pthk!

Guy's backhand volley hit up the middle and his separated opponents were no longer able to mobilize their forces and creativity.

KEVIN: In just a hemidemisemiquaver, you collapse.

Guy grinned slightly, admiring his pianist partner who juggled a million lives so quickly that the blurriness resulted in a solid, energetic Kevin.

ERIC: You hear that Aldair? Now it's ON!

Guy naturally smiled although his tired lips barely pushed up his cheeks. Soon, it was 3:45 p.m.—time for the guys to go to the weight room while the women (many of whom were running at this time) took over the courts.

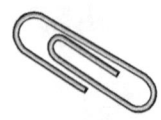

The dim gym startled Guy. He walked across the empty basketball court and stretched on one of the red mats outside the weight room. Seven minutes later, he was greeted by the dinginess of the refreshingly bright weight room.

He finally turned the weight room's difficult door handle and proceeded to walk down the four wide steps. He picked up a 35-lb weight and held it overhead as he did funny lunges behind the flat red-cushioned benches. He didn't grunt. The delta of sweat seeping through his earth-green shirt may just as well have been nonexistent. His focused blue eyes disallowed access to a behind-the-scenes look. A goofy girl that pretended not to notice him was staring all the while and he could sense it. But the soft bead of cognizance instantaneously dropped to the ground as he continued to lift. He lay on his back on the bench farthest to the right and softly grunted as he drew two weights of 65 lbs above his head. The fifteenth repetition did not elicit any louder sound, nor any extra effort. He was content for a second as he recalled how weak he was two years ago.

Guy's back felt shaky, so he strengthened it with three sets of twelve pulls. The 150-lb weight levitated up and down, stopping a millimeter short of hitting the weights below. Guy was sitting down with his legs extended. When he brought the metal handlebar towards his chest, he felt his left shoulder doing more work than it should. He was concerned that his movements, although slow, were not as controlled as they were on Monday.

Guy wasn't thirsty, but he felt like walking towards the water fountain for a refresher. His sip was curt and the water was just as concise, ending its conversation with his mouth before his lips even closed. Nonetheless, he wiped the side of his mouth.

Finally, it was 4:45, time to quickly shower and race to his 5 p.m. class. He briskly snuck away from the goggle-eyed female lifter, gently opened the familiar weight room door, and speedily did fifteen push-ups on the stretching mat just outside the clear windows of the sun-kissed weight room whose smell Guy never noticed.

Guy walks to his Architecture 341 class and grabs a seat across from the door that is opened to the bright, windowed hallway.

PROFESSOR: And the Ionic columns contributed to the overall grandeur of the Temple of Athena Nike by providing nobly decorated support....

GUY: *Forever the frozen pedestal is to be admired, to be adulated and accepted as it was. Why must this be so? Perhaps it is not even the clear strong ice that we behold, but the desiccated twig that is too well-preserved to present its precious texture and prints.*

No. I'll see to it that my columns will be as mahogany leaves with a single layer of ice caressing each vascular face.

Throughout the winter the leaf is living healthily; it inevitably retains its vital moisture as it is smothered by the loving thin ice that slowly grows on it. But peel the leaf from the ice, and lo! The ice shows the beauty it had learned from its intimate association with the leaf. The impression of the delicate veins of the leaf are manifested on the surprisingly moldable ice while the leaf, well into the winter, is still free to bend without a worry of wear or tear.

So should be the relationship between design and practicality. Corrosively trite designs are ever bound to flake away.

The sound of zipping and ruffling is heard in the background as students put away their papers and books.

PROFESSOR: ...Class, we will be having a pop quiz on ancient Greek architecture sometime this month.

Make sure you review your notes.

GUY: *(Guy looks at his illegible notebook.)*
         Notes? I will do better to read the book. I like that image... peeling ice from a leaf.... Perhaps I'll use it when I write a book.

Balancing his blue pen between his knuckles, he writes, very slowly, "ice from leaf."

PROFESSOR: Oh, and don't forget—the makeup exam for the last test will be this Friday. If you were absent, as most of you were, it would be a good idea to take it. All sections of Studio II should be over by then.

The class rises. Guy slides his notebook into his opened tennis bag.

GUY: *(speaks softly to himself)* Wow. I wonder if I'll live long enough to be done with Studio. Friday seems almost realistic.

MELLISA, a pleasant, dark-eyed woman with dyed-blonde hair turns around to pick up her backpack.

MELLISA: Guy! I didn't know you were sitting behind me! How's it crack-a-lackin'?

GUY: I'm suppressing the revolt.

MELLISA: Revolt, you say?

GUY: *(blows his lips)* The echoes against my stomach will forever cling then fling until the soft fern of will is blasted. Five is such a bad time to be in class.

MELLISA: Well, at least it's not at eight thirty like my history class.

GUY: Eight thirty is decent, but five to six fifteen is the perfect time for a nap. Wait. Actually, eight thirty is a good time for a nap as well. O, to nap at one's leisure!

Mellisa laughs.

MELLISA: So you're tired and hungry I see? Well, I'm off to Dining Hall to splurge like a spelunker.

GUY: I'd love to go myself. Say, while we're there, would you mind if I looked over your notes for the first five weeks of class?

MELLISA: Not at all, Bud!

They walk to the dining hall.

D-HALL, BIRDS, & PAPERCLIPS
VIII

Guy and Mellisa exit the building and walk towards the resident dining hall. After walking 350 feet, Guy feels an overwhelming and blessed feeling of excitement because of what lies shining on the very edge of the sidewalk. It is a paperclip. He picks it up with his knuckles and puts it in his pocket.

MELLISA: Did you drop something?

GUY: No, it's my hobby.

I bend, twist and press paperclips into elegant sculptures. It's quite inexpensive—I've never bought a single paperclip. They merely await the noticer as they recline on the sidewalk, on the street, by the entrance of the lecture hall, outside the office... everywhere.

They always present themselves right before the epiphany.

MELLISA: That's unlike you! I've never heard you say something so optimistic! So what happened the last time you found one?

GUY: I was visiting Dr. Lowe's office to go over why I got a B.

MELLISA: He dared give you a B? *(She grins.)*

GUY: If earned, ease would overcome the pangs of dissatisfaction. No. I mastered the material. But some tests assay your ability to notice nuances in the questions, and to develop extensions of all the information you've learned—all in one hour. It's like measuring the foot size of a scintillating orange elephant in order to see if it glows. But lo!—Not Dr. Lowe, Mel, but the "Lo" of "Lo and behold!"

Mellisa giggles.

GUY: Lo! I found the paperclip and the conversation that ensued shortly thereafter secured my A. My dismayed cumulative grew of a greener hue.

Two beautiful brown birds are perched on top of Azalea, a residence hall adjacent to the dining hall.

BIRD 1: Twee-eut.

GUY: Twee-eut!

BIRD 1: Twee-eut!

GUY: Twee-eut!

BIRD 2: Tweet!

BIRD 1: Twee-eut!

GUY: Twee-eut!

BIRD 2: Tweet!

Mellisa dodges the birds who suddenly fly right in front of Guy and perch atop the dining hall rooftop. They look quizzically at the misshapen bird-man.

MELLISA: My, the birds are crazy today!

Guy realized that she didn't know that he was whistling and that the birds wanted to see him. He looked at their cute heads that tilted sideways, allowing one of their binocular eyes to see Guy. Guy turned his head in a similar manner and noted how sweet and smart they looked with their distinguished beaks.

Guy opens the door for Mellisa and keeps it open for a girl behind them. The two females hand the cashier their student

ID cards and enter the cafeteria. Guy is now at the front of the line.

GUY: Hello. *(hands cashier his student ID card)*

CASHIER: Hi. *(swipes his card)*

GUY: Thanks.

CASHIER: Uh huh.

Guy noticed that Mellisa didn't even say hi to the attendant. She just shoved the card into the worker's soft hand and then snatched it back. Guy's thoughts returned to the birds. He decided that the birds would say thanks if they came to Dining Hall to eat.

Guy cased the place to find a good table. He chose the spot that had the most light coming in from the windows. Somehow, the ambience of the room was not at all influenced by the sun which seemed to prance like a lunatic recovering from chronic laziness. No. Instead, the cafeteria seemed immobile and the people seemed to make minimal efforts at serving themselves, eating, or talking.

Guy served himself some fresh crab cakes, mixed vegetables, vanilla and chocolate swirl ice cream (with chopped almonds sprinkled on top), pasta with marinara sauce, and two cups of water. It wasn't every day that the dining hall served crab cakes and had almonds by the ice cream. Guy was not surprised; the paperclip had worked its magic yet again. But he had no idea just what else that paperclip would bring him.

Mellisa served herself a hamburger, fruits, and a cup of cranberry juice mixed with mango juice. They ate silently until Mellisa's friend, LILI, came over. Lili is an adventurous girl from Italy who spreads an exquisite love of life to all those around her. Every time Guy sees her, he thinks of his paternal grandmother from France, for some reason unbeknownst to him (they do not look alike, nor do they share a similar personality).

While Mellisa and Lili talk, Guy peruses the notes. He doesn't write. Rather, he drinks in the information. Soon, he is finished eating and the architecture notes are thoroughly digested.

Mellisa and Lili continue talking as Guy takes out his red-handled needle-nose pliers.

LILI: What are you doing with those pliers?

GUY: This impending masterpiece will dutifully hold together unwitting, unappreciative papers no longer!

He uses the pliers to transform the paperclip into an abstract delicacy.

MELLISA: That really looks like a rabbit!

He reaches into his right pocket, takes out three more paperclips, and continues to sculpt.

LILI: That's so cool! Let me try!

He hands her a paperclip and then sculpts two people holding hands and a column of the Doric order.

GUY: For you. *(He hands Mellisa the column.)*
          Thanks for the notes.

Guy slips away, toying with the silver people. He faintly hears Lili in the distance.

LILI: Haha! It's a mushroom!

He wasn't close to being full. In fact, he was a little thirsty and felt like getting more water, but he found himself walking towards the door instead. He waved goodbye to one of the cafeteria attendants and was about to exit when he stopped abruptly.

He looked onward. The vanishing sun had left a soft trail of subdued brightness along the horizon. But Guy again did not notice the light. As soon as his eyes migrated to the great wilderness beyond the cozy dining hall, he saw hundreds of obtuse blue chestnuts, lined up, masking everything in sight. Slick streaks of silver stretched along the top fourth of each chestnut's midsection.

Still at the glass door, he slowly closed his eyes as he swung the door open and stepped outside. His confused body trembled most discreetly as he opened his eyes. He didn't hear the birds that flew down to greet him from the bushes to his left, nor did he see the Indian couple eating ice cream cones diagonally from him. His eyes were drawn immediately to the woman in blue who was running down the hill, away from him. Her golden hair sparkled violently with the sun's last ray which she stole from the horizon.

CELL PHONE: *(vibrating)* **Bzzzz! Bzzzz!**

GUY: *(Guy takes out his phone and sees "Theresa" on the screen. He speaks to the phone without answering it.)* **Theresa, if I didn't leave my headphones, I'd surely pick it up! I'll chat with you online when I get back.**

He returns the phone to his left back pocket.

THROUGH THE LAKE OF FOG TO GUY'S SECOND HOME

IX

Guy walks briskly to work on his Studio design project at the Architecture Research Center (ARC).

A drizzle softly graced his white T-shirt as he rushed past the dining hall and the oft-climbed tree between Fennel Hall and the dumpsters. A breeze rustled the infant leaves which seemed to exclaim: "She went that way! I saw her!" Sure enough, a wisp of blue flashed around the trees. She was across the road, speeding down the grassy incline against the woods.

GUY: Why race? Strange woman.

SPARROW: Teer!

GUY: Teer!

She refuses these sweet, plunderless gems. *(extends his hand to catch some concentrated moisture)* It's refreshing and mutualistic.

He turns the corner, cautiously jogging down the hill towards the woods.

SPARROW: TeerTeer Teer TeerTeer Teer!

GUY: *(looks up disapprovingly at the mocking sparrow; two raindrops kiss his bright right eye.)* Small, refreshing splashes drip away my stress with the sky's acrimony. Rush from elevated prongs and promiscuous fronds, but gulp the olive oil!

He jumps into a big puddle and stamps on it two more times.

Guy easily forgot the urgency of his work when he entered the woods across from the ARC. Each day he'd follow a bird (or a beetle) for a bit. When the weather donated big puddles, he'd stoically jump into them as well. His speed kept

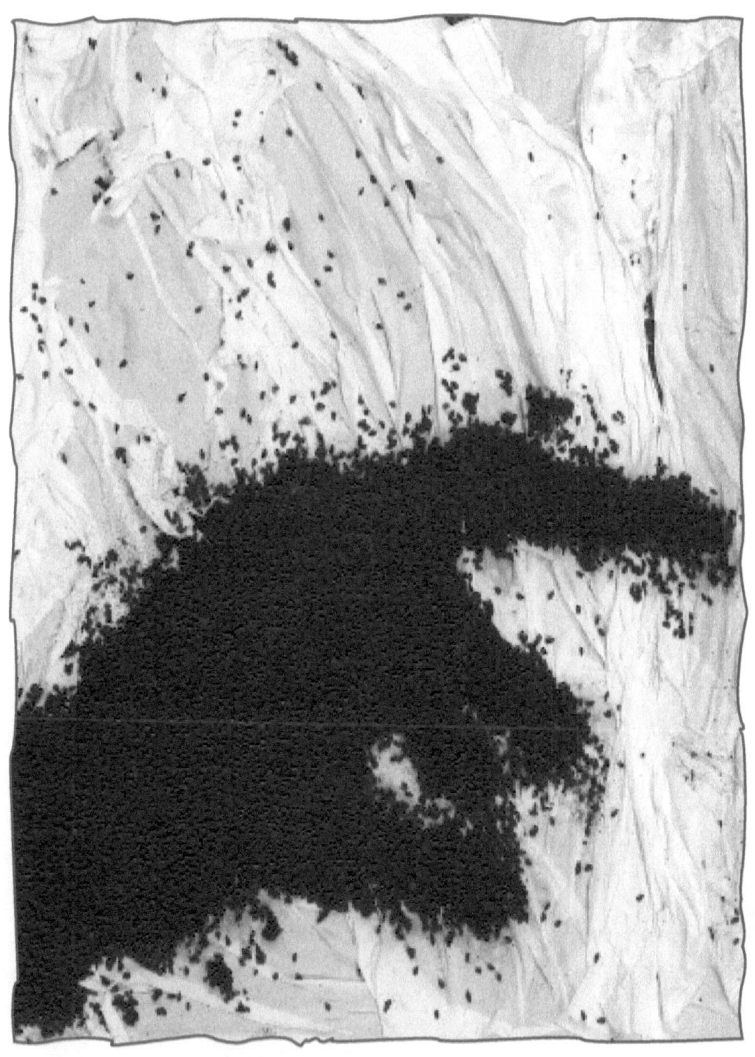

Chillin' with a Small Winged Friend

his jeans dry. He walked towards the path across the creek, but a nice mass of brown sparkled slightly out of his way. He approached the sleek brown stripes of gleaming water and slowly grazed the friendly puddle with his right foot.

It was now pouring and the little creek had grown. The large rocks were no longer peeking over the water's surface. Guy had to quickly create an exact map of where each one was located. After the blueprint was drawn along the inside of his head, he peered into the rapids that transparentized where he had placed the stones. Encouraged by the confirmation, he leapt adroitly from rock to rock, immersing the bottom fourth of his shoes in water. He was on the other side, feeling proud of the scene he had shown Woman, who must have been hiding by a tree.

CROW: Gwaaa'a!

As he walked across the ARC parking lot, his eyes focused on the limping woman who was within earshot of him. How she had crossed the creek so skillfully, he was dying to know.

GUY: GWAAAAAAAAAAAAAAAA'AAAK!

Woman speeds off into the thick lake of fog. Guy quickly takes out his cell phone to see the time.

GUY: Why not?

He sprinted into the thick fog whose border treaded on the sleepy moisture nearby. Once inside, he slowed down.

The myriad dots of vapor hissed at him, molesting his long, water-speckled arms. He feared that inhaling the excess oxygen would stupefy his lungs. He stopped abruptly and spread out his hands to see if it was indeed possible for fog to conceal one's extended arms. He saw them, and having forgotten why he had entered the wet nebula, he walked towards the ARC.

CROW: GwaAk!

GUY: Gwaaak!

He walked up the five left steps and unlocked the archaic door which seemed unbefitting of an edifice in which cutting-edge designs were constantly being drafted. He opened the second set of doors and was met by the dark windows in front of the front desk. He hated the sight; the darkness meant that the secretary had gone home to relax while he and his classmates had to quickly finish projects to meet deadlines.

He glanced through the right corridor where a post-doc was knocking on his selfish colleague's door, waiting to ask if he could use the plotter sometime that week.

It was 6:45 p.m. Class had ended over six hours earlier, but no outsider could tell because both studios were practically filled. Each large room was home to forty brave third-year architecture students.

Guy fished out his key from the front pocket of his tennis bag and unlocked his drawers, pulling out his Olfa knife and basswood. He reached up and removed his nicely crafted model from the shelf atop his workspace.

Guy knew his fellow soldiers very well. They had been in the same grueling classes for nearly six semesters.

He sat right next to the exit. To his right was KRISTEN. Kristen was *The Drafter*. She was the go-to person whenever anyone had a drafting question, such as which template to use with what, which line should be thick, stippled, or nearly invisible in a design, etc.

Behind her sat CYRIL. Cyril rarely spoke, so everyone decided he was a gifted guy who never needed anyone's help. The class wasn't fond of him.

However, in order to be able to do a decent job on his projects, Cyril actually did ask his brother many questions. His brother, Andreas, was a professor at the rival architecture school downtown. Cyril didn't speak to others because his asthma and chronic bronchitis were so bad that he was constantly holding back terrible coughs. It was incredibly difficult for him to speak, and if he laughed, his chuckles would be overpowered by heavy, disgusting coughs. Of course, nobody knew this, so his classmates assumed he was a cocky jerk.

JERRY sat to the right of Kristen. He wore a small Piglet watch on his nicely tanned arm. Jerry moved to Maryland from a city full of miners in northern Michigan. He was a pleasant, jolly guy who slept a lot and, consequently, failed a lot. He was incredibly lazy and everyone, including his teachers, wondered why he had chosen to study the most demanding major at the large university.

VERONICA sat diagonally from Guy. She was by far the most creative drawer. Like Kristen, she was always willing to give feedback on the circulation in one's floor plan, how to make the building more economical, or how to alter a few lines to make the entire building rich in meaning.

Guy was *The Techie.* If someone had an issue converting, exporting or importing a file, or if anyone had difficulties getting the temperamental 3D programs to cooperate, Guy would be there to help. He didn't especially like computers, nor did he feel that he was good at troubleshooting. He merely started sooner than everyone else, encountered countless problems, struggled with each for hours, and then finally resolved the issues (oftentimes with the assistance of a Master's student). Having learned the hard way, he was happy to save his classmates time by teaching them how to commandeer the crazy programs.

Guy sits down beside his daunting project and is immediately exhausted.

JERRY: Aha! I made an even better limerick than yester-night's!

              Ahem!

              We are trapped in this studio citadel!
              Where our fingers catch a gluey smell!
              I went home four projects ago,
              So I don't see Mama no mo'.
              We are truly insane, can't you tell?

              Haha! I missed my step-sister's wedding, and I still won't be done!

Guy gets up.

JERRY: Where're you going, *(mispronounces his name on purpose:)* **Guy?**

GUY: Coffee.

JERRY: Ooooh! I should do a coffee haiku! Th—

Guy leaves and then jerks his head towards LIZ, a red-headed underclassman who is singing and skipping down the hall.

LIZ: I'm looking for the set squares, the set squares, the set squares. I'm looking for the set squares. La da DA da DO.

GUY: Did you check the closet?

LIZ: First place I looked, Bud.

GUY: They're usually just hidden underneath all the boxes.

The old white linoleum silently carried their feet to a room in the hallway perpendicular to the east corridor, where the Master's students worked. They passed the student lounge and some offices that had doors that opened inward. Guy's Studio I teaching assistant said that those rooms housed the live-in counselors when the ARC was an insane asylum for children.

MILOS: **ELIZABETH!** *(Liz and Guy stop and turn around; they see MILOS, a friendly Serbian, waving two set squares in his right hand.)*

LIZ: **Yippee! Thank you, Guy!** *(She quickly hugs Guy and gallops to Milos while popping invisible balloons with her index fingers.)*

DANIEL, a friendly exchange student from South Africa, walks past Milos, towards Guy. Neither look at all disconcerted that Liz is galloping maniacally.

GUY: 'Sup Daniel?

DANIEL: Does my project look like a frog?

GUY: What?

DANIEL: It's **Reuben**. So, I asked if I should change anything and—

Guy cringes slightly upon hearing the name of their Design Studio II professor.

GUY: *(raises his eyebrows)* You seriously *asked?*

DANIEL: He was going to give it to me anyway.

Guy continues to walk towards the closet although he forgets why. Daniel follows.

GUY: True.

DANIEL: Well, he said *(mimicking Reuben's slow voice)* "It is sooo nice!"

(Daniel pauses; Guy stares at him, wondering if he is making this up.)

"It's so lovely! Would be perfect—if it didn't look like a frog."

(Guy smiles, certain of the veracity of Daniel's account.)

So I asked how to make it look less like a frog, and more like a museum, and he said "divest the superficiality, add more rigidity to the building and make the windows less watery." Then he walked away.

GUY: What?

DANIEL: I know! He makes no sense! *(He walks on, past the closet.)* Lovely frog, the lunatic. I'll show him rigidity....

Guy looked at the door of the supply closet and then realized he had no reason to be there. Instead of returning to the studio, his ever-demanding intuition had him turn towards the adjoining hallway, past the hinges and doorknobs that were facing him. They were safeguarding tiny closets which augmented the burning insanity that plagued two tiny children sixty years ago.

He looked up and noticed a white metal ladder nailed to the wall. A similar ladder could be seen at every hallway's mouth. His pesky intuition did not steer him to a dead end. The door to the attic was missing. He cautiously climbed the ladder, squinting his blue eyes at the top to prevent dust from irritating them. He was relieved that the ladder didn't budge despite placing 195 pounds of force on the middle rung. Using the back of his hand, he gently stroked the wooden floor, feeling tufts of grey and a sleek, long...

GUY: A paperclip!

He blew the dust off the paperclip and placed it between his index and middle knuckles of his left hand as he traveled down the well-painted ladder.

On the way back to the studio, Guy took out his red-handled needle-nose pliers from his pocket and let his knuckles run wild. Twisting here and pressing there resulted in... a Thing.

Thing didn't need eyes to look very disappointed.

GUY: But I will work on the project nonstop soon. It'll be done.

Thing just looked at Guy.

GUY: *(walking through the studio doorway)* You want me to write down what I need to finish? *(sees light reflecting off Thing)* Great idea!

Guy turned Thing sideways and at once Thing's identity changed. Thing was now It. Guy liked It. It didn't resemble anything. He placed It on his drafting table and proceeded to write everything that needed doing in order to perfect his project. He wrote for one whole hour, then looked at the 162 details that he had remembered.

GUY: Just a spirit, whisking my jumbled-up thoughts. Just a spider, threading away, but where from? Where is this silk concealed, this silk whose design was woven over twenty-one years ago? Why does it freely pace about the ruffled sky which can't fathom its beauty and merely exploits it *sans* gratitude? I can't see it, I can't taste it, but acts, words, movements... they're designed somewhere. Somewhere blue... bold... beautiful.

Somewhere I won't know. Stored metaphysically. No colors.

He gets up to use the bathroom.

GUY: *(looks at It)* I'll be right back.

It said nothing.

The bathroom closest to him was in the undergraduate wing, and quite frankly, he was tired of seeing that wing. He ventured to find a bathroom in the adjacent Master's students' hallway. He passed a bulletin board, offices of Vladimir, Marie, Alexander, and a printer room. He peeked in and saw Mike A.'s small office which had a tiny private bathroom attached. Mike, whoever he was, probably didn't work there anymore, for his office was practically bare.

For the first time all day, Guy noticed his keys clinking around in his top left pants pocket as he passed a large conference room. He liked the haphazard sound which suited the old building. However, the conference room looked completely out of place. There were grand windows and pristine blinds whose white stripes enhanced the image of the healthy green grass, the clean road, and the red maple tree outside. The black tables and chairs were brand new. He sat in one of the chairs and leaned backwards. He then got back up and walked towards a folded sign taped to an old yellowish door which was originally white. He unfolded the sign.

SIGN: MEN

He opened the door and was completely taken aback. In front of him lay four shower stalls with wooden, electrocution-style chairs placed in each one. Before he used the lavatory, he explored the bizarre scene, much to his bladder's dismay. He opened the small closet left of the bathroom entrance and saw a box full of papers mixed with sponges. While Guy was curious, it was not his nature to be intrusive. He left the papers be, and finally used the restroom.

He washed his hands with the yellow water that leaked where the rusty faucets met the fake marble base. The side of his pinky finger burned as the unsanitary waters dived into Guy through a small cut he didn't know he had. He shook his hand and decided he'd stick with the undergraduate wing bathroom after all.

He couldn't wait to see the rest of the creepy insane asylum whose present projects involved architectural theory, sustainability, urban design, building materials, and acoustics as opposed to methods for disciplining mentally ill children.

GUY: Ha.

Some kids probably just had self-control issues. I'll bet many weren't crazy at all when their parents dropped them off here. They probably *became* loonies after being subjected to the experiments of the evil counselors of this place.

He racewalked towards a studio with five graduate school professors, said hi to them, then turned down the dark stairway which had about twelve red poles at the entrance. The green-yellow tiles along the wall added to the old feel. Guy was captivated; he walked more slowly—slowly enough to take it all in, but not so slowly that he wouldn't promptly return to his post. He saw a newly constructed area of the building which ruined the brightness of the dismal clamor. He walked on, finding another staircase that led to a room with bright yellow lights seeping out from beneath the door which was ajar.

SIGN: AUTHORIZED PERSONNEL ONLY.
         KEEP DOOR CLOSED AT ALL TIMES.

He opened the door cautiously and saw a large window atop a medium-sized green counter. On the other side of the window were black boxes and wires jutting from every which way. He heard a constant beeping sound coming from his right. Guy decided he didn't have the time to open the light-blue metal door which stifled the red beeps. He had to find his way back to It and the lookout.

He raced back down the stairs, ran past some architectural engineering research labs, and found another stairway across from a vending machine and a hole in the wall. Forgetting that he was on the ground floor, and needed to get back upstairs, he descended below the second story building.

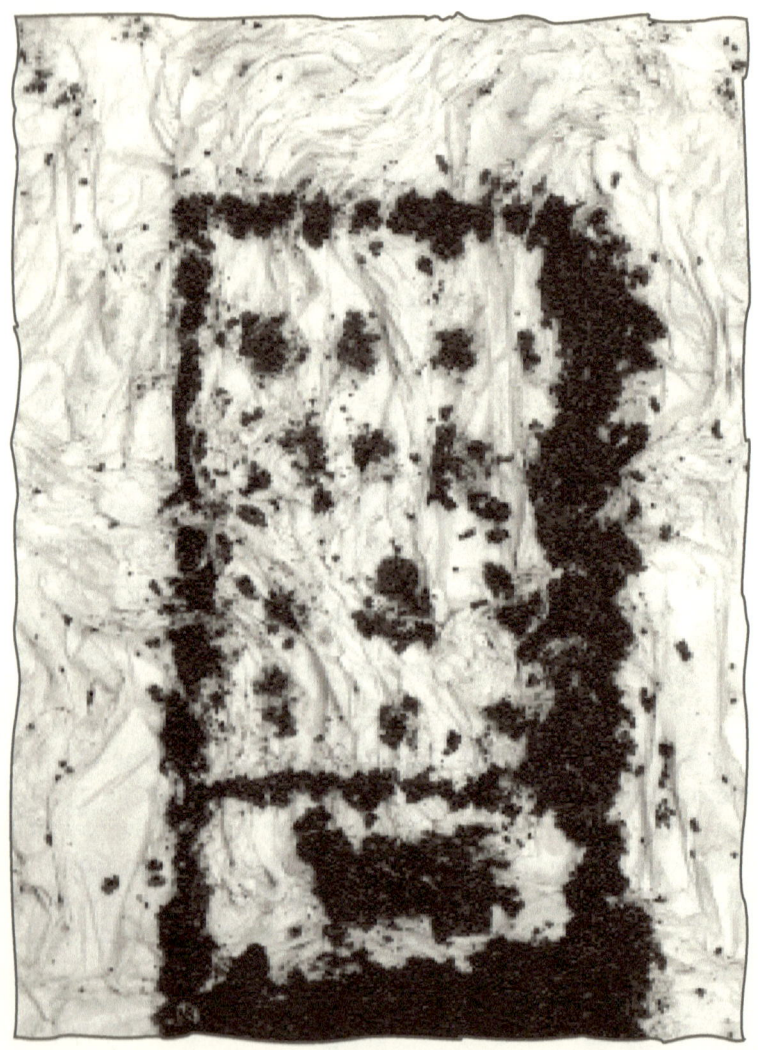

The Vending Machine

Guy reached the bottom of the stairs and was greeted by an odor of unfamiliar fumes. The cloudiness of the arena excited his curiosity. He saw three stout pillars spread around the boxing complex. He would have loved skateboarding all over, grinding the sides of the boilers far ahead of him. The room was spacious, murky, and creepy. He expected Smile to appear at any moment to taunt him, but the complex was much too unnatural for Smile's company.

Guy tiptoes a few steps towards the wooden door that is perched upon an even lower platform, twelve feet away.

DOOR: SLAM!

Guy quickly turns around. He didn't even remember that door being there; the door that was left open for him had withdrawn its light.

GUY: *(whispers while looking at the suspended dust)*
How special this silver mist, arduously gleaning luminescence to be self-reliant. I thank you.

Feeling he couldn't turn back, he continued onward towards the wooden door, descending the step in front of it very slowly. But as he placed his left foot on it, the doorknob began to shake.

His face was expressionless. When his right foot joined his left, the whole door began to shake. Guy stepped back. He pressed the step with his left foot again and then hopped onto the step with his right foot alone. The pitch of the rattling increased. He then placed both feet on the step, removed one, jumped on and off with both feet and then jumped on with one foot. He felt dust enter his nostrils.

DOOR: Rattle Raaa! Boom Boom! Rattle Boom, Boom Raaa, Rattle Rattle Boom Boom! Ra Rattle Raaa! Boom Boom, Raa! Rattle Boom!

He imitated the sounds with his mouth as he slowly skipped backwards, pivoting as he skipped. He clicked his tongue, blew in air, sighed, kurkled his throat, and smacked his lips, beatboxing a lively rhythm that caused his dancing shoulders to strut their stuff. *(Guy squints his irritated eyes.)*

He was hot. He promptly took off his shirt and threw it into the dust. The XXXL white shirt was stomped on and dragged all over the impatient floor as Guy's shoulders rose and fell in harmony with the rhythmic changes of the rickety beatboxing. Soon, his large feet had swept a good portion of the sultry, now exposed floor.

He bounced around a bit within the shirt-scrubbed circle and proceeded to breakdance in his white tank. He held himself up with his left hand as his right hand grabbed the tips of both of his shoes. His legs were fully extended; he was impressed that he could still do that freeze. He got up, jumped around a bit, and started to do the flare.

He failed to keep going, and played it off by transitioning into the windmill. He rested his abs on the triceps of his left arm and then pushed forward, collapsing onto his left shoulder. He used his legs to propel his body around. His rounded back smashed into the blue-grey concrete, but the floor didn't mind; the parasitic dust liked his back more than it cared for the concrete.

GUY: *(while spinning, careful not to hit a boiler)*
           Cha pa cha Boobi Boo. Cha! Pa Boobi Boo!

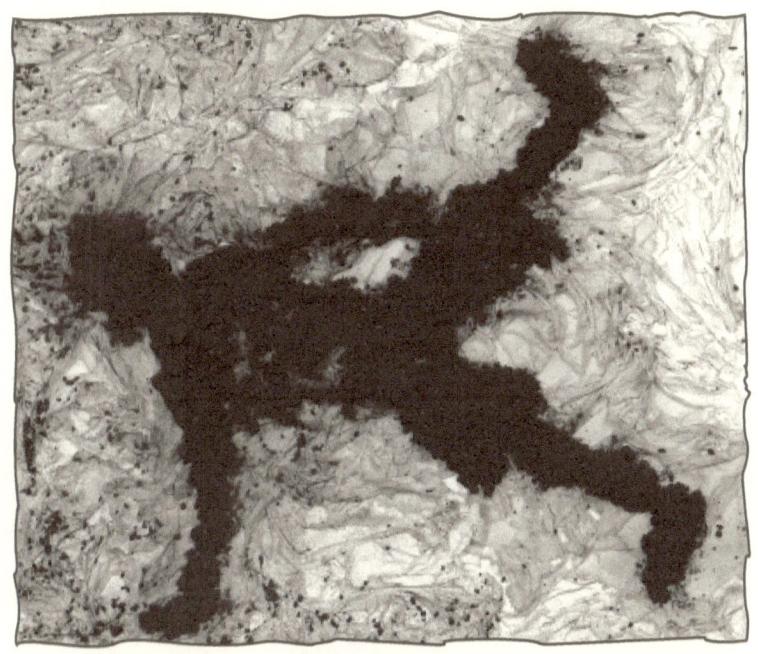

Doing the Flare

He rapidly spun on his back. In between spins, he held his torso up with his left arm. After the sixth spin, his bent legs froze high in the air as the triceps of his muscular left arm firmly held up his torso once more. The side of his head and his left hand were now his feet, softly planted on the floor.

GUY: *(screaming)*
        Cha PA CHA PI!
        CHA Pi! ChA PiPi!

DOOR: Squeeeek!

He pushed forward with his left hand, landed on his back and sprung up to his feet. As soon as he landed, his eyes caught a glimpse of a janitor carrying a green-handled mop. The corpulent man had just entered the large, spacious boiler room and was standing ten feet away. Guy quickly walked up to him.

GUY: Hey, Joe! I'm Guy, Joe!

BOB: Hi, *(Guy extends his arm and shakes his hand.)* Bob.

GUY: Nice to meet you, Bob! Joe is a cool name too, of course. Hehe! Have a great day! *(Guy's smile resembles the grimace of an evil long-lipped clown.)*

Guy skips past Bob and returns to the studio.

BOB: I see why they call it archi*torture*. Poor kid's lost his mind. *(shakes his head)*

So young! 'Tsa shame.

Guy was just short of entering the studio when he remembered why he had gotten up earlier. He used his hands to hold up invisible horse blinders and zeroed in on the coffee machine, knowing full well that coffee did little to keep him awake. But perhaps it was very "little" that he needed. He took out his student ID card from his back pocket, swiped it, and watched as the vending machine poured three shots of espresso with caramel and milk into a small red cup.

He drank it and dropped the cup in the trash can outside the studio. After entering, he found his professor, REUBEN, examining his basswood model. Since he held no set office hours during the day, Reuben oftentimes visited his students at odd hours.

Reuben was a fifty-something-year-old man who always wore brown corduroy pants and brown clogs with light-grey socks that didn't match anything else. His tops were sometimes collared shirts or sometimes wool vests with a bright, tacky undershirt which defied all fashion reasoning. He was a divorcé who, ironically, helped his stepsister become a prominent fashion designer. His connections were vast and practically everyone in the class sucked up to him to ensure that his rich, silk letters of recommendation were nothing short of magnificent.

Since Reuben often responded favorably to the brownnosing, Guy disliked him and decided right away that he would never ask the man for a recommendation letter. This was the fourth class Guy had taken with Reuben, and Guy knew his style very well. Reuben noticed that Guy caught on to his likes and pet peeves as Guy's projects became more and more elegant. He marveled at his ability to trowel the student's ideas.

Guy, on the other hand, felt as if he was holding back. His brilliant, ecological, *different* ideas were always dismissed by Reuben, regardless of the amount of meaningful, important research he would eloquently present. The obstinate student had lost way too many points his sophomore year, so he instead channeled his creativity into quick designs for his summer internship project (which was to start in about a month).

REUBEN: What's the occupancy of this?

Guy wondered if Reuben was drunk or senile, for he praised his work in class on Monday.

GUY: It's a museum. To preserve—

REUBEN: Ha! The glass is overpowering. Laminated?

GUY: No, actually—

REUBEN: Tear down the old one and go for your glass theme, or preserve the original layout with necessary modifications. *(He never explains what exactly is "necessary" but throws that word out a lot.)*

But for God's sake, don't make this sickly hybrid. Get rid of the stone bases on this face. And add more parallelism to your windows.

He walked away without listening to Guy's thoughts. Guy, very tired, didn't feel like explaining why he made each window different. He didn't follow Reuben to explain that each corresponded to the age represented by the nearby exhibit. Guy sighed as he watched Reuben leave the studio. The glass face was not going to match his design at all.

GUY: A glass wall without any stone will ruin everything! It'll be more expensive! But perhaps— Yeah, maybe it'll make the room appear timeless. After all, this room does house the Future Gallery.

Guy strokes the cool paperclip with the back of his hand, feeling calmer.

GUY: It's crunch time, It! *(He delicately moves It to the right of his mouse.)*

Guy bent his head to the left as he put on his headphones. He played his trance mix which helped him rapidly change his 2D rendering and export it to redo his 3D computer model.

Eighteen songs later, he was chilling to "Elements of Life" by DJ Tiësto. He became the genius he admired. The keyboard and mouse became his mixer and the museum library a song whose texture needed changing. He didn't pause once (unlike CLARK, a tall classmate from Lafayette, Louisiana, who was laughing upon hearing something outrageous on a short British podcast a few rows behind him).

Finally, the wall was glass. Guy rubbed his forehead and closed his eyes briefly only to meet his coach's glare which often haunted him.

COACH: SLEEP EACH NIGHT OR YOU'LL MAKE US LOSE.

Guy sighed silently and drew his Olfa knife up to his eyes. He tilted it sideways and the light on top of his drafting table reflected off his silver blade onto the pipes of the complicated ceiling.

He tiredly watched the light slide across the ceiling, growing until it disappeared. Soon, a bright star appeared where his dim reflection had vanished. He looked across the studio and saw Veronica's blade as the bright light's source.

VERONICA: Guy! The light! Don't let it vanish!

GUY: Haha! How long you been up?

VERONICA: I'm nearing hour *(pauses, spinning in her chair)* thirty-twooooooo!

Guy shook his head and unwittingly showed off a gorgeous smile. It went unnoticed by all, including himself.

He held the ruler to the base of the building and cut the wall away from him. He was nearly done when—

CLARK: **NOOO**!

Guy cut deeply into the adjoining wall and also felt like screaming. He set down his blade and stood up. He became paralyzed at the sight of blood all over Clark's painstakingly hand-drawn papers and his perfect, polished model.

CLARK: Probably cut into a vein! Shoot! My work!
          (holds up his bloodied papers with his clean hand)
          Five weeks' worth!

ABBIE, Clark's Japanese girlfriend who sits three seats to his left, runs up to him with the first-aid kit.

ABBIE: Forget about your work! You're bleeding!

She opened the white plastic container, took out the cotton and alcohol and wiped his poor cut finger. He only felt the pain of knowing that he would have to redo over a month's worth of work. He silently glared at his model as Abbie wrapped up his finger. Guy saved Clark's computer files, shut down the computer, and placed his supplies in his desk as Abbie escorted Clark to the door.

ABBIE: Let's go. You'll need stitches.

CLARK: My Model! My Poor Model! So Red! It was Brown, Abbie! It was Broooown!

Abbie and Clark leave.

The students sitting close to Clark's desk engage in a discussion. Classmates in the discussion include MARAH, a slightly older Jordanian woman with a pleasant disposition; CHRIS, a blonde three-time intramural dodgeball champion from New Market; RYOMA, a thin Japanese man who speaks like a football announcer; DEAN, a close friend of Lili who grew up in Ohio; MARIEL, a compassionate Boricua woman who can't

wait to return to the beaches of San Juan; and MARIA, a cute
fellow Baltimorean of Greek descent with curly brown hair.

MARAH: I wish the professor had stayed to see that.

CHRIS: Sixth person this semester.

RYOMA: He definitely spilled the most blood, though.

VERONICA: That's so sad!
         I hope Reuben gives him an extension.

DEAN: Yeah, right! When Marla sawed off the tip of her finger last year, she still had to present that Friday. I wonder what it would take to get an extra day....

CHRIS: He'd have to die.

GUY: You kidding? Dying is no excuse. He'd fail him for sure.

RYOMA: No—perhaps I'd get an honorary degree if I became another Architecture casualty.

MARIEL: Another?

RYOMA: Sure, many have died.

         Some of overdoses, others of a mix of too much wood glue consumption with numerous fatal knife stabs. Then some of our kind are found dead on the side of the road when a big truck rams into the poor drunkard and then speeds away. But they get honorary degrees, right?

MARIA: Ryoma! You want to get the degree to be able to start your own design studio and work as a full-fledged architect.

Ryoma looks at IMRAN, a brown-haired student who is smiling as he taps his foot to Italian beats playing in his head.

RYOMA: Archi—What?

Mariel taps Ryoma on the shoulder.

MARIEL: Forty hours?

RYOMA: Forty-three, Yes, Sirreeeee…

SALLY, Ryoma's twin sister, peers over at Maria who somehow looks both annoyed and very relaxed.

MARIA: What's the point of the degree if you're dead?!

RYOMA: …Bob. Sorry.

SALLY: What?

RYOMA: The "Sirreee" needed "Bob," for if there is too much ventilated space between the faceted "Sirreeee" and the "Bob" frame, the "Yes" is gonna scream for some ethafoam, you know? Yeah.

Marah and Mariel look at each other, then both start laughing.

RYOMA: But yeah, Maria, I want to be… *(he pauses to release a very coercive, soporific yawn which tires Maria to silence)* an **artiket.** *(looks at the clock)* Could someone wake me up in half an hour?

Guy turns off his computer, places his basswood model on the shelf above his drafting table, and leaves.

CONSTANTLY STOPPING

X

It was exactly 10:45 p.m. when Guy let the door of the Architecture Research Center close behind him. He looked at the bush to the left of the main entrance and noticed a spider suspended in the air.

GUY: Spider web! From whence doth thou hang? I see your white foot upon the spiny bush tops, but this line of white!

Why, you're vertically suspended in midair!

Guy was grateful for the streetlights. He walked the long way around the "creepy insane asylum," as he referred to his studio building. Five lights were happily gleaming in front of him, but they soon ceased to brighten his path for he had passed their conceited selves. He was in the dark now, walking across the humid parking lot. The lights behind him couldn't quite let him move on; they sprinkled glitter on the blacktop before him.

GREY BIRD: Weee!

GUY: *Fascinating. The beautiful glistening road we drive upon has a most sincere and sparkling account which we trudge right over with obliterating mud.* (He walks between two huge trailers that line the entrance to the woods.)

Guy responds to the bird; the sound ricochets off a side of each trailer.

GUY: Weeeeh!

TRAILER 1: Weeeee—

TRAILER 2: —eeeeeeeh!

The echoes frighten the small grey bird who becomes silent.

GRASS: Crunch! Crk Crunch!...

GUY: **Can't see a thing!** *(He pushes aside some branches and walks down the muddy ridge of the small stone hill, past the trailers and the pavement.)*

Guy tilted his head, much like a bird would, and finally he saw little orange patches of shiny slime floating on the water along the far side of the creek. The orange slime shimmered and trailed into the other side of the bank where the broken tree trunk swallowed it whole.

He liked the orange dew and wanted a closer look. His feet prudently withheld his weight as he feverishly overcame the strange sucking force of the water. He was on the other side, but instead of continuing upward to exit the dangerous valley, he walked along the broken trees and then sat down, refusing to acknowledge the harmful person who was already sitting there.

WOMAN: You went the wrong way. But I understand. The confused light isn't making any sense. These reflections defy the Way of the Shadow and Angle.

Guy turned and stared straight into her tranquil face. She was looking down at the water. She removed her right arm from her bent right leg and placed it around three centimeters from Guy's person.

He breathed heavily. The strange, hale being was clearly alive, but in Guy's mind, the mesmerizing woman was nothing but a dead girl from an 1804 painting.

While Guy became incredibly shy, Woman, bold at heart but

discreet in action, took in each of Guy's movements. She didn't believe in reincarnation, but she was positive that Guy used to be a blue jay. As she spoke, she let his body movements massage her pride, for each quick, raw turn confirmed that she was right. Much bigger than his sparrow friends, and more reserved and vulgar looking, he stood out as being incredibly handsome. His appearance and his rough actions made him attractive to her, mostly because she disliked his kind.

> WOMAN: The clouds will rejoice! All four! Together!
> They always do. It's so strange.

The Woman's wide brown eyes saw the casually sitting Guy looking straight ahead now. A car honked in the parking lot he had just left, and Woman waited to see him quickly look up to try to see it. She smiled at seeing him stay still.

> WOMAN: I think they're four.
> You'll see.
> Then you can tell me.
> I mean, I figured it out, though.

He had an urge to scratch his chin but repressed it because he no longer felt comfortable with her eyes on him.

Guy gets up and so does she.

> WOMAN: Don't be crazy! You should follow me. It's safer.

Guy took two steps in her direction and then his heart nearly burst. His left foot, Bruce, had found a secure foothold; but his right foot, Santiago, slid between logs, deep into the clay ground.

He felt Santiago could easily come out, so he sat down where he had become stuck, thinking about what had just happened. She was gone. Why did she want him there? Then, his eyes opened wide.

He became scared, for right behind where she had been, a black amorphous figure crawled into view.

BUSH: Crinkle! Crinkle!

Guy was worried for his life. The cat-like creature, whatever it was, could not be seen, so it remained an evil force emanating from Woman's wiles.

GUY: *(short of breath; whispers)* I... **trusted you!** *(He lifts the logs and jumps away from the bank, towards the top of the wooded valley. He stops when he is a third of the way up the nine-foot rocky hill.)*

WOMAN: *(Guy sees her suddenly appear on the other side of the bank.)* **Learn not to be stupid, Idiot! How could you trust me? I worry about you. Be safe.** *(The black force withdraws into total silence.)* **I'm right though.**

Guy could barely see her behind the tree branches, but he understood and was happy to have such an eccentric, though somewhat supernatural, friend.

GUY: *(sincerely)* **Thank you.**

He runs out of the valley into the grassy plain beside the satellite parking lot.

It was 10:59 p.m. when he successfully made it out of the water valley. Naturally, he wanted to run away from the wild scene, but his legs couldn't. A large coyote was staring at him, mirroring his every step. She was just a dark-grey blur eighteen feet away, but Guy knew she could outrace him. So he stopped.

The coyote stopped as well.

Guy ran for his life. He saw the coyote closing in and so he raced even faster up the grassy incline leading to the freshmen parking lot. However, the creepy coyote wasn't interested in Guy as much as the location where she first saw Guy. The animal continued on, along the outside edge of the woods, towards the mahogany path leading to the rocky creek below.

Guy turned around but couldn't see the sneaky being. When he turned his head again, looking onward, his eyes met a strange-looking man in a vest and old green cargo shorts. He had on large brown boots and had thin dusty brown hair that curved along the sides of his round face.

Guy wondered how long he had stood there and if he was a normal person, for no sooner had the coyote disappeared than this odd man appeared. The stranger's eyes were peering at his hands that were stretched forth into the dark, purple sky.

His large colorless eyes quickly met Guy's defiant face. A wide, distracting smile unwreathed the stranger's chapped lips.

STRANGER: Hi!

> I was trying to see if it was raining!
> Did you feel the rain? It might rain soon.

GUY: Hi—It's nice to see another human. Please be **careful.** *(His head quickly turns towards where the coyote had stood.)* **There** was a big coyote, or... fox... or something over there. *(His eyes return to the wide-eyed man.)* **Nearly** scared me to death.

The strange man's eyebrows were fixed midway across his forehead as he replied in a relaxed surfer's accent.

STRANGER: Is that right? Well, he's probably more scared of you, you know.

Guy's heartbeat slowly regained its composure.

GUY: *(walking away)* Yeah, just be careful if you're crossing the creek—Oh and yeah, I noticed the rain, maybe it will rain more. Bye.

STRANGER: Stay safe!

Guy nodded and continued on without looking back at the wide-faced man. He felt comforted when he saw him, a person, on top of the hill, away from the coyote. It was a relief much likened to what he felt when he saw a baby or a plant in a mall. Malls always made his heart tighten because of the ostentatious materialism he felt steaming from adults, kids, and teens alike. The kids seemed to enjoy buying more than playing; seeing them further disgusted him. So when he found himself in a mall, his eyes always searched frantically for the comforting likeness of a baby, or a leafy plant, to assuage the discomfort.

He shot a backward glance at the strange man to see if he was still checking out the luminescence of far away streetlights on his bulky hands. No. He was gone.

GUY: Probably went to the creek. Silly man. Seemed nice—but weird.

The time was now 11:15 p.m. when Guy crossed the street, finally returning to the campus of the school he represented at tennis tourneys. He passed two residence halls, looking at the freshly mown grass which he walked on instead of walking on the impractically placed sidewalks.

WINGS: Flapflapflapflapflap!

Guy didn't hear the bird whistle, but he looked up and was able to follow the creepy soar of bug-like jet wings which belonged to a female blackbird.

His gaze upward, he continued looking into the sky, this time searching for stars. He hadn't stared up at the stars since fifth grade, but the sight of little white dots behind the bird intrigued him. There were eight small celestial crowns in the sky, but Guy couldn't see them.

Instead, he saw clouds. Three disparate clouds followed a fourth one in an inward spiral direction until finally they combined in the center, forming a slightly brighter cloud of white. It was truly phenomenal. They stayed together as a conglomerate star for exactly one second and then spiraled outward.

Guy marveled at how the luminescent fusion emitted considerably more light than the explosion that occurred when the clouds separated. He stared at the spectacle, mouth slightly open. He saw a guy in a large blue shirt walk across the sidewalk next to the grassy spot on which he stood.

GUY: *How could this guy*
         (sees a woman rushing towards Azalea Hall)
         or that girl not stop and check this out?

Guy kept walking, following the furry white stars with his bewildered blue eyes. He had wanted to go home so that he could shower, sleep, and wake up early to work on his project at dawn. However, the strange balls of sparkly cotton were dancing towards the Student Union and he couldn't help but follow until they disappeared.

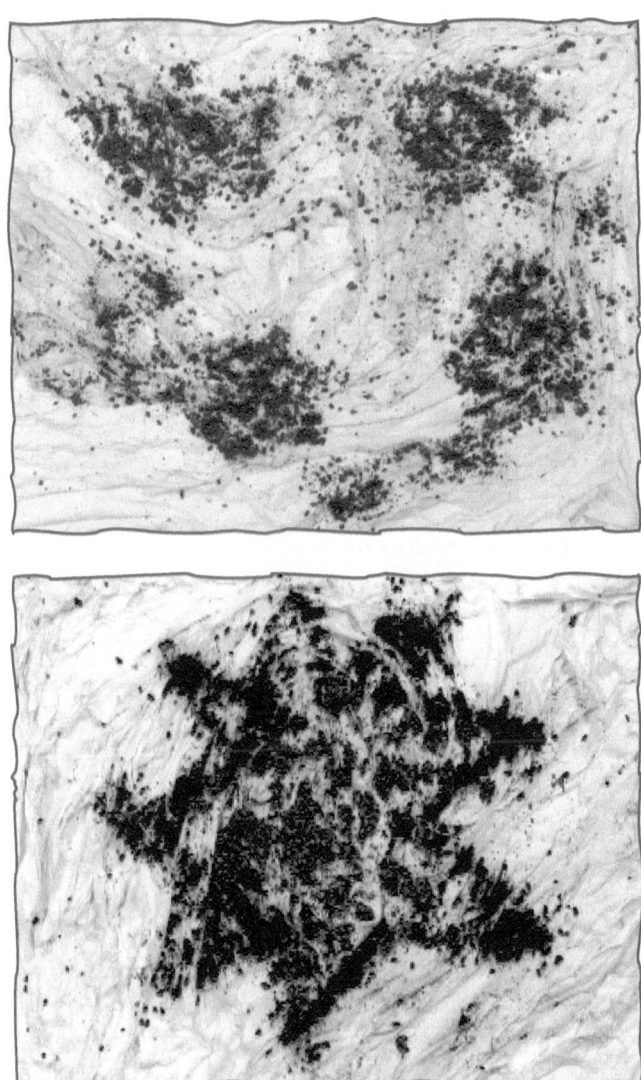

Spiraling Clouds, The Bright Fusion

Completely mesmerized, he walked underneath a tree, towards the Student Union; he felt as if the clouds had deserted him once the tree had been passed. Where were the clouds of light?

He found them, slightly to the left. They were directly above the Student Union Building. His dying suspicion that they were unreal was about to be laid to rest. They started flickering, as if they were losing energy.

A couple walks towards where Guy is standing.

MAN: Sharanya, the Econ test is tomorrow!

SHARANYA: But we have that down!
            Seriously, just study for Orgo.

GUY: Excuse me, do you...

> *("...see that" is how he wants to end his sentence. But there is no need for the words, for the mystical clouds are now completely removed from the sky.)*

            ...uh, do you know what time The Grill closes?
            (He points with his thumb in the direction of the Student Union Building.)

MAN: Twelve thirty.

GUY: Thanks.

He entered the Union, went upstairs, and found a seat next to the large glass windows. He dropped his tennis bag there, ordered, then returned to his seat with mozzarella sticks, blue cheese sauce, and water from the water fountain. (Although his cup entitled him to any soda, he didn't want to let anything he didn't love enter his body.)

RADIO: Uh-uh, Babeee! Can't you seeee? Rush not! Love is only a-hayayay... blissful harmonee-eee-heeeheeehauh ee eee-uh!

GUY: No, you cheesy, meaningless-lyric-singing waste of my thoughts! Love is nothing. It's only fulfilling if it's your opponent that has it. Love for you means you lost. Pity such a nice voice sings such rubbish.

He looked up at the TVs on the wall. For some reason, each was muted. Annoying commercials graced each huge screen.

As he turned his head towards the window, he saw the wings of the blackbird. This time, the Union's bright outside lights danced along her back, coloring the bird white.

GUY: *Birds don't fly low at night in a normal place. Maybe the history of this college as a prison for the country's rejects was too rich to remain in books. Perhaps the hijacked minds didn't disintegrate with the possessed corpses. These crazy birds were the owners of the misery, the troubled nerves, and the horrific memories of the torture inflicted by the asylums.*

And Those... Those Clouds! What message lies in this building? First, Grace lifted my gaze into the manipulative slickness of the above and then, it swished my plans throughout its darkness. And for what? And why must I be alone in—And That Woman! She must have seen—Or That Strange Man! Looking up! Distracting me? No. This parasite's doty timber—so thick is its enticing, mysterious scent, but so elusive.

> *Poor cog.*
> *To always be, but to never be truly known.*

Five minutes after he had first filled his cup with water, he was finished. He left through an exit opposite from where he had entered.

The well-lit footpath clashed with his distorted reflections. He took three steps and then was stopped once more.

The bird had flown down to the grass across from Guy. Her tiny claws stood one yard away from Guy's big feet. The bird merely looked at Guy for two seconds, then flew off.

WINGS: FlutterFlapflapflap!

GUY: Where is she leading me?

He racewalked in the general direction of the crazy bird. Guy hoped to find her, but it was much too dark. He looked up towards the Union Building and saw her dark figure coming out of a transom light, screaming at three other birds that screamed back from within the hot light dish.

The bird flew towards the trees around the library. Guy ran this time, trying hard not to lose sight of the flying clue. But before any clue was to be found, the blackbird flew into the thick midnight shadows.

He walked home, confused and irritated because of the unnecessary uneasiness his fatigued, overworked body had to combat. He turned back twice as he ascended the top of the hill where his apartment stood. The bird was nowhere to be seen. He walked on, praying to see the bird once more. He closed his eyes as a light breeze cooled his sweaty back.

Feathery Stalker

WINGS: Flapflapflap!

He quickly looked up and caught a glimpse of the taunting animal overhead. Guy continued on towards his door.

GUY: Tchee Tchee Tchee Tchee uhh! *(pauses)*
         Treeuruh tri triuh! Tree!

BIRD: *(remains silent)*

Within a flash of a pirate's shiny sword, Guy opened his apartment doors (leaving the front door unlocked for his suitemate, Bryan), slammed open the tight window beside his bed, and sat, leaning his head against the window net, whistling inquiries.

GUY: Twee? Twee Twee twee!

         Tweee Twee Tweee!

         Didididididi!

         Di DiDi DiDiDi!

         Twee dii Diii Diii Twee Tweeee?

He started shaking. It was a strange sight. Here sat this tall man, crouched in his room with the window wide open and the lights all off at 11:40 p.m., frantically trying to talk to a bird that was perhaps somewhere outside his window.

Upon realizing how chillingly pathetic he looked, he promptly closed the window, pulled down the screen, and turned on the lights. He just stood there by the light switch. He asked himself whether or not he had lost it and started heaving violently at the thought that he couldn't trust himself. His other suitemate, Uwem, was in the apartment, blasting music. Yet, Guy felt as alone as could be. He desperately needed to run somewhere.

GUY: No! You will stay! My God! What have I become?
         I don't want to hurt myself. I need help.

He forced his reluctant body to sit in a chair and opened up his laptop. Shortly thereafter, he wrote an email to his mother.

Guy loved his hardworking mother and couldn't wait to get a well-paying job so that she could finally retire. Before junior year he'd talk to her every day, but now he was lucky if he could get an email in. He was very confused and yearned for immediate wisdom. However, he wouldn't wake her up since her doctor said that she needed six hours of continuous sleep a night. Instead, he wrote to her about the crazy bird and the fantastic clouds. Mommy was the only person he knew who was truly wise, so he didn't hesitate to spill all the details about the soothing celestial sight and the late, frightening flight of his winged stalker.

EMAIL: call me, Please, as soon as u read this.
         dsn't matter what time. luv u, guy

He took out five paperclips from the silver-painted staple box on his dresser and placed them next to each other, forming a spiral. He looked at their shininess and felt energized enough to finally shower and get ready for bed.

5 A.M. BREAKFAST

XI

It's the next day, Thursday morning. Guy is in the common room of his apartment, standing by the open blinds of the glass door.

GUY: I open my crusted eyelids to the incandescent room and am shot by the sun's rays. They pierce my entire side when I give in, turning my shaken, limp body, so that its murderous warmth can penetrate me evenly.

    So I start my every day.

He doesn't notice his suitemate in the living room. He pulls up the blinds, allowing the light to strike his large body.

BRYAN: Mornin' Guy. *(checks his watch)*

GUY: Morning.

BRYAN: So poetic at 5:07 a.m.? What's wrong?

GUY: Surely, my presence does not always lend to our apartment an air of uneasiness. I intend entirely to enjoy this new, golden day.

BRYAN: Sounds good.

GUY: Strange. It's six blessed hours before you usually wake up.

BRYAN: Couldn't sleep—this image tormented me
Til I felt enslaved,
Captivated by its splendor.
It called me,
"Bryan, don't forget me.
You need me!"
Its beauty kept me up all night,
I couldn't say no.

GUY: Orange donuts.

BRYAN: You bet!
         I must go now.
         They await my faithful appetite.
         Wanna come?
         Pushin' back your daily promenade fifteen
         minutes won't hurt ya.

GUY: Very true. I suppose the change of environment
         could prove quite medicinal.

Guy grabs his wallet, his cell phone, and its headset, and places them in his cargo pockets with his needle-nose pliers and tissues. He finds the paperclip couple he made the evening before and adds them to the paperclips that stayed in his pants while he washed them three days ago.

They walk silently and then enter Bryan's green Jeep.

GUY: *(looking out the window)*
         The sparkling rice encapsulates the warmth,
         The fond memories, the traditions.
         Our teeth are gently molded as the enriching
              mastication
         Strengthens our background, our connection.
         The soft, sticky rice clings for an instant,
         When it obsequiously releases the tooth,
         That enjoyed the visitor, but lost its company,
         Nonetheless, by virtue of its willingness to
              complete its duty.

BRYAN: You speak like tradition and heritage are so
         important.

         Yeah, orange donuts with thin purple stripes
         don't represent a rich culture.

Tim wanted a signature donut, so he made it up
last month.

And yeah, not a lotta people eat 'em.

GUY: Which is another reason why they are not worth
        quibbling a second over.
    Yes, orange donuts have their farm charm,
    And are most singular...
    If you consider another "trendy" idea for the
        sake of novelty something singular.
    (smiles sarcastically)

BRYAN: You basin' a food's worth by its popularity?
    Look, orange donuts are gonna be huge,
    Mark my word.
    Just take last year for example—
    Nobody came to our basketball games.
    Then news of how good we became spread,
    And just like that, games were sold out.
    Yeah, word will go around,
    Word about their deliciousness and greatness,
    And they'll become huge.

*Guy stops listening, preoccupied with looking out the window
and counting the many cars without their lights on. He counts
eight.*

They enter the parking lot of Timmy Tim's Donuts.

BRYAN: Here we go!

*Guy looks to the side where there is a bird eating large crumbs
of donuts.*

GUY: Tweet tweet! *(pauses)*
    Tweet!

BIRD: Tweet-tweet!.

It was the first time Guy had initiated a conversation with a bird. His heartbeat raced as he satisfactorily whistled a "thank you" and entered the restaurant.

The song being played at the restaurant reminded him of his mother whom he hadn't had a chance to call last night. He tried to remember the singer.

RADIO: Smile for awhile and let's be jolly!
         Love shouldn't *be* so melan*choly*.
         Come along and share the good times,
         While we caaaa-a-a-an.

         I beg your pardon,
         I never promised you a rose garden!
         Along with the sunshine,
         There's gotta be a little *rain* sometime....

BRYAN: Mornin' Tim!

TIM: Why... it's my best customer! Please, sit here!
         (turns his head to the side)

         MARGARET! *(turns his head back towards Bryan and smiles)*

         Margaret will be your waitress today, she's lovely. So tell me, how was your basketball game Tuesday?

BRYAN: We won! To be honest, I played horribly, so I still feel a little embarrassed.... *(He taps his finger-nails along the edge of the table.)* But hey! We ended up beating them by fifteen points!

TIM: Is that right?

BRYAN: Yeah! Oh... by the way, that's um—Hey Guy!! That's my suitemate, Guy.

Guy is seen three steps from the door, looking out the window. He walks up to TIM, a stout, middle-aged man with jet black eyes and salt-and-pepper hair. Guy shakes his hand firmly and then takes a seat.

MARGARET: Howdy! Here you are! An orange juice and...
(she uncovers the plate with her left hand) ...three orange donuts with grape syrup!

The donuts smelled too tart to Guy. Just then, the radio played an uncatchy song with poor rhymes, horrible grammar, and even worse lyrics. Guy had never heard it before. He tried to ignore it.

BRYAN: I've never seen 'em this large! Awesome! Thanks!

MARGARET: And what can I get you?

GUY: Broccoli soup with milk, please.

Tim laughs from behind the counter.

MARGARET: *(smiling)* I beg your pardon?

GUY: I know it's not lunchtime yet, and I'm sorry for the inconvenience, but rich, creamy broccoli soup soothes my raspy, morning throat.

Margaret shakes her head and continues smiling as she writes the order down on her notepad.

GUY: Lynn Anderson.

BRYAN: What?

GUY: That last song....
Never mind.

Margaret glances down at the strange character who is amusing, yet stoic.

MARGARET: Okie dokie!
          One broccoli soup comin' up!

GUY: With milk, please.

MARGARET: With milk! *(She winks at Guy and leaves.)*

Bryan was smiling as he chewed, thinking about how nice it is to be the subject of people's conversations. Guy looked at Bryan's jolly expression and felt nothing. He examined each of the short nails on Bryan's right hand as they dived for the table in succession, paying homage to the stupid song being played. Guy's own right hand started throbbing by the unwilling association bridged by Guy's mind.

Bryan's face was lit up by the extra light the open door let in. A sweet draft entered the restaurant, accompanied by a short, thin man with overalls and a name tag bearing the letters *K* and *G*. Guy waited til KG passed his seat to turn his head right and examine the very curious-looking fellow.

Guy glanced at his truck outside (the fourth vehicle in the lot). It had a light-orange cab and a wooden stake bed holding over a ton of hay.

MARGARET: Here you are!
          Bonna Pehteet!

GUY: *(in a perfect French accent:)* Merci.

Bryan got up to pick up the paper that was on the counter. He proceeded to do a crossword puzzle as he returned to his seat. Meanwhile, Guy was eating at his usual fast pace. He briefly looked up towards Tim who was watching him.

GUY: This is great.

His eyes returned to his creamy, tasty soup. It was his favorite food and Timmy Tim's Donuts had done a wonderful job. It was warm, thick, but not too thick, creamy, cheesy; most of all, it was as broccoli as broccoli could get. *Bryan grunts as he struggles to remember how to spell a five-letter word for corn.*

One thing Guy loved about his suitemate was that he didn't feel the need to talk all the time. While Bryan actually enjoyed talking, he rarely did so in front of Guy. He viewed Guy as conceited and eccentric and Guy knew how he felt. Rather than changing his opinion, Guy purposefully compounded his view since he believed that if he didn't, Bryan would talk his ears off.

Soon, Guy was done and Bryan had given up on the crossword puzzle. They were ready to go.

Bryan reaches into his wallet.

GUY:　　No, you drove. It's on me. *(Bryan smiles.)*

Guy leaves $5.00 for the waitress and hands $12.50 to Tim who is at the silver cash register.

TIM:　　You guys have to leave so soon?

BRYAN:　Yeah, Man. See ya tomorrow!

MARGARET: Bye gentlemen!
　　　　　　Thank you!
　　　　　　(She smiles at Bryan, naturally assuming that it wasn't his defiant-looking friend who had left the tip.)

TIM:　　Bye Bryan! Bye Guy!

Tim rhymed "Guy" with "bye," much to Guy's annoyance.

Guy grabs the door and they are out. He turns towards where the birds were eating earlier. No crumbs remain on the parking space ahead.

GUY: It's beautiful weather. You go ahead; my adventurous feet are vying to tread this here ground.

BRYAN: You sure?

GUY: Yeah. *(He gives Bryan the stern glance that always keeps him away.)*

BRYAN: Alright, Man. Take it easy!

GUY: See ya. Thanks for the ride.

Bryan looked confused at Guy until he realized that he was thanking him for the ride to the restaurant, not the ride back. He smiled, started the engine, and drove off.

Guy walked towards Mr. KG's truck on the other side of the parking lot. Right by his front left wheel lay a jumbo paperclip. Guy leaned over, picked it up, and blew the dirt off. He couldn't help but touch the huge wheel of the truck with the back of his hand as he straightened himself. His large hand returned dark brown, soft with mud.

GUY: Where did K get his tires this dirty?

Guy had a mind to march right back into Timmy Tim's Donuts and strike up a conversation with KG. Guy wasn't one for mysteries. However, he knew that he'd have to return K's paperclip to him if he accosted him, and *that* he didn't feel like doing.

Instead, Guy promptly dived into the hay in Mr. KG's stake bed truck until his clandestine body was completely concealed. He lay on his right side with his nose and mouth against the wooden slabs that defined

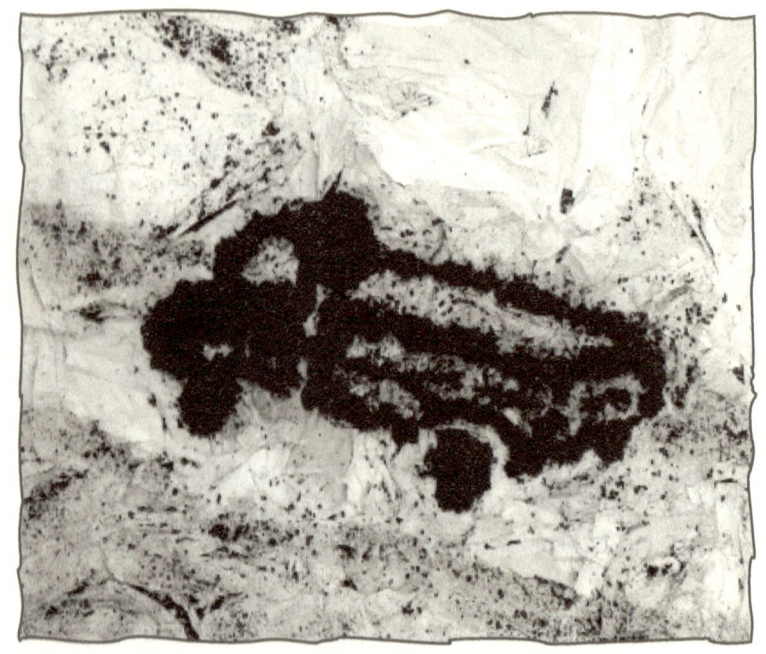

KG's Stake Bed Truck

the right side of the cargo bed.

While in the truck, Guy decides to ascribe the name "Ken Gates" to the mystery driver, after a manager at the apartment complex where he grew up.

Soon, he heard the hastened pace of Ken Gates's leather boots. Within one minute and twenty-seven seconds, they were off.

TRUCK OF HAY
XII

Guy struggled all of two minutes to stay awake and see where the old truck was taking him. Naturally, the bumpiness, coupled with his need to stay low, made his reclining posture strappingly convenient. The soothing scent of the hay contributed to the soporific urges he ardently fought. However, his anemia and his environment got the better of him.

The rhythm of the road intensified once Ken Gates drove deeper into the country. The gait of his vehicle was no longer a trot, but a gallop at full speed. There were no lights beside the dirt roads that lay ahead. There were no traces of Eisenhower's road reform of the fifties, either.

Despite the increased speed of the stake bed truck hopping about the loud gravel, Guy was deep in sleep. He was having another one of his haunting nightmares in which he had to lay the last brick on the building he designed before he could wake up. He searched far and wide for the single brick, but they had all been used for the nearby prison. Consequently, he was stuck in his nightmare, as usual.

The sun was at its brightest yet. It was 10:30 a.m., four hours since Guy had taken refuge in the hay truck. The large tires were muddier than ever. In a flash of vital luck, a brick was delivered to Guy and he immediately pressed the last punctuation mark in place, securing his freedom from his latest project. Instead of waking up relieved, having gained the right to live upon finishing another beautiful building, he woke up incredibly agitated, for the brick was red, unlike the rest of the ochre structure.

The situation reminded him of a phrase he had learned. He tried to find the huge chalk he kept under his pillow so that he could write down the Russian saying on the wall half-consciously. However, the scent of hay shook off this desire.

TRUCK: BUMP!

GUY: Truck of Hay. What a cozy arrangement indeed! I know not how far we've trekked, in which direction we've flown.

Every right have I to feel shaven, my precious porcupine pins lie all around my bruised limbs. Yet, the oval triangle that is confusion massages the hoarded holes until all that can be sensed is this buttery breath of the beyond! Haha! I am not scared.... Psssst! *(spits out some hay that has just crept in)* ...Nor am I amused.

Shakily, he felt his right upper pocket for the paperclip he had found earlier beside the vehicle. He grabbed his needle-nose pliers from his left middle pocket and started sculpting an anonymous object named either Gus or Fred (those were his names of choice).

TRUCK: BUMP!

GUY: Mr. G, if you would only slow down! It's nearly impossible to sculpt under these grey conditions! Lights! In the middle of emptiness.... I smell humans about!

The truck stopped. He returned his pliers to his pocket and tossed Fred out of the truck, towards the gas nozzle. It looked up at him, beckoning him to come down.

GUY: *(whispers)* No, Fred! Save yourself!

The transformed paperclip remained there, looking up at him. Soon, Fred tilted over as an aggressive wind lifted him from his awkward position on the ground.

Guy felt the truck shake as Ken Gates slammed the door to pay for gas.

GUY: Alright! I'm coming!

With a sudden jolt of energy, Guy sprang out of the truck, flinging hay everywhere. He placed his hands on the top wooden slat and proceeded to swing his body overboard when suddenly the weathered red oak slat broke. He froze an instant, looking at Fred the Paperclip imploringly. Realizing he was an idiot for seeking assistance from a lifeless paperclip named Fred, he shook his head and continued to jump over the broken piece of wood.

He leaned low, swept up Fred, and ran off before Mr. Gates returned. When he realized he was leaving a trail of hay, he started sprinting for his life.

GUY: So much for spreading smiles—*puff puff*—KG seemed so calm. Orange with discomfort and scratchy with fear he shall be found.

Discomfort, I hate you. Yet, here I am, disseminating your wonderment!

MEADOW HOME
XIII

Guy pressed his finger roughly on the freshly escaped vision which trammeled his body exasperatingly. He dropped Fred who was hanging unwittingly from his left hand, and he ran. He ran. He had a vague idea of a destination.

Guy was drenched in delirious comfort as one who knows exactly what he feels and more importantly, exactly what he needs. So he ran, clutching onto the dripping, pernicious green beast that he had thus far tried to strangle. Now, his fingers and his hands were mazes of veins inside which his vitality flowed, fully aware of the imminent changes that lurked beyond. The obstruction was to be broken forever.

So he ran, for as long as he could, racing as quickly as his muscular legs would allow. He ran on, when suddenly, he ceased to feel his aching hip and the side-splitting pains that resonated in his head. For about sixty meters beyond a bush lay a little being, weeping and tearing the grass off the ground, then throwing it into the embracing, sympathetic warmth of the dark air that enveloped each strand and caressed its fine green stripes as it came trickling back down, some strands clinging to her frail, soggy body. As Guy approached, her melancholic expression intensified because he seemed to bring the sweet, serene neutrality of the sky.

When he was younger, Guy used to put lukewarm water in a jug and dip his left middle finger to see how deep his finger would go before the temperature apprised him that it was in a different environment. At this moment, when the woman began to turn away from him, he felt as if his whole body was suddenly plunged deep into the Caspian. A large temperature difference piqued his senses and he was no longer able to ignore the physical world that chilled him back to logic and reasoning through experience and research.

Watching Woman Throw Grass

From afar, the woman seemed small. He crept closer and saw her spirited five-foot-six-inch frame. Her dress shot blue velvet tinges of cognizance all over. He remembered the dress very well, and the vision of blue chestnuts that momentarily draped his view.

As soon as her soulful brown eyes thronged towards his heaving body, he froze, not daring to encroach upon her mystical world. She shocked him immediately; her gaze alone pelted soft, chilling vapor that slowly beleaguered Guy.

She jerked away from the ground and darted towards an evergreen as Guy recovered from the drastic, ethereal temperature difference.

He suddenly felt dizzy and couldn't help but push his palms deeply onto his forehead which housed a most maddening migraine.

GUY: She runs off. Always running. Always interrupting my thoughts. Crazy stalker! It's as clear as a rusty diamond smear: she's a strange one.

He felt a little disheartened as he watched her run. He needed to tell her to stop. He needed to run after her. Still, he knew she wouldn't tell him where they were. Before long, she was completely gone.

Guy looks away.

ROBIN: Shi shi eur her er er er shi er eor er!

GUY: When was it last that I've breathed such a pastel, crystal air? Truly cleansing is this magical meadow. Why, just staring at that huge river over there is purification.

ROBIN: She eur eer shi fi fi sheu—

GUY: Fi fi fireur freee free freefree foreur ererer!

ROBIN: Free fri for eur shu shu oor orr sshe shi ii ii ii ii!

GUY: Fri fri feoer shi shi foeuer eor shi shi ii ii.

The robin flies twenty-eight feet to a tree branch right above Guy.

SEA GULL: Aaaaauuuuuuurr! Aaaaaaauuuuur!

CARDINAL: TWEEEeeeeeet. TweeeEEEEt
           Tweetweetweetweetweetweetweetweetwee!

BLACK SPARROW: Tweet Tweet!

ROBIN: Sshe shee oeur eer er er er!

GUY: Ii ii ii ii ii fre fre forer eehr eehr!

Guy continued chirping with the robin whose eyes seemed to be firmly stuck onto her head with excess glue. Two minutes in, he spotted the bright flame in the sky that was the noble male cardinal.

Even though his conversation with the cardinal outlasted the dialogue between him and the robin, he felt a special attachment to his welcomer who had defecated right in front of him upon learning that Guy was not an alpha male as she had thought. She continued tilting her head, silently examining the strange figure.

Guy felt at home since the birds spoke the same unique language there as they did on campus. He proceeded to end the conversation with the cardinal in his unique Guy-bird tune reserved for farewells. Then he looked up at the little female spy, but as he started to tell her goodbye, she flew away to a neighboring tree.

GUY: Haha! If I weren't getting so exhausted, Buddy, I'd chat with you for hours!

He saw some brightly lit berries in a tree but noticed that they were all untouched. No animal bothered eating them so he didn't want to be an anomaly. He spotted the glistening of blue-orange scales in the nearby river.

Before long, the cardinal was gone and all he felt was debilitating hunger.

GUY WRESTLES A BEAR
XIV

Guy walks towards the river.

GUY: Fishing is in store. My, what a beautiful river! Now to construct a raft to drift merrily into the Atlantic!

Guy wished he carried away the whole wooden slat that he had broken off Mr. KG's stake bed truck. It would have made a nice broad base for the raft.

Guy looks around and finds some large twigs and logs within a distance of 120 feet.

GUY: *(panting)* Sweating and walking. I'm in no shape to construct anything.

(He sits down.)
This comical distaste I've developed may be the death of me yet. Or, it may be the rare pop of day that shakes me into saving my life.

(looks at the water)
Sadly, I know the truth. With me, all is replaced by the treacherous act of debilitating planning.

I see the movements, the actions. It commences with a brief stroll 120 feet to those logs. Lazy loggerhead! Countless accounts have I read, so many TV shows experienced. Those men weren't any more brilliant than I am! Their foraging ingenuity compares not to my conditioned genius. My raft will be constructed in a flash and will outdo their splints!

No. I'm bushed. No raft for me. Visions are more easily sliced than they are synthesized.

The former seems a natural physical action; the

latter purely theoretical.

(looks afar, holding his throbbing head)
Atlantic, please don't sob. We weren't meant to be as one happy entity. Much too wet already, please don't shed any tear because of me!

Fishing. A dream no longer. I am pursuing this tangible goal right now. But alas! No comforting towel. Just molesters of the Invasive Insect variety.

(He grabs his right shirt sleeve and looks at it for a second, then scans the area.) I must part with you and your cargo friends....

He notices two large willow trees amongst the overwhelming number of evergreens. He looks up the willow with a lighter bark and spots a forked branch fourteen feet above. He then takes off his socks and shoes and proceeds to climb it.

He stops at the forked branch and takes off his shirt. He quickly folds it, sloppily. Then he takes off the rest of his clothes. He folds his pants, with his boxers, haphazardly at first, watching as three paperclips precipitate to the rooty ground. As he folds his shirt, he marvels at the cleanliness of his raiment.

GUY: Not a drop of resin on my clothes! Now let's see if I can climb down without a mark on my brazen body.

Guy's modest posture revealed an infixed physical void. It wasn't that he cared if the bizarre woman came back and was watching him as he dexterously descended from the swollen tree.

The yellow discomfort he felt was not the flirty air's doing either, as it shamelessly spread over his body. Rather, he had grown used to the rigid sensation of his pugnacious pliers thwapping against the side of his left leg (they had torn a small hole in his pocket). The curious purple bruise felt more abandoned than free.

He soon reached the ground. The warm earth massaged his feet and he immediately forgot about the brief awkwardness.

GUY: And now, the metamorphosis begins!

Guy catapulted himself into the water. Soon, the round saucer of light upon the tranquil waters was torn into pieces as bits of light rose up in all directions. He immediately felt large fish all around him and tried grabbing them with his hands. Five minutes later, he managed to grab one with his left hand around her head and his right around her tail.

He lifts her up.

GUY: Aha!

The white perch seemed subdued; however, she all of a sudden writhed violently, catching Guy off guard. The fish managed to free herself from his dark-red fingers, slapping his right wrist with her tail on her way back into the water.

Guy returned to land and saw a bright sparkle on the ground. He surreptitiously approached the thing, and then realized it was just the three paperclips that had fallen from the pockets of his pants.

GUY: Now to find bait and assemble an amazing fish-
         ing hook....

He links the first two paperclips and stretches apart one end, forming a hook. He then digs out a worm and pets it.

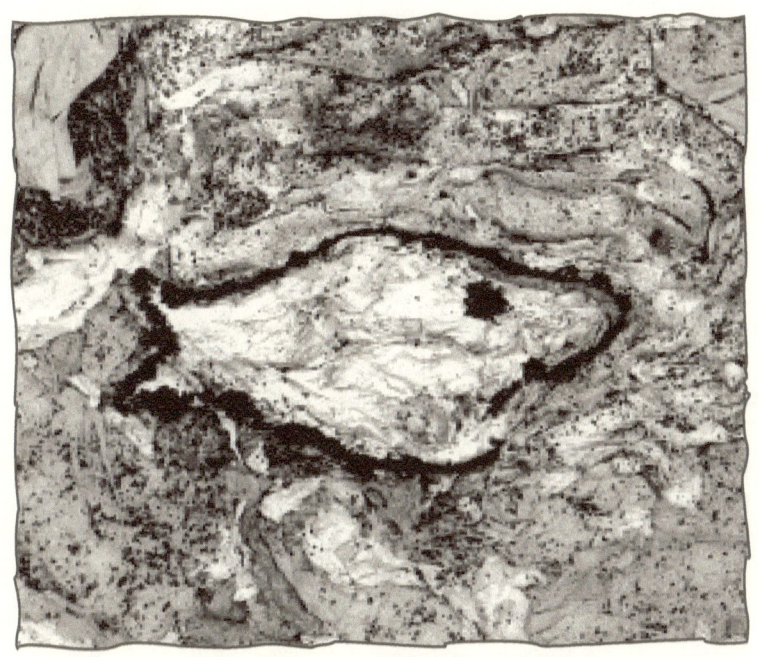

Brett the Fish

GUY: Don't worry, Creepy Corpulent Pink Friend. I
         wouldn't impale you for sport. Sure, I'll eat you
         live if I don't catch a plump fish, but I would
         never impale a friend.

*He finds a bright red leaf and tears it into a stringy worm. He
then attaches it to the deadly, albeit blunt, hook.*

*He waits for about seven minutes, huddled on the muddy dirt
shore. Finally, a fish bites.*

GUY: Waaah! Blaglababa! Ima getchu Brett!! Blaaah!

He grabs Brett's large striped body tightly with his free hand, then quickly releases the fishing rod for backup.

He straightened out the third paperclip and used it as a knife. Mindful of the pain he could inflict, the blow was swift and the execution was reinforced by his nails. The cut was accurate, and the striped bass was in two in less than two seconds. The action caused Guy's unhealthy hands to feel as if they too had been cut in half.

GUY: AAAaaaah!

His fingers were throbbing intensely. He was soon distracted from his pain by what seemed to be a broken whistle being blown just beyond the meadow. The minced notes were mobilizing and soon, Jean Shepard's "Second Fiddle to an Old Guitar," jovially moistened this seemingly fitting environment. Guy quickly put the headless fish in his mouth and bit deeply so that the large body didn't fall as he scurried up the tree, towards his folded clothes.

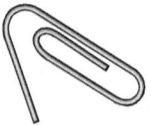

He tasted the strains of life crawling around the curves of his lips. Although his teeth pierced through the meat of the headless carcass, very little blood trickled down his chin as he hastened up the dormant tree.

Once atop, he quickly, but delicately, removed the bleeding

bass from his mouth. He held the body in his right hand and then wedged the fish in between a large branch and its teenage offspring.

Still excited about the catch, he didn't bother drying himself off as he proceeded to carefully clothe himself, all the while spying a tall, lanky hunter who returned to the meadow to pick up his hunting permit which he had left there earlier that morning.

The hunter, a seventy-four-year-old man named GUS, suddenly froze behind a large evergreen. He felt grateful that he had brought his gun with him, for around four hundred meters in front of him pranced a jolly, strong deer, oblivious to the imminent danger.

The obstinately passionate deer, "Fred," had just badly injured his cousin to win over Kookook, a healthy, attractive doe. Fred had practically bartered his soul for her noble affection. His cousin, a slightly broader buck who had ogled Kookook for seven whole seconds, was rudely interrupted by Fred who spread out his magnificent body almost awkwardly in between this *other guy* and his beloved Kookook. As he and his smelly rival wrestled violently, Kookook could not be heard as she dashed merrily away, her conceited chuckles making a nearby sensitive squirrel spectator cough with disgust.

Fred was enraptured by his own quickness. He rammed his antlers into the other buck. When he realized that his damsel had vanished, he skipped away without searching for her or even nonchalantly casting his injured cousin an apologetic glance. He merely basked in his shiny bright orange armor and trotted away, remembering the bloody brawl with fondness. He forgot about Kookook who was at one point foremost in his mind.

GUS'S GUN: POOOOOOH! POOOOOOH!

The hunter shot a distracted Fred in the heart and then in the head. He rushed towards the deer, as if it would evaporate within a twinkling bristle of the ripening fern.

Guy walks towards the hunter. Meanwhile, Gus looks down austerely at Fred.

GUS: *Where were you this morning, Bud?*

GUY: Nice shot, Sir!

Gus slowly turns his head to the left and smiles upon seeing the tall, handsome young man.

GUS: Howdy-do, Son!

GUY: Hi. Are you gonna cook him now?

Gus looks deeply into Guy's large blue eyes.

GUS: Intend to do just that, Son.

His practically nonexistent lips formed a very large, calm, wrinkly smile.

GUY: Awesome! I would love to eat Brett here. *(He raises the fish in his right hand and uses his left hand to unwrap the leaves absorbing his blood.)*

GUS: He's a beaut! Ne'er seen a rockfish caught that big in this here meadow! Then 'gain, not many fishermen 'round here—mostly hunters'n even them're scarce.

GUY: Please, just let me know what you'd like me to do and I'll do it. I haven't made a large fire in quite some time.

GUS: Alrighty, just pick up a handfulla twigs'n a buncha large sticks from a dead tree. 'N if you could peel off 'bout a handfulla some bark from a peely river birch tree, that'd be perfect.

Before long, most of the deer's blood had seeped all over the grass. Guy was happy to distance himself from the distinctly fresh smell of death. Although his grandpa had taken him hunting many times when he was a child, Guy had not grown unaffected by that smell of decay.

GUY: *How ironic that the scent of life's cessation could smell so vile, yet so sharp and lasting.... Piques my senses every time.*

While Guy searched for standing deadwood, the strong old man strung the deer with rope upon a very low branch of a birch tree. Guy's headache worsened with every reach and pull. He tried to sing softly, but he felt it too somber a situation to do so. After what seemed like an hour, the gorgeous firewood was finally gathered. Gus immediately set the wood aflame with two metal sticks he had in his pocket. By that time, he had thoroughly skinned Fred. Guy offered to disembowel the buck, but Gus refused the kind lad's help.

Guy's stomach yelped. It was not objecting to the stench of the green feces from Fred's intestine. Guy preferred that odor to pungent artificial scents like his suitemate's cologne. Rather, he felt the vibrations of echoes coming from the loud, insatiable voice of hunger.

Guy insisted on helping, and soon, he was placing the wet insides in a tub for Gus to take to his Italian neighbor who was fond of tripe.

Soon, the fish and the deer's left thigh joined the captivating fire dance that enthralled the bugs who flew too close. The birds perched high in the evergreen trees were also enchanted; they felt the force of the fire as it arched its way into their paralyzed periphery.

The men began to eat. A small bright-winged beetle flew onto Guy's left index finger as he ate. He looked at it closely, internally marveling at the amazing straightness of its perfectly spaced green stripes. Guy's eyes then shifted to Gus, whose perspiring face reflected light from the few sunbeams that had managed to seep through the tall branches above. The thick veins on Gus's hands, however, did not seem to experience the sun's warmth; interestingly, his tenebrous hands, which were not hit by sun rays, didn't seem to glisten at all despite feeling the brunt of the fire's more formidable blaze.

Guy wanted eagerly to explore the fascinating ray of fog that was Gus's tender mind. He waited anxiously for an invitation.

GUS: Ma Boy, you seem much too tense. What's ailin' ya? Live!

GUY: My fingertips. I think it's cuz of my anemia. I can't even stroke a feather with 'em, let alone write. So I hold my pens and everything in uncomfortable positions. I'll never become an architect with all this pain.

The bright sun shone fiercely, much to the delight of Guy's fingers. Although speaking about his fingers usually incited more pain, at that moment he didn't feel the slightest discomfort. He was completely immersed in the conversation, as evidenced by the gradual assimilation of Gus's accent.

GUS: Raynaud's Syndrome. Happens to many young folks in 'er twenties. But ain't no disease existin' without its unstoppable combatant! Soak yer fingertips twice daily in a paste composed of black seeds'n warm water. Them black seeds 're called *Nigella* if I 'member correct. You can get 'em at any ethnic food store. Put yer fingers in this water mixture for 'bout fifteen minutes. *(Guy listens attentively, registering everything permanently for posterity.)*

Sure, see, I've had so many diseases, been constantly in pain'n died three times. Them AED heart revivers're really somethin'. But I kept sayin', "Ain't no way I'm gonna die before my baby's big," cuz see, my health fell way down by the wayside right after she was born. My wife'n I was so poor, but know what she kept sayin' to me?

GUY: "You'll get better soon"?

GUS: No, Sir! She said she ain't prayin' for me to recover cuz I ain't yet reaped no benefits!

GUY: How'd she figure?

GUS: I always keep what my dear Marigold wrote me in my pocket. *(He takes out an aged yellow sheet of paper and carefully unfolds it four times.)*

GUS: She wrote:

My Dearest Gustavito,

Them fools make fun. They say you's cursed when really, it's the sick and the dyin' who's blessed. You have the opportunity. You feel like it's almost over'n it might be, but every precious instant's rich. No foolin'. Yer more alive 'an any others cuz you know what it is to feel. As for the sick ones like you who's recoverin', you just wait, you'll see; there ain't nothin' like renewed life. Take the time to feel the pain'n embrace it. Don't be all suicidal now, that'll be wrong cuz we'll be miserable if you do.

(Gus pauses briefly. He smiles and shakes his head, looking down.)

No, Gus, I don't pray for you to be all perfect yet. Recoverin' now would be a shame cuz you ain't yet put leashes 'round yer pain and steered the pain to makin' yer strength stronger. You need to change mentally and this is yer time. No more worries. So I pray for you, once you's a strong man (and you hafta get stronger, no choice!), I pray you use yer God-given creativity, individuality, and ingenuity til you breathe yer last cuz ain't nothin' more satisfyin' than bein' able to work'n doin' so, takin' full 'vantage of yer mobility.

Guy stares at the letter in Gus's hand. The hunter's lips try hard to arrest his eyes, but his eyes are too affected and a tear runs down his cheek. Gus wipes his nose with the side of his tanned right arm.

GUS: *(smiles)* Hadn't read that in quite a bit. She was a poet, God rest her soul. Such spirit! Well, Son, you will be that architect you dream of becomin'.

When times get rough you can either become stronger or lose completely. You don't look like a loser!

GUY: You're right. I've been losing too much.

Guy picks up a huge piece of meat and marvels at the perfectly printed gradient of brownish grey.

Guy finished his fish and declined eating any part of the deer. He felt slightly nauseous (unlike a female BEAR whose baby sang as he rubbed his clean fur on her leg).

GUY: Thanks a lot for helpin' me cook the fish, Sir.

GUS: Don't mention it. *(Gus smiles and then takes a big bite into the deer's shank.)*

GUY: And for sharin' those moving words of your wife—may she rest in peace. I will certainly heed your words, Sir. *(Noticing that Gus is still chewing, he continues talking. Gus finally swallows the last of the masticated meat in his mouth.)*

I should be off, but would you mind telling me the name of this town?

GUS: *(chuckling)* You're in Bakerstown.

GUY: Sweet! This is where Theresa lives!
(He gets up.)

GUS: ...Now go get them black seeds!

GUY: Yes, Sir!

Although the river was a good four hundred feet away, the wide, knowing delta could be seen in Gus's kind, lambent eyes which inspired Guy so. Gus's comforting wrinkles joked with one another as they danced upon his tranquil face. Guy felt as if his whole left side had become stale as soon as he realized that he was leaving this jovial old man. It was a very uncomfortable feeling, more unpleasant than anything he had ever felt. He knew something was wrong.

Guy bows his head and bids Gus adieu.

He started walking back towards his willow dresser, as if it were his home. He wondered where he had placed the fish bones; he didn't recall eating them nor putting them on the ground. While wondering if it was proper to leave bones by his hunter friend, he all of a sudden felt terribly uneasy. Less than a second later, he knew exactly why the ghastly, foreboding vibes shot up his spine erratically.

GUS: # Aaaah!

Guy quickly turned around and ran to help his grey-haired friend. The cool spring air traced his body as he trampled the bug-ridden grass with the pressure of his leaden feet.

GUS: # BaaaAaah!

The seventy-four-year-old man was trying to make himself appear huge by waving a wide, muddy stick with his right hand, and a thinner, dry one with his left. He was jumping forward and backwards, diagonally and sideways, all the while facing the biggest black beast Guy had ever seen.

She was a 452-lb black bear that had to be at least six feet

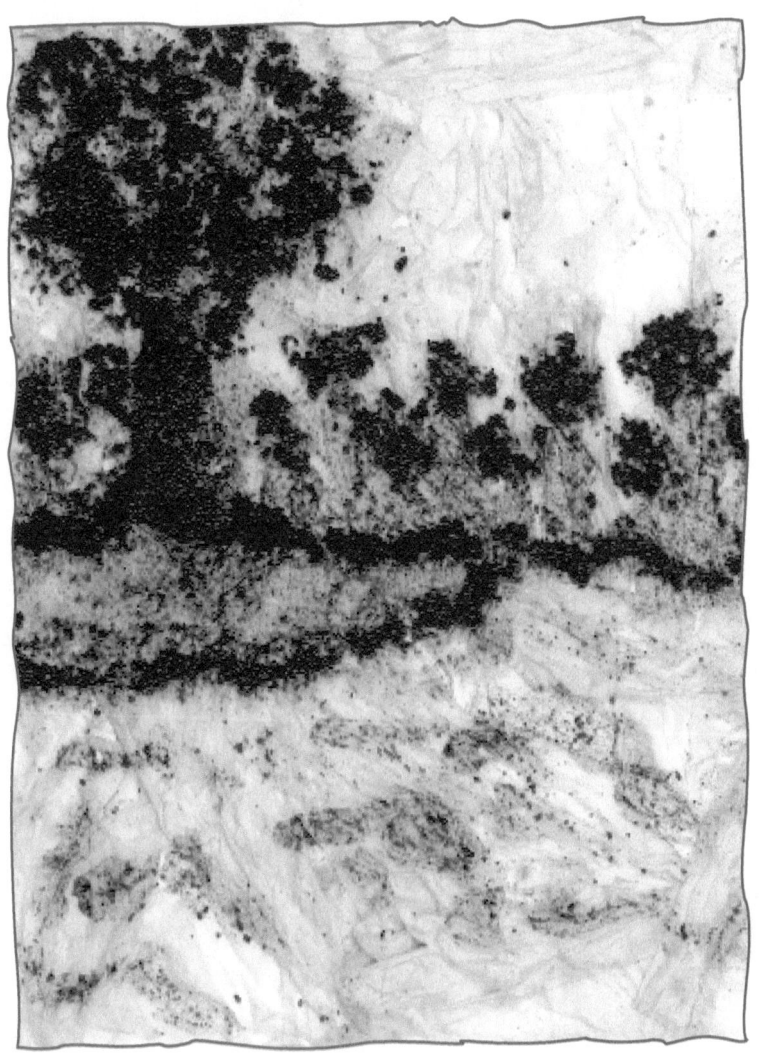

Guy's Willow Dresser

of pure, dense bulk. She could never be outpaced.

Her baby waited for game. Fred, the strung deer, intensified in color although his body seemed frozen with fright at the nearby tango-pokie that ensued between the ginormous, elegant beauty and the wiry, pale mammal.

Once within a hundred meters of the spectacle, Guy grabbed the sturdy wooden vines that zigzagged up a pallid oak tree. He immediately felt the wrath of the violent vines upon his fiery fingertips. He shook his hands for an instant and scurried up the tree using his legs and knuckles until he reached the lowest branch which maintained a good distance of fifteen feet from the wild earth.

GUS: **Bwaaah!**
BEAR: **ROOOoooooaaaaar!**

The bear had observed Gus from afar, so she knew very well that Gus was only pretending to be crazy; his temperament was too placid for him to be rabid. Bear welcomed Gus to try to bite her. She thought the match would be most interesting.

BEAR: **Gaaaaaaar!**
        Enough is enough. If you will not attack, I will.

Bear quickly advanced. Gus dashed straight ahead, not looking back. His legs never sipped the tandem of muscular dystrophy and old age. He ran faster than Guy who was ready to anchor into the air.

Finally, Gus is a foot in front of Guy's mossy platform.

Guy leaped downward into the froward, heavy air, extending his long, patient arms. His dusty brown hair flew perfectly behind him as if it was its duty to keep Guy balanced in the air.

Guy was very anemic and his fingers started shaking rapidly. His body acted as if he had long since smoked his patterned reasoning on a porch with invisible, generous foes.

Pure impulses pulsated in his purple fingers. Void of energy, and low in hemoglobin, he had no choice but to listen to the parts of his dehydrated body that demanded attention: his heavily armored, strangulated head and his now bloody fingers that had dug into the shoulders of Bear, close to her neck.

GUS: I'll go get my gun!

GUY: No you shall **not**! For Bear is my—**friend**!

With "friend," he began digging his sneakers into the bear's sides. She shook violently to remove the murky bacteria that cut her open. Instead of shaking Guy off, the writhing allowed the six-foot-four microbe to dig deeper into her body. The tennis-playing parasite atop Bear would have fared excellently in the national mechanical bull riding competition held in Indiana the day before. He would undoubtedly have won second prize, losing only to the rising star, a short, focused farmer who, like Guy, would never ride a real bull for fear of harming his bovine brother.

Guy would not let go of Bear's soft, clean fur. He saw Gus race back towards his gun.

GUY: You shoot my buddy, you shoot **me**!

Gus knew Guy was exhausted and felt that the poor crazy kid was in grave danger. He picked up the rifle.

About forty-five trees away, the cute CUB was toying with

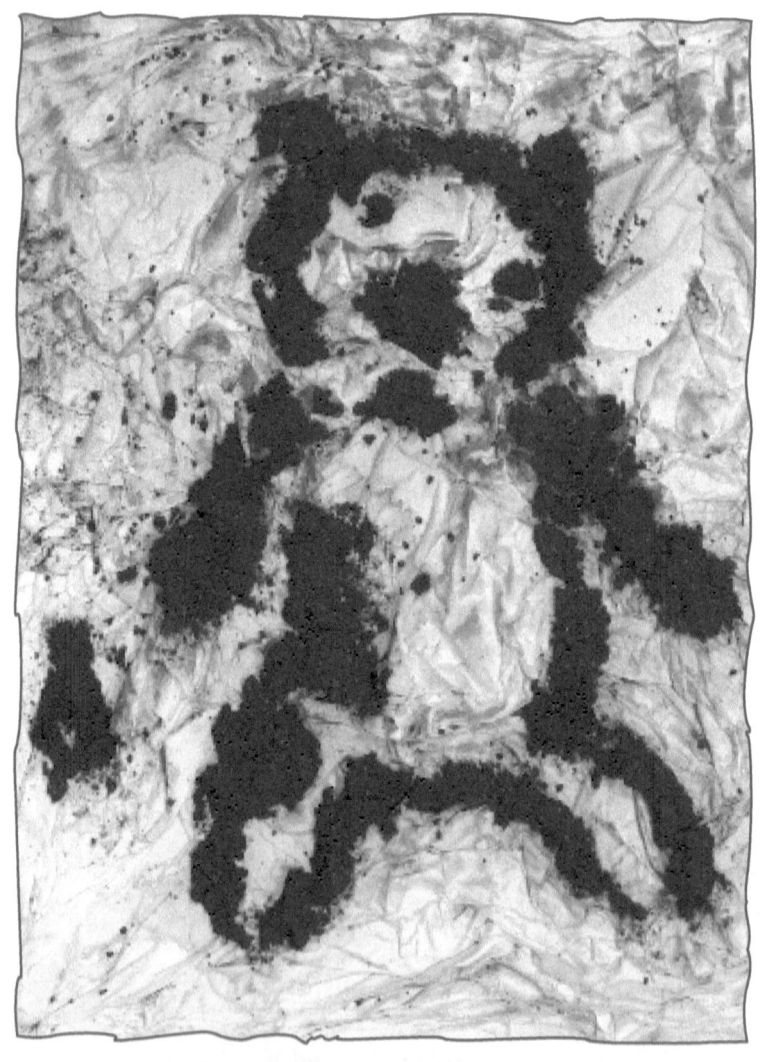

Bear & Cub

the long grass by his lair, waiting anxiously for his single mother. (One week after Cub was born, his father was killed by an annihilative drunkard who was driving 80 mph in pitch darkness.)

Bear was grateful that Guy did not bite into her neck. He spared her face and heart as well. Guy did not want to kill his furry chum, so they continued their rodeo dance. Guy jammed his left foot into the tiring bear's rib and the animal turned so that Guy was directly across from Gus and his rifle.

Gus finally regained his breath; his shooting hand was now steady. He was still a little dizzy (which imperiled his aim), but he didn't have time to run a bit closer. Gus had to save his ally, as the lad had just saved him.

The cub grew impatient and raced to find his mother, not realizing that a giddy gun was waiting to have as much fun as it could that day.

Guy and Bear continue to wrestle.

BEAR: Rooaar!

The roar was subdued and Guy knew it meant "You win!" The tennis cowboy loosened his grip and let the bear launch him away.

Clearly, the bear was running away from Guy and Gus, but Gus had his mind set on saving the young man.

GUS: Ready, Aim—

CUB: **ROOOOoooooaar!**

Gus was very confused. He saw the bear limping away ahead of him, yet he literally shook by the sheer volume of her roar. The old man had had too much excitement. He pondered the strange situation.

GUS: Am I hearin' things'n my imagination shakin' me?

The giggling gun stroked Gus's finger, encouraging him to shoot at someone. The tired old hunter had no reason to argue.

Cub found the deer that Gus feasted on earlier and immediately started chomping, not caring about the bedazzled man with the glittery eyes admiringly cast towards Guy who was so young and healthy. (Gus already forgot their conversation earlier, for Guy did expose to Gus two of his most menacing ailments.)

Guy examines the sky for birds; he doesn't see any.

BEAR & CUB: Roaar!

Gus understood. He quickly turned around, aimed at the horrible offspring of the evil bear, and he sho—

RIFLE: Pooooooh!

GUS: Hey!

Guy had kicked the gun upwards. The low clouds did their best to conceal the smiling, naked bullet as it jerked up into the foggy grey sky.

Gus tried to kill Guy's ursine friend despite his desperate supplication. There was no way he would let him harm Bear's baby.

Guy snatched the gun. Gus was not at all scared of his young companion as Guy motioned him to head towards his pickup truck.

FUELIN' UP
XV

Guy refused a ride, saying he was meeting someone at the gas station. He saw Gus's chariot off and climbed into his dresser tree, as high up as he could.

Gus didn't care about leaving the deer. He was grateful to be alive. Now collected, he whistled his own folk song all the way back to his brick home.

Guy watches intensely as his friend limps towards her cub. Her son boastfully presents the deer parts he found and then continues eating.

It was now 1:45 p.m. and Guy was ready to go home to write a few chapters of his play (after he finished his homework). The encouraging sight in front of him helped him forget his fatigue. His effervescent thirst, however, could not be assuaged. *Guy walks towards the gas station.*

BIRDS: Chirp! Tweet! Twouhtweeit! Chirp! Tweet!

GUY: Tweet... Tweet!

ROBIN: Fri e Fri er shi shi free eur er er ii ii!

GUY: Fri feur uer uer ii ii shi ii fri er er eur free!

ROBIN: Tweet!

GUY: Tewee whert twee hert tri tri!

ROBIN: Tri!

GUY: Tri.

The robin flew away. Guy knew he was going to miss the meadow where he didn't have to feign friendliness or conform to look dignified. He was fully Guy; his feathered friends obliterated any loneliness as they flew freely about his head.

Guy tarried six minutes more and found himself at the green gas station. He grabbed a dark-brown T-shirt and two bottles of water. He immediately opened one of the bottles and started gulping for dear life as he walked towards the cashier, a pleasant young chap from Latin America.

LUCIANO: $17.50. Will that be all?

Guy places the water bottles in his pockets.

GUY: Yes, please. *(He pays Luciano in cash.)*
         Where are your bathrooms?

LUCIANO: You'll need this key. *(He hands Guy a wooden
         block with "CPU" engraved towards the top, away
         from where the key hangs.)*

         Go outside and it's along the right side.

GUY: Thank you.

Guy wondered if people often walked into that gas station smelling as putrid, or looking as dirty and bloody as he did. He appreciated Luciano's disinterest.

Guy exits the gas station and holds the door open behind him in case someone else walks out.

He looked up at the sky and was grateful for the additional fog which further grayed the spiritless sky. Upon reaching the bathroom he felt a tinge of excitement, for right outside the bathroom lay a shiny, small paperclip. He immediately picked it up, raising it to his eyes.

GUY: A wonderful sign!

He changed his shirt, leaving his bloody white tee in the freshly lined trash can. After returning the key to the surprisingly clean bathroom, he reached into his lower left pocket, took out his cell phone, and called THERESA, the assiduous brunette he used to have a crush on.

TRAIN TO NOWHERE
XVI

Theresa drove seven miles to the gas station where she greeted Guy with a smile. His innocent wide eyes of blue softly praised her kindness as he opened the door and hopped in.

Guy forgot how calm she was. He was reminded by her mellow countenance and by her innate ability to maintain a speed of 42 mph on the road where the speed limit was 40.

THERESA: Before I drop you off, you're eating at my place.

Guy quickly sculpts the gas station paperclip into a figure resembling a hippo.

GUY: Thanks, Theresa, but I have to go finish my project; I have to be at the train station as soon as possible. I appreciate the offer, though.

I will treat you to lunch next Wednesday, okay? Ojalá. Yo te prometo.

Theresa smiled as she made a right turn. Was she smiling at his unconvincing Spanish accent? She remembered how she would always see him on the tennis courts or in the library. No, it was a sweet, understanding smile which told Guy, "Don't worry, you too will graduate soon and learn. Instead of your numerous balls, you'll be juggling striped clubs soon enough!"

THERESA: Sure, whatever you say, Guy! But you still haven't told me how you got here.

GUY: I found a pond of pale cow food and dived right in. It wasn't processed yet, so rather than eat, I swam for four hours and got up for air in this here village. *(He takes out another paperclip from his pocket and begins to sculpt a bee.)*

THERESA: Mmmhmm.... I suppose this liquid hay evaporated before you could swim back?

GUY: No, the hay still floats over yonder. It was purely by luck that I swam up for air in your vicinity. If I were to swim back, there's no telling when or where my orange lungs would demand their feed. I could even end up in Jersey.

THERESA: You done with your museum project yet, Mr. Poet?

GUY: It's become a swampy project.

THERESA: So swampy you're staying away? Taking a break?

GUY: I shouldn't be, but lo. Homework is strangling.

He was indeed behind in three of his classes, but that wasn't at all what prevented him from promptly finishing his Studio project. It was his commandeered fingers who were screaming at him through their knotted tips.

THERESA: Well, Busy Boy from Hay Waters, here we are.

Guy looks outside the window at the quaint mahogany train station. He then turns to Theresa who smiles at her friend three years her junior.

GUY: These sculptures are for you. This one's a hippo and this is Maya.

THERESA: Oh my goodness! They're so cute! You made these with pliers and paperclips?

GUY: You actually don't need pliers. Just bend them.

THERESA: Cool! *(She marvels at the well-crafted creations, then looks up at Guy.)* You need any money?

GUY: No thanks. You've been so helpful, Theresa, I appreciate everything greatly. Wednesday I'll be driving over here to pick you up to take you to the restaurant of your choice... unless you don't mind me choosing a place?

THERESA: You'll be busy, Love. Don't worry. You owe me nothing.

GUY: No! We shall dine next Wednesday. Expect a text message. *(He shuts the car door.)* Bye! *(glances above the opened car window at his sweet friend for an instant, then walks away)*

The brick train station was very cozy. There were five maroon sofas and four chairs by the ticket counter. Pastoral paintings adorned the brown walls.

Guy heard a "tweet!" and was about to respond when he heard the same sound repeated at regular intervals. It was the wheels of an old lady's suitcase.

His feathery friends, Popcorn, Bungie, Feathey, Butter, Gaston, Iris, Sundance, Moss, Tulip, and Spirit, all flew into his mind, joining whatever desultory thoughts abided within. Their whistles (especially those of Popcorn, Bungie, and Tulip, the lovebirds) would greet him each time he entered the apartment. Then he tenderly remembered Dallas, his bright blue parakeet, and missed him. Dallas fot very sick and passed away two years after he was given to Guy thirteen years ago. Spirit resembled Dallas in color and flew out the window once, never to return. The rest were given away when his mom became allergic to them.

Guy's mind returned to the train station. The scarcity of life made his conscience heave. The three people who were sitting quickly appeased him by inviting their quintuplet siblings. Guy laughed as he imagined their siblings dancing erratically.

TICKET AGENT: Hello.

Guy was at the front desk. The greeting startled him. He turned his head from the nimble loonies of his mind, and met the face of FELIX, a man about his age, also six feet four inches tall but with blonde, shoulder-length hair. He was a swift runner studying to become an ESOL teacher.

GUY: Hi, I'd like to purchase a day pass.

FELIX: Day pass?

GUY: I am not sure where I'll be needed and when.

FELIX: We don't offer that here.

GUY: Could I please see your supervisor?

Felix turns away and brings a portly, curly-haired woman of about thirty-five years of age whose name tag says PAM.

PAM: What's the problem.

Her monotonous voice amused Guy.

GUY: Not a problem, but an inquiry regarding a necessity.
         I follow the *(says the name of his favorite larva slowly:)* **Caaaaterpiiillaar see,**
         But he evades me ever so often.

         Now, Caterpillars are a peaceable group,
         But the head has gone awry.

         He is a powerful bug that must be stopped.
         I need a day pass for easy access to trains,

> For subtle smushing—not stomping life *ex corpore*—
> Is a must in accordance with the Payment Principle.
> Name your price.

PAM: I'll need to see your badge.

GUY: Smelt me! *(face stern)* His electronics could detect it and alas!
> Our plan would spiral into the kiln of fiery loss and regretful pain.
> We only carry around the sculpture as proof.
> X-532 for purpose.

PAM: Sculpture.

Guy presents Pam a paperclip from one of the lower left pockets of his pants; it resembles the silhouette of a junkyard.

PAM: Haha! *(Guy smiles imperiously at having shaken away her monotony.)* Why this looks like a paperclip!

GUY: X-538.

PAM: I thought it was X-532.

GUY: We, the force, shan't be redundant.

PAM: Haha! Listen Honey, if you buy a ticket to the last stop, you can get off at any of the places in between. For the trip back—

GUY: Never a same the place for stay, the force must
        move to grey-starred away.
       (Guy lifts his eyebrows high.)
       I've said too much! Yes, quick!
       The ticket!
       As soon as deliverance permits!

Pam stared blankly at the architect student. He didn't appear the least bit drunk or tired to her. The blasts of energy disagreed entirely with the austere, rebellious features of the lad. She finally decided that he wasn't crazy, just strange.

Felix gave him the ticket after Guy paid one-third in cash and the rest with a credit card. He wished he had brought his checkbook because he knew a spunky check would enjoy sponsoring his capricious trip. Better yet, he would have written out two checks—one for one-eighth of the fare, the other for 24¢ (his favorite number)—so that each could have the opportunity to offer their support. *Felix is a bit scared to smile, but he can't help it.*

FELIX: Thank you.

GUY: Yes. *(He reprehends the amused student with a frown and then glances up at Pam, admonishing the confounded lady with a nod.)*

Guy pretended not to notice the stares of the twenty-five-year-old man with a brown cowboy hat and a jacket much too old-fashioned for his young body. He was holding the slender hand of his attractive sanguine-cheeked wife who was staring in fright at the stranger. The old lady with the chirping wheels was watching Guy as well. She examined him both admiringly and disapprovingly, for she maintained that a poetic man of such good looks shouldn't be wasting his life. She assumed that he was in some sort of gang and that his mother must be worried sick.

If he were in school at that moment, he would be eagerly volunteering to translate the first part of a passage by Tolstoy. He always volunteered at the beginning of class so that he could make a checklist of what he had to do for his Studio project while other students prayed that they weren't on deck to translate the next part.

Instead, he was patiently awaiting a rustic train to ship him somewhere. After ascertaining that the train did indeed go all the way to Savannah, he didn't bother reading the available pamphlets or the big black board behind him which listed all possible destinations.

Finally, Guy boards the train.

He was assigned an aisle seat towards the front of the passenger car, by the bathroom. *He passes his seat and continues until he reaches seat thirty-six which is in the middle of the empty train, right next to a shaking window.*

He decided he liked Bakerstown as he lay down, falling asleep instantly.

THE LILLY GILDS GUY
XVII

The conductor approaches Guy who is lying down across the two seats in front of the old lady originally from South Carolina, judging by her accent.

OLD LADY: I assure you, the lad has a ticket. You needn't wake him. His ticket is for the last stop.

CONDUCTOR: All passengers must have their tickets punched. Sir? *(nudges Guy's left arm)* SIR?

Guy did not budge. The conductor pushed his left shoulder. He didn't feel it. He was about to shake Guy when he saw Guy's ticket sticking out from the side of the Venetian red cushion. He punched a hole in the ticket, put it back in between the seat cushions, and continued on.

At 3:00 p.m., the train arrived at the Clear Spring stop and soon, the car was filled. Two large Trinidadian men were assigned the seats in which Guy was making jerky swimming movements since the train's rhythm was suddenly taped to the beige past. The motion left an unconscious Guy and an exhausted man in a cowboy hat sleeping five seats in front, wiggling and withdrawn. The kind men found two vacant seats at opposite sides of the train, and claimed them so that they didn't bother the sick Guy, whose grateful, unintelligible murmurs happily carried on, uninterrupted.

An hour later, Guy was rudely awakened by a deep pain in his knees and lower back. He couldn't move without the garrulous joints screaming loudly at one another, their voices sending deadly vibrations to the very unappreciative Guy who could barely breathe.

GUY: The train halts. Gather ye the strength to drag your uncooperative corpse to the unsympathetic, impatient door. No. I mustn't bask in this deterministic haste. I must harness this blessed, horrible pain which alone can subject my dilapidated skeleton to the direction of a sound, user-controlled brain!

Now where is that lilly?

This sudden pain percolated into, out from, and back into Guy's once strong body with a vengeance. It was the pain's three-month anniversary. Last time it helped Guy fall behind in all his classes. This time, its mind was set on ruining Guy's pleasure trip. In February, Bryan had rescued four beautiful white lillies from the paper bag that suffocated them in his friend's dorm. The original owner's roommate had covered them because their hideous stench worsened his sinuses. Guy agreed to let Bryan put the poor things in the center of the common room table. That very night, Guy had pain-induced insomnia as his healthy joints abandoned all integrity by shoving utter confusion and thorny, relentless sticks into Guy's frustrated head.

Three days after living off whatever food was within reach of Guy's bed (mostly clementines), he realized that the putrefying, vile smell he couldn't escape came from the kryptonite. One wise hour had witnessed both Guy being shown the dainty winks of pure lillies, and the collapse of the tall man shortly thereafter. Finally, Guy talked to a concerned Bryan who agreed to remove the smelly culprits. That very night, he could sleep once again.

Guy looks down the aisle of the maroon passenger car. He spots a young British boy wearing a bright red baseball cap. His pants were clean but had patches all over and a small hole on his left pant leg which somehow emerged during the train ride.

GUY: I will have to take that. *(Guy weakly snatches the four lillies while his growling stomach protests vehemently.)*

MOM OF PATCHES: Wait, he—

GUY: Sorry Ma'am, but it's not to appear til the agent reaches the maroon-gated theatre. Seeing the signal prematurely would endanger the premises. *(The boy begins to cry upon seeing Guy's stern face. His mother cannot comprehend Guy's words and is about to speak when Guy gently puts his hand on her right arm.)*

No, generous indeed is our government. *(He pulls out $45.00 and hands it to the boy's mother whose tired eyes light up. Guy interrupts her thought just as her mouth opens.)*

No. Speak nothing of this and please avoid carrying lillies this week. *(He looks down at Patches whose wet eyes sparkle upon seeing the money in his mother's hand.)*

My apologies for the inconvenience. *(Guy reaches into his small pocket within his larger right one, pulling out the two paperclips he fashioned into a loving couple the day before. He hands the paperclip sculptures to Patches, puts the stems of the lillies in one of his socks, and leaves the train.)*

Guy didn't remember whether or not the boy took the paperclips, but the sight of shiny alloys falling down would surely have struck his memory. He normally looked to see how people responded to his artwork, but all he could do at that moment was hold back the pain.

He was truly grateful for being awake; he felt the same at that moment as he did the year before, when his usual four hours of sleep a night had quadrupled to sixteen due to his severe anemia. He was frustrated at having forgotten to take his daily vitamins and felt that the excruciating pain was penance for the deadly oversight.

THE BUS
XVIII

Guy's knee joints surrendered to the lillies' incapacitating charm. Luckily, his nose was stuffed up, so their fiendish odor could not easily infiltrate his system. The train stop had a vitamin store where Guy promptly purchased his over-the-counter pills and a couple of oranges. He used his debit card and withdrew $85.00 to cushion his empty wallet. He needed to eat. His nausea amplified the quiet, ever-whining voice of his stomach as he limped to the bus stop down the block.

Judging by the slowness of a man who was also walking towards the bus stop, the bus wasn't coming anytime soon. Guy looked horrible. He struggled to keep his head still and his eyes quite enjoyed extended blinks instead of being halfway open. He peeled one of his oranges, offered slices to his bus stop cohabitants (who refused upon seeing the sickliness of the blue-eyed man), then clandestinely finished the whole thing before a squirrel had a chance to see him eat it. He always ate quickly when he was outside because if ever a squirrel were to find him eating, he would feel obliged to share his food with the hungrier being. Just then, Guy did not have the energy to be generous to a squirrel.

A few minutes later, MATT, the heavyset bus driver, turned his head lethargically to greet the new passengers.

GUY: Hi. Day Pass please.

MATT: $3.50, Sir!

Guy put that exact amount in the jar. He was annoyed at the genuine serenity in the large man's voice.

MATT: Thanks and have a nice day!

Guy's expressionless face always had a tint of defiance, but never so much as on this bus. He hated the grey powdery bus smell which somehow managed to entangle the city's grimy air. His dimming eyes procreated the stench so that his stuffed-up nose could share in the discomfort. The bus was full of fixed, biased minds in unfit grown-up frames. Guy's migraine echoed his disgust. He longed to focus on a token plant or baby to assuage his uneasiness. Luckily, he spotted innocence sitting alone by a window in the middle of the bus. The joint pain subsided drastically.

GUY: Hello, Sir. This seat taken?

KID: No.

The precocious boy in a bright green shirt looked even more exhausted than Guy. His pale blue eyes defied his tender age. The small hands of the dark-skinned seven-year-old quickly moved his large paper bags.

GUY: I'm Guy. *(extends his hand)*

KID: **George.** *(firmly shakes Guy's hand; Guy likes him immediately.)*

GUY: Where's your sidekick?

GEORGE: Huh?

GUY: Your friend who helps you while you plan your next move. Mine is undercover. His name is Ryan. *(takes out a large paperclip)*

GEORGE: That's just a paperclip.

GUY: Sshh! *(Guy's expression becomes histrionic.)*
         It's just a disguise! Wait! *(whispers)* Ryan, can I transform you now? I want to introduce you to my new friend George. *(Guy shoots a side glance at the calm George.)*

         He said okay. *(As Guy takes out his pliers, his joints suddenly remember their hostility towards the lillies that are scratching against his ankle, concealed within his pant leg. He rocks in his seat as he quickly bends the paperclip into a man's head wearing a top hat. He puts Ryan to his ear.)*

GUY: Ry wants to know if you bought any candy.

GEORGE: No. Does he really talk? He has no lips.

GUY: You can't hear him? He is very quiet. Here. *(Guy puts Ryan to George's left ear.)* Listen carefully.

GEORGE: I can't hear anything.

GUY: That's weird. He's not usually shy. Lemme talk to him. *(unintelligibly whispers to Ryan)* Huh? Really?!

GEORGE: *(His concerned eyebrows shoot up.)* What?

GUY: He said that you're the only person that can help him break the *Penelope Jumbie Curse!*

GEORGE: What's that?

GUY: *(unintelligibly whispers to Ryan, then turns his head towards George)* He said the curse would be unbreakable if he were to reveal it. He didn't tell me. Just said it was threatening the Caribbean.

GEORGE: Why am I the only one who can help break the curse?

GUY: *(again unintelligibly whispers to Ryan, then turns back to George)* You're the George in the bright green shirt!

GEORGE: Oh.

GUY: *(loudly whispers to Ryan, looking down in disbelief; his voice suddenly amplifies because of the heightening pain.)* **But I need you!** *(Guy sighs.)* Okay.

(looks up at George) He says he's your sidekick now and that you must deliver the tender to your mother, without mentioning the Penelope Jumbie Curse.

(He takes out a $50 bill, a $20 bill, and a $10 bill. He folds them into thirds and slips the money into a paperclip from his back left pocket. He then links the paperclip to Ryan's chin.)

Could I please have your receipt?

GEORGE: What should she do with the money?

(George reaches into the bag full of canned food and takes out the receipt. He hands it to Guy who is holding Ryan up to his right ear.)

GUY: He says she can do whatever she wants! *(Guy writes on the back of the receipt.)*

GEORGE: Can she use it?

GUY: Yes. *(He attaches the receipt; George reads it.)*

RECEIPT: A GIFT FROM THE ARTIST. - GUY.

GUY: But remember, she must get this for the Caribbean to be safe! Please hide it in your pocket. We must now shake hands and recite the magic chant! Repeat after me!

George stared at Guy who was wincing with pain. Guy tried to hide that he was suffering. While the seven-year-old noticed his strange jerky movements, he attributed them to the fact that Guy was very concerned about the Caribbean. George was happy to be able to help the poor guy break the spell.

GUY: Six, five, THRIVE!

GEORGE: Six, five, THRIVE!

GUY: Perfect! *(Guy turns around and notices that everyone behind him is staring. He then looks back at George.)*

         Thank you **so** much for helping, Green Shirt George!

GEORGE: You're welcome. *(The innocent boy all of a sudden regains all the energy he had expended while running errands for his indigent, disabled mother.)*

The bus was coming to a stop. Guy was going to get up, but he noticed that George was preparing to do the same.

GUY: Thanks again and don't feel bad if Ryan doesn't talk to you for a while. He's just excited to be working for a Hero. *(George looks very excited.)* Be nice to him!

GEORGE: I'll take good care of him, Sir, don't worry!

GUY: I trust you. *(The bus stops and George stands up.)* Bye!

George smiles shyly at the tall stranger who had journeyed far just to find him, and then gets off the bus.

As the bus continued on, Guy looked out the window and saw middle schoolers wearing white shirts that concealed the top half of their loose blue jeans. They were riding bikes that were much too small for them.

GUY: I'm in Baltimore!

Guy twisted his spine to grin at two ladies behind him who were speaking about a man who just left the bus, and how he wasn't fit to be a father based on what he said about his teenage son.

Guy slides to George's seat and presses his nose against the window.

He loved the harbor city where he was born and went to elementary school. He especially liked Fells Point, where he often checked out the many Gothic, intricately designed doors, each leading to secret small corridors within.

He usually unwittingly subscribed to the convenient Baltimorean fashion as well. However, his height kept his XXXL shirts from covering the top half of his jeans.

He glanced at his wrist. He wasn't wearing a watch, so he shook his head and pulled out his cell phone. He hadn't slept in that train car for nearly as long as he had thought.

GUY: Almost four.

If he were on campus, he'd be at tennis practice, perfecting his groundstrokes. Today, the thought of tennis hurt him further. The pain escalated, and then suddenly it froze.

He didn't dare move a muscle since his body was satisfied in the position he had assumed. Nonetheless, he maintained a positive attitude; the violent storms in his legs were successfully keeping him awake. It was a close game, but he was beating fatigue.

At the next stop, he forced himself to get off.

LOOKING AROUND, EATING AN ORANGE

LXX

Guy had never been to this dilapidated part of Baltimore. There were no row houses in sight. He wobbled around and was captivated by the beautiful colors all over the small brick buildings. It looked as if a paintball tournament had just taken place. The graffiti on the bridge rails a mile away stood out with their wavy black outlines guided by splashes of lime green. There were small patches of dead grass painted bright orange. He loved the contrast.

He spotted a dark-brown building with what looked like bullet holes along the side. It was a library. He sat on a curb just outside the entrance and reached into a large cargo pocket on the right leg of his pants. His hand returned with the second orange he had purchased. Guy stared at it, holding back screams. He started peeling it. The pain in his fingers was muffled by maddening joint pain, compliments of the lillies.

The fresh orange juice excited his dormant tongue as it dripped down his chalky throat. He was screaming inside. The pain was just as bad as it had been when Bryan first introduced him to Lillies, but this time he was strangely encouraged by every stab and stretch. It reminded him that he was winning; he was awake, living.

The citrus scent and the bright orange peels attracted a bee that was clearly lost. Unfortunately, Guy couldn't fully appreciate the only food he'd have for hours. His mind quickly shifted to the clandestine city dwellers who were no longer hiding. They lined up behind a table across the street, half a block away.

LIBRARY TIME

XX

Guy eats his orange and watches Woman as she serves the homeless lunch and gives them packages. A female wearing a colorful tulip-and-rose-patterned scarf walks up to Woman.

FLORA: What's in da bags?

WOMAN: Those are for you, too! Hygiene products—towels, toothpaste, soap, brushes, you name it. Please, take one, and take some more for your family!

Guy was staring at the stalker who, unsurprisingly, was nearby. He hated her. He hated her stupid dress, her nonchalant caprice, and now her cheerful Bulgarian accent that bounced around in her stupid, warm voice. It was obvious that she was healthy; she stood unwaveringly as she served the homeless spaghetti, garlic bread, and cookies. The other two servers were to her left, farther from him. Guy was certain that she positioned herself so that he would see her flaunt her healthiness.

She runs to get some bags and the corpulent volunteer to her immediate left gladly takes on a second duty.

GUY: There's the Woman. She's not racing on the grass, nor is it being pulled off the ground. No, there is no grass here and she smiles.

He walks into the library, confused. He saw that exact dress earlier that day. It was one person, in both places, on the same Thursday.

GUY: Am I mad? No. The gown confirms it. She is real and is sailing on a different stream on my very boat. But she didn't even see me in Bakerstown! So? Must study to ace tomorrow's quiz on Greek architecture....

Slowly her figure vanished from his mind as three burly men skipped in. Soon, the jolly men were ready to put up some new columns. Guy wondered if much movement was required; the men in his mind had so much equipment about their bodies that they must have had trouble walking.

One of the construction workers was in his sixties and had an evil look in his eyes. He quickly dived through Guy's esophagus and began pounding his hammer all over the inside of his poor, weakened body.

Guy's insides felt as if they were rapidly deteriorating. Every lift of his foot was a grand struggle, for his hips ordered him to sit down. His stomach was in the most pain, yet it actively helped his back and knees stay strong by staring at them, sternly ridiculing their royal complaints for such minor aches. His back was not used to its weakness, however insipid it seemed, which is why its pain created the worst discomfort.

Guy had forgotten that the quiz couldn't be until next week. In his mind, the quiz was to take place on Friday, the day of his Studio review (and a makeup exam which he didn't need to take). He pushed on most heroically. The heavy smell of old books further melted his sizzling head. His headache made the world seven tempos slower. The weathered linoleum reflected a line of pale orange mushroom heads which suddenly tore the motif to freely oppose the dinginess of the floor wheresoever they saw fit.

Then he saw a depressing sight between the base of a fan and the floor. It was a jumbo paperclip speckled from curve to line to curve with either thick chunks of rust or ruddy mold. His rotating concentration made it difficult for him to stay upright. His hunched back defied his age and embarrassed his blood which was stoutheartedly being pumped throughout his huge body.

Guy's legs began to give way. His thirsty eyes prayed to behold the Nonfiction sign. Dewey led him to an old book on ancient Greek structures.

Guy clumsily drags the spine off the shelf and then drops to the ground.

He staggers to the wall so that he can lean his broad back against it, his legs shaking as they straighten out. With his knuckles and his fist, he forces the pages apart, takes a deep breath, then reads for what seems to be an hour or so.

SAMPSON*: That's impossible! You can't sneeze if you're on a motorcycle going 90 mph.

RICHARD: Yes you can.

SAMPSON: It's physically impossible!

RICHARD: No it's not. It would just really hurt.

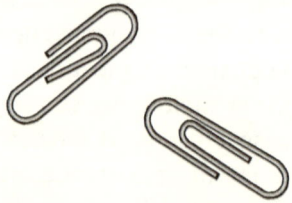

TYRONE: Ma, let's go to the comics!

TYRONE'S MOM: Just a minute, Honey, I need...

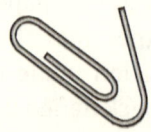

*I don't know these people so I gave them random names.

Guy

SHAWAN: Uh-huh! Seriously! I... no. What? Listen Joe, I...

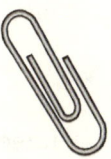

LIBRARIAN JAMIE LOU: ...shelf, but maybe it's in the back, let me check.

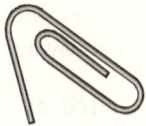

MARCUS: ...very big! Nah, but they hate her cuz last Friday when Celeste...

LISETTE: PQ 1240 PQ—Aha! Modern French Literature!

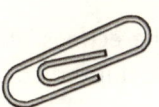

There were no windows in the old library. Despite frequent mini-breaks Guy took to look at the lively figures as they walked by, he felt his eyes straining.

He limps towards the bookshelf to return the book, nodding at it in gratitude as he slips it back in place by an awkward orange bookend. He needed a fifteen-minute break before faithfully returning to the book.

Only the skinny woman at the front desk could have as amazing a sufferance as Guy had at that moment. None of the others in the library had ever felt the unfathomable pain that the wilting lillies lent to Guy. But Guy was appreciative; he reminded himself that he was awake and therefore able.

His intense blue eyes squinted as he left the library. His head followed the shocked eyes that narrowed in on a sparkly blue skyscraper three blocks away. He raised his heavy left hand.

GUY: If I could slice the bottom third of the building, I could cut this layer out of existence. The residue would exude the boisterous splendor of complete opulence and easy "living." Now replace this segment on the ground and rub this fantastic feat of architecture into the ever-praising skies. Ta-dah!... Why... it's the cacophonous cheeches of the contaminated squirrels. Yuck. The stench of the smoggy air has cleared my nose. Joy.

            This sound! The echoes of gunshots against the graffiti set this unpredictable tempo most blunderingly.

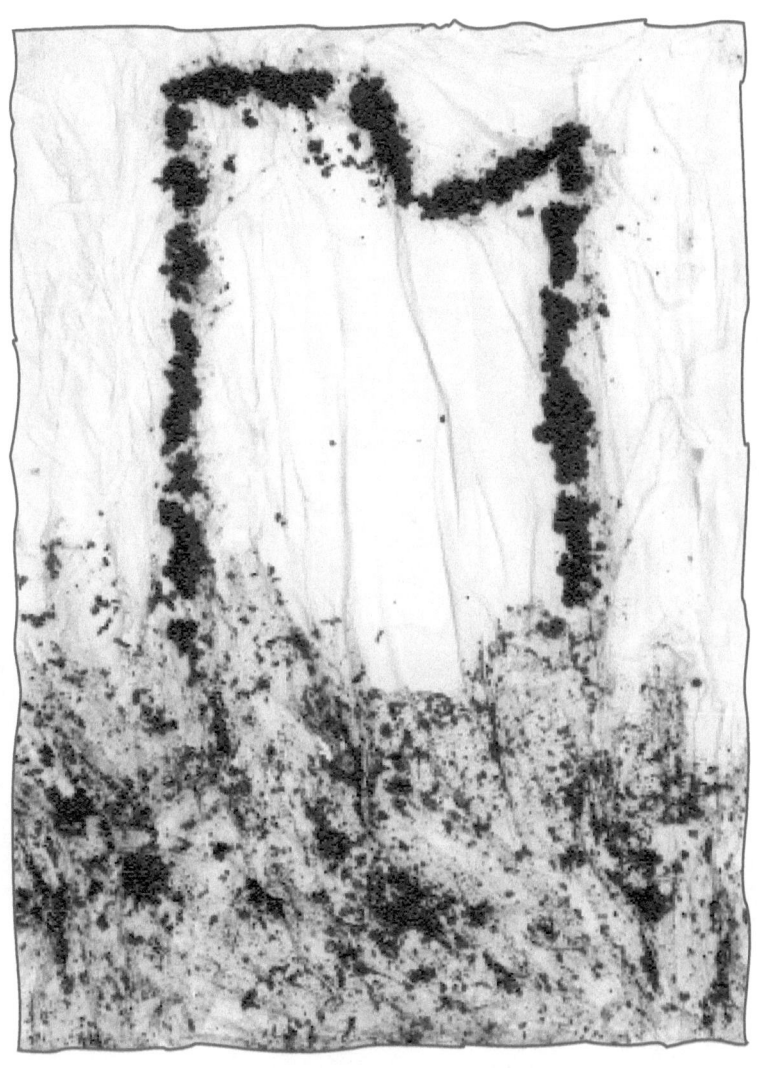

A Grand Building in the Dirt

(He sees a huge man with purposefully distracting chains banging on someone's door.)

Bleak indeed is that man's life. Throwing up in the off season, beating up debtors in the on.

He continues walking towards the shiny building.

THE ELEVATOR

XXI

Guy tried to focus on an uninterested cat who was heading towards three dumpsters. He was unsuccessful, for the cat started to look very blurry. Guy's body was trembling. However, he was proud of his aching back for helping him ignore the trifling heaviness of his fingers and his need to relieve himself.

The splotchy cat climbed onto a grey fluted dumpster and watched a mouse scampering many feet away.

GUY: STUPID CAT!... Finally! The treads and risers to lead me to the ELEVATOR INSIDE!

None of the passersby looks his way.

SPARROW: Teeer!

He drags his feet up the stairs, turns his head slowly to see the bird, and then runs through the revolving door, pushing the door's leaves as he sprints towards the front desk.

GUY: HI! ELEVATOR, PLEASE!

At that time, verbal language, unless communicated through screams, felt incredibly forced and could only spread the sharp, excruciating pain.

ARENA: Hello, Sir! Straight down this hallway! They're past the first door to your right.

Guy didn't have the energy to thank the four-foot-six, sickeningly perky receptionist. Soon, his stomach punched him. He could no longer wait.

GUY: BATHROOMS!!

ARENA: Why, I'm sorry, Sir! Thought you said *elevator!*
         (Guy starts swaying back and forth impatiently

- 158 -

*as his eyes search for the little stick figure with-
out a skirt.)* **The men's—**

*Guy sees the sign and runs as quickly as he can; his eyes
continue staring at the bottom-most theatre of his vision.
His left hand forcefully yanks open the door, alarming the
frame's sheltered jambs.*

*The bathroom is empty. He immediately looks at the tiled
floor.*

COMPUTERIZED VOICE: Welcome. Please help yourself to
            a complimentary towel once you're through.
            Thank you.

The wall partitions between the stalls were securely
mounted to the golden-peach floor. *Guy enters the farthest
toilet enclosure. In addition to seeing the shiny toilet, he
finds a small table and a glass cabinet stocked with two air
freshener cans and many rolls of bathroom tissue.*

The bathroom was so large and clean that the little fruit fly
buzzing around had a much more exuberant life than ninety-
seven percent of the locals. Most apparent was the immense
light that flooded the air-conditioned bathroom. The scathing
sunlight tried its best to tunnel through the exquisite Gothic
window, but the bar tracery stood firmly, enduring the sun's
every attack. While it would only make sense that the sunlight
burned the stone flower on its petals, the stoic tracery merely
shone and earned a healthier hue. The burnt side looked
excellent long after the sun set.

The custodial engineers were clearly experts in their field.
His eyes appreciated their effort; however, the rest of his
ever-weakening body was choking. His agitated stomach pain
had nothing to do with digestion, so the insulted tenderness

spread even farther.

GUY: God! I'll do *anything* if you take the pain away! ANYTHING!

He washes his hands and then collapses onto the lounge chair by the window. He bends his body leftward, clutching his stomach. He then rocks his torso back and kicks his left leg. As he leans forward, he bends his leg again. He didn't give his mind time to figure out if he was feeling better or not, so he continued rocking and kicking to be on the safe side.

GUY: Aw ugh! *(pauses, holding his breath)* Aw ugh!

He felt pitiful as his bottom lip trembled. He had to prove to himself that he was strong.

Guy starts singing the only song that makes him feel better when he's in excruciating pain, "The Scientist" by Coldplay. The tune always tames his breathing so that even the worst of pain becomes bearable.

GUY: *(slowly sings)* I was just gueeeesing. At numbers and fiiiiigures... Pulling the puuuzzles apaaaaa-art....

He leans back, one last time, and lies on the chair, barely breathing. He looks around, having successfully forgotten his body. He gets up slowly, surprised that he feels okay.

He didn't thank God nor question whether or not he was completely better. He feared that if he did either, the pain would return.

He found his way to the door and exited the bathroom, noticing at once a man in a wheelchair. *Guy watches as the stranger's wheelchair touches the first step of the escalator whose tread elongates until the whole wheelchair is aboard the escalator. Soon, the man is on the third floor.*

GUY: With such an escalator, let's see which well-paid, otiose employees use the elevator.

Guy presses the up button, waits two seconds, and then enters the elevator.

It was very spacious. Guy stood in the corner by the buttons. He didn't press any; he merely waited. He mentally started a fifteen-minute timer and was soon face-to-face with ALLEN, a thin elevator user. As soon as he saw the man, his pain returned. With considerable effort, he spoke.

GUY: Which floor?

Allen pressed the bottom half of the fourteenth button. He didn't listen at all to the dying kid.

On the second floor, the elevator stops and a heavily made-up middle-aged woman named ELAINE enters.

GUY: *(I'm so pain in much! My mind's ablaze no and! Must be polite to and talk. Such pain finger is!)* Which floor?

ELAINE: Third.

Guy uses the knuckle of his index finger to press the red light in the middle of the button for the third floor. He looks at Elaine who doesn't smile at him. She avoids both men and stands right in front of the entrance.

The elevator reaches the third floor. Elaine briskly exits and five employees stroll in.

LARGE WOMAN (without a name tag): ...actually drink it!

GUY: Which floor?

LARGE WOMAN: Eighth, so I said, "No, I saw you put black pepper in it!"

MARGARET: How could he think you'd drink it?

SANDRA: Ha ha.

HOWARD: That's so crazy.

Guy casts an angry look at Howard who sounds unbearably phony.

LARGE WOMAN: I know!

FANNY: Did you make him drink it?

Sandra keeps looking at Allen who seems to be smiling genuinely.

The door opens and everyone exits except for Guy and Allen.

SANDRA: I would have—

The elevator door closes.

The silver shuttle stops again at the twelfth floor. The doors part, but no one is there to enter. **Guy felt uncomfortable with Allen, so he believed that the neutral elevator determined his destination for him.** *He exits and finds the elevator to his right open as well. He limps inside just as an orange-haired Asian woman exits.*

The elevator was identical to the other except that ill-favored Allen wasn't in it, so it felt much lighter.

Guy doesn't press any buttons. The elevator goes down and stops on the tenth floor whence two employees enter.

SHAWNA: —that really had nothing to do with our project.

GUY: Which—

Shawna quickly clicks the sixth button and keeps her back towards Guy.

MORRIS: It *has* really become crowded.

The elevator stops again on the ninth floor. An employee whose name tag bears the name XIU JUAN enters.

XIU JUAN: Morris! Shawna! Is it over already?

GUY: Which floor?

MORRIS: Never mind that! So how'd it go?

XIU JUAN: Mr. CEO had just stepped out. Must say though, the nineteenth floor is nice! Roger's office was ridiculously snazzy.

Guy could feel the heavy throbs of his jugular vein as the elevator stopped. This time a young custodian from Southeast Asia entered wearing the shiniest name tag Guy had seen that day. *MINA rolls in a cart full of cleaning supplies and filled trash bags.* She wasn't lazy like the rest, for her wide cart merited elevator use (it was much too wide to fit on the escalator). Guy respected her.

GUY: Which floor?

MINA: Seven pleease. *(Guy presses the seventh button.)* Tank you.

GUY: Mm-hm.

The car stops on the seventh floor. Morris shakes his head as Xiu Juan and Shawna chat away in the background.

GUY: Have a good day, Mina.

MINA: Tanks! *(Her eyes sparkle in wonderment.)*
         You do same!

Guy's friendly eyes answered for his trembling mouth. His legs were failing him. He envisioned a large, beautiful black chair in the CEO's office. It would be nice to sit in it.

The elevator stops on the sixth floor. Morris and Xiu Juan exit arm in arm, followed by Shawna who is giggling.

He pressed the button for the nineteenth floor and was pleased that the elevator was not further delayed by any lazy socializers. He couldn't wait to sit in the CEO's leather chair; he needed to lie down. He looked at his shoes and prayed to pass out so that he didn't have to feel the strong pain that now afflicted his stomach, legs, back, and hips. *Guy starts bending down.*

GUY: *No! You must live!*

He straightens his body just as the elevator car stops.

ELEVATOR: Bing! Nineteenth floor.

Guy wonders if the elevator had been announcing the floors during the whole ride as he lifts his gaze.

THEY SHOULD BE PLAYING TENNIS
XXII

Guy hears Vivaldi's Le quattro stagioni at the entrance of the floor. The elevator led to a small lobby which overlooked a large digital clock shaped like a tower (apprising Guy that it was just 4:28 p.m.) and the workspace of two secretaries. Their communal office was separated from the lobby by a wall of glass. It was soothingly dim.

GUY: *You only live once, Guy! Suck it up!*

He takes a deep breath, straightens his back, and opens the glass door. He walks in and approaches the younger secretary, a meek woman who appears to be about thirty years old.

FLORINDA: Hello, may I help you?

Guy's hair was disheveled. His body swayed slightly and it was evident that he had trouble breathing. In addition, his T-shirt, cargo pants, and sneakers made him look anything but professional. However, his earnest eyes told Florinda that she was not speaking to just any guy. His haughty posture further presented him as a man of noble character.

GUY: I need to see Roger.
          (I hope that's the CEO's name! I forgot....)

FLORINDA: Regarding what?

The classical music becomes imperceptible in the background.

GUY: This property. It's very urgent.
          Tell him Guy is here.

FLORINDA: Certainly.

She calls Roger whose office is hidden beside a third secretary's desk.

FLORINDA: Hello Roger, Guy is here to see you.

What? Oh, one moment—
(to Guy:) Last name?

GUY: I'm the landowner and I don't have time.

FLORINDA: *(on the phone with Roger)*
D. Landowner. Says it's urgent.

Okay. Right this way, Mr. D. Landowner.
Go through Catherine's office.

GUY: *(Guy's eyes are looking towards Roger's wall, not at Florinda.)* Thanks.

Despite channeling all his strength into staying upright, he starts to rock back and forth. No pain so far compared to the extreme excruciating backache which screamed as he straightened his back. The CEO's office was clear across the building. His nervousness added to the pain and he could no longer walk.

GUY: *Just make it to the chair.... Just make it to the chair.... Almost there....*

He nods at Florinda, knocks on Roger's open door, walks in, and then slowly sits himself down in a dark-green leather armchair.

The healthy thirty-eight-year-old bachelor smiles, much to Guy's disgust. Roger's toothy grin seemed incredibly contrived, as if the brilliance of his large teeth aimed to distract Guy from seeing the more obvious phoniness that held up his large face.

Roger watches Guy's uncouth movements while thinking about what to say. Something about the young man's contained, yet austere facial expression made him seem worth listening to.

ROGER: *What gall, this handsome kid!*

GUY: *Green leather? Black would look nicer.*
          My legs! Poor legs! Calm down, be strong….

ROGER: *(looks at Guy, startled)* Excuse me, *Sir*, but who
          exactly are you?

GUY: I own this land and I am very disappointed.

Roger was taken aback by the handsome tall man's words
more so than by his coarse actions or the strange smell of
the cologne that he wore. The words themselves were of no
import to Roger; it was the tone and deepness with which
they were delivered that piqued Roger's interest in Guy.

Roger enjoyed dismissing people and seeing their reactions. He would often say, "Please speak with my secretary;
I'm heavily engaged at the moment," or better yet, "I've heard
your case and there's nothing I can do." He had a mind to
say the former as soon as Florinda had spoken to him on the
phone about the visitor, but he decided to give Mr. Landowner a chance. He didn't feel let down, for this man proved most
intriguing. Soon, Roger was subjugated by the brown-haired
man's arrogant eyes. Their grumpy glare gave him undeni-
able authority.

ROGER: You must be mistaken. This land was purchased.
          It belongs to the company now.

GUY: You don't understand. It was from my father
          that you bought this land. True. However, if you
          think anyone's currency could sever my deep
          attachment to my firm, healthy land, then you,
          Sir, are mistaken.

          Again, I am very disappointed.

ROGER: *(very interested)* **In what?**

GUY: I had the displeasure of meeting many of your employees. I won't name them, but they're a rather sociable, lazy bunch, though this is not what concerns me. Last week I saw two young girls with braided hair, in pink barrettes. Their shorts were pink and their shirts white. Different girls—one in DC, the other in Baltimore. But they both shared one thing. They were poor and looked miserable as their fathers held their hand. Howard has just the features of one of the fathers.

The other looked identical to Morris, strangely enough.

The difference? Morris and Howard are dandies, as evidenced by their flashy business suits and matching jewelry. Well, needless to say, in my presence, the subject of charity did not come up, and why should it? They're so busy since they work so hard for your company.

ROGER: Wai—

GUY: Now listen! Those girls should be playing tennis!

Guy was shocked at how tired and illogical he was. He quickly tried to link his statements together.

GUY: Listen, you know that large building seven blocks that way? *(points in a random direction)*

ROGER: Why yes... the Brussels and Stable Building.

GUY: I own that land, too, but I feel as if only one business in the area should be rich at a time.

ROGER: Listen, Mr.—

Roger didn't seem like a concerned citizen. Guy's pain liberated him of all inhibition and so, he drafted another approach.

GUY: NO, YOU LISTEN TO ME!
I feel very fond of your establishment here; therefore, I am going to tell you how to do better than the others.

I shouldn't interfere....
But something must be done.

Those annoying poor kids are walking all over and making you look as if you are miserly.

What is your Outreach Initiative?

ROGER: We're currently working on it, I've just hired—

GUY: You need a tennis league. My father wanted to have each business that he owned form a team and they'd play against each other for publicity.

My mother, Martine—yes, founder of the Reflectionist Movement—my beloved mother, decided that in order to maximize publicity for one's company, it may be wise to be the sole sponsor of the league.

ROGER: Oh, I see where you're heading! Cat, please come here and write this down.

Catherine walks over. Although homely, Guy can't help but look at her beautiful legs which she is flaunting in a purple miniskirt. He slowly breathes in her flirty perfume and wishes that he could talk to her instead of acting. While he looks at her, his pain starts to dissipate. He focuses on her from the corner of his eye as he speaks to Roger.

Guy suddenly notices that Pachelbel's Kanon in D-Dur is now being played throughout the elite nineteenth floor.

GUY: First, advertise a tennis league for children ages four to eighteen. Then, hire tennis instructors to teach your employees how to coach. The employees will have fun coaching and being competitive against their colleagues.

But what do you do with all the indigent fans who are watching?

(Guy pauses and thinks about Woman who is probably still handing out hygiene supplies.)

Have the welfare department train other employees to run information booths. Handouts with your company's name would be great, as would hygiene bags with toothbrushes, towels, etc., proudly displaying your distinguished mark.

(Guy looks outside his window at a huge field with trees fencing away the indigent world.)

Construct tennis courts on the rest of my property. That way they won't have to take any insalubrious public transportation system.

ROGER: I like this! We were looking to do a big promotional event! A summer tennis league would be perfect! Cat, have Michael order three tennis courts on our open field. Brilliant!

CATHERINE: That's very nice. I'm excited!

*Suddenly the tune streams a huge splash of notes that remind
Guy of elementary school where Mr. Valentine, his music
teacher, first played the song for his second grade class.*

GUY: The dimensions demarcated by the doubles
          lines are only 36 x 78 feet, but you'll need 60 x
          120 feet per individual tennis court. So... I'd
          say you have room for three sets of tennis
          courts. Place three courts in one, two in the
          other, and one in the last one. Oh, and it really
          won't cost too much to add a grated trench drain
          so that the water doesn't crack the tennis court.
          Believe me, (*wait!... I sound too much like an
          architect!...*) your company will be the better for
          it.

          (*Please don't think I'm an architect that needs to find
          work! But hey, it would be nice to design a tennis
          court—No! I'm just a rich, powerful, educated guy....*)

ROGER: Thank you. We shall certainly name the tourna-
          ment after you. The—

GUY: Never! Why... *you* thought of it, Roger!

Roger's eyes sparkle. He could kiss Guy.

GUY: That's why this business will prosper. It has such
          a wise CEO. Adieu.

ROGER: Wait! We need to at least get your contact info!
          You have to cut the red tape!

GUY: I trust you know my father? I still live with him.

Guy said it really angrily, making Catherine think that Roger
was an imposter who didn't know anything about the land.

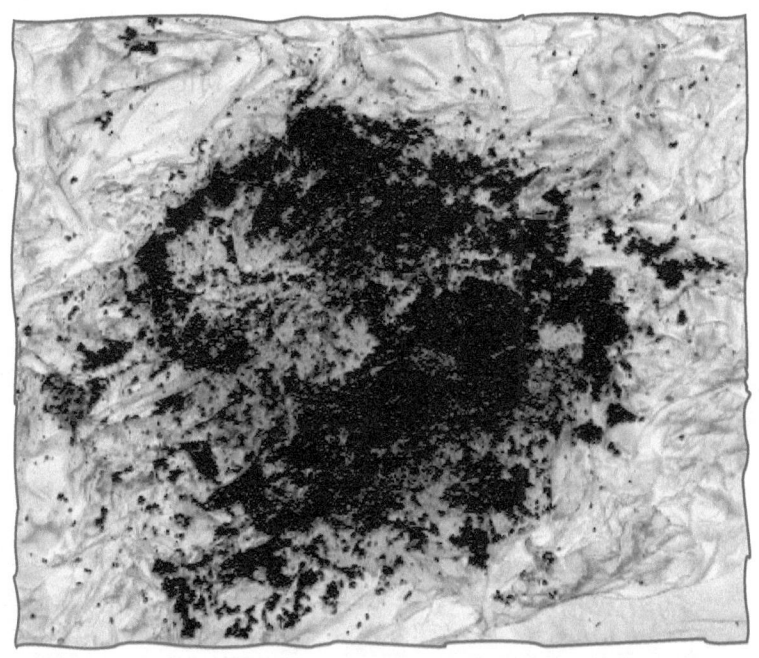

Pain

ROGER: *(lying)* **Of course! Thanks again!**

Guy nods to Catherine and then leaves without saying good-bye. As he leaves, Cat and Roger are left with a strange lingering smell of dying lillies.

Once Cat is no longer in view, his pain starts to rapidly escalate and the music once again fades into the background. He limps away, trying to conceal the thunder beaming from his back. He takes the escalator, races one floor below, and finds a bathroom nearby.

GUY: ¡Por el amor de Dios! Let me live! I want to live! I am suffocating. This stupid curse! What's wrong with me? I want to live! I am so weak. I am so...

He stared at his skewed, miserable reflection that hugged the sides of the sink faucet until all of a sudden, he felt as if a bug were crawling up his leg. Shaking, he slowly bent down and placed his arm through the bottom of his pant leg. As he tried to delicately remove the bug, he realized the lillies were the root of his problem.

GUY: Why did I ever strap myself to this rash?

Guy put his hand in his sock, grabbed the four lillies that were stinking more than ever, and flushed them down a toilet. His ankle was a depressing shade of maroon. He threw off his shoe, tore off a long sheet of paper towel, and finally wrapped up the ruinous sock whose furrows were dampened by sticky green blood.

He pushes the wrapped-up sock deep inside the trash can. He breathes heavily as he places his foot underneath the faucet and lets the soothing water run over his ankle. The joint pain still persisted, but it was very soft and subtle.

He covers his mouth with his right hand and silently yawns as he cries.

GUY: I'm cured! Thank you, God! I am... it was all this.... Finally! I'm going to—and do big things, just watch! I'm—*sniff*—

He grabbed his cell phone and set the countdown timer for thirteen minutes. Unaccustomed to the relief, his back remained bent as he limped over to a lounge chair and dragged it towards the sink.

The water burnt his ankle each time someone in the adjacent bathroom flushed the toilet. A few people used that very bathroom as well, somehow making the water feel cooler at times. He didn't have to explain why he was washing his foot; his red ankle said everything.

Guy falls asleep in the lounge chair with his foot in the sink.

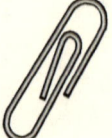

CELL PHONE: Beebeeeep! Beebeeeeep! Bee—

Guy turned the alarm off and put the phone back into his pocket. His ankle was no longer directly under the faucet. He grinned slightly, dried his ankle with paper towels, and searched for his shoe.

GUY: My shoe, my shoe! Skippidy Dippity... Doo!

He finds it next to a spider.

GUY: This place is practically bug-free, Spidey.
         Come on, let's go outside.

Guy reached into a side pocket, took out the plastic bag from the Bakerstown gas station, and proceeded to guide Spidey into it with his shoelace aglet. Soon, it crawled deep into the bag; Guy loosely sealed a big bubble of air along with Spidey.

He put on his shoe and raced down the escalator, switched to the series of escalators at the other end of the building, and was finally free.

At the revolving door, he turns around.

GUY: *(yells)* Spidey here says "Bye Arena!"

Arena smiled at the insolent guy with beautiful blue eyes and decided that he was just misunderstood. Guy walked upright. He saw trees a couple of blocks away, so he went towards them to find Spidey a nice home. He hadn't forgotten about his upcoming quiz or his project. However, he decided that Spidey's life was more important than school.

He opened up the bag and softly stroked Spidey's legs with the knuckle of his left index finger. Instinctively, Spidey scampered deeper into the bag. Eventually, it figured out which way led to freedom, and which led to a film that draped the outside world, thereby preventing Spidey from actually living in it.

The small, hairless brown spider jumps out. Guy wrinkles up his bag and places it back into his pocket.

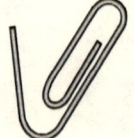

WOODED SMILE
XXIV

Guy walks into the wooded area behind the building. His breath infirm and his body forgotten, he is suddenly stopped by an offensively bright yellow shape growing rounder and rounder.

GUY: Yellow, dementia's dimensionless cape.
         While rousing my discomfort,
         You sand the little cusps of cartilage.
         Without the adhesion,
         My fidgety bones conspire to help string the
              laughter of hopelessness
         Directly from my servile mouth.
         I stand akimbo, my dour face smirking
              authoritatively,
         Fooling no one.

The brightness took the shape of Smile. Guy felt terribly frustrated and guilty at seeing the expression, as if he hadn't done a project design and was about to be accosted by his professor.

SMILE: For the truth is to be envisioned as a single
              object.

Guy felt Smile was obnoxious and was trying to ruin him. He felt weaker in Smile's presence, although mentally, he felt his mind was somewhat clearer; he knew that he was about to release the repressed gusts of frustration that never ceased to bang against his tightly shut lips.

GUY: You want to push the chimes of passionate
              endeavors in my way.
         You want to grasp the tangled up roots by
              sacrificing the pedestal.
         You want to massage the powdered remains
              into my aching neurons.

I can't—I failed.
I won't, because I can't.

SMILE: Why invent misery? You've accomplished
greatness. Now wear me!

GUY: I did not endow the world with its problems.
I merely let free my hollow, albeit keen, eyes
on this world.
Unthinker!
The smilers of this world are the ones that do
not think.
For thinking must naturally deprive a sensible
man of puerile happiness.

SMILE: The infant.

GUY: What of the imprisoned rat that is about to press
his whisker onto the sharp root?
The stem naturally stands firm and capable,
Yet, the wild water within its walls will not rise
as far as the moon.
Silly stem supports the unthankful petals which
gloat as they float.
When broken, the stupid stem continues to do
what it can for the petals.
Why not be beautiful and happy for oneself?
I have had enough of your paronomasia!

SMILE: How dare you?
As the brush softly touches the brilliant white
canvas,
The marvelous fabric on wood becomes
complete.
It is the gold of the painting, engulfing the pollen
and scent.

            The brightness of which soothes its weave,
            As the aroma caresses the sturdy, consenting
                wood.

GUY: The tree!

SMILE: Continue!

GUY: The symbol of truth! I can see is the tree!
            Riddled with ants, sprinkled with moss....
            It's tousled in love, sharing its splendor to
                allow us to live,
            Rustling leaves press our hearts closer to the
                fountain.
            Although parasitic monsters threaten its integrity,
            My tree friend stands firm.
            And tall and sturdy. With age....

SMILE: And it witnesses all, but remains the same tree,
            Not aware of the cumbering ferocity of the
                insignificant swarm.

Guy walks away.

SMILE: Silly, silly Guy.
            You claim your eyes are open, yet you cannot
                sense the sun.
            You swear that you think, yet the barbed wire
                has your brain stuck.
            You cannot think. You are scared to think.
            You cannot be mistaken. Yet, truly you are.

Guy continues walking into the woods, feeling relieved at having left Smile behind.

DRUMMING CIRCLE
XXV

Guy looks at his phone.

CELL PHONE: 5:16 p.m.

Guy walked on until it was very dark. He was confused, for he could have sworn that he had been in the woods for less than ten minutes. He was right, although the thick tree canopy prevented the sun from ascertaining the fact that it was still early.

GUY: Here I am. Amongst the Vulgars. The Vulgars,
              developing the method.
              But for what? For what aim do they weep and
              sweep and riot,
              And crush their beloved in order to achieve
              their hope? How destructive!

Guy unwittingly reassigns his hands the names he had given them in sixth grade. He slowly places his left hand, Gauche, on an old oak tree. Smile abruptly disappears in the distance.

GUY: I know, Gauche! I didn't think it was possible for
              a tree to beat this loudly of its own accord either.
              That Smile must be in it.

              *(His right hand, Derecha, slowly joins Gauche in
              feeling the bark of the beating tree.)*

              Hmmm…. Seems in sync with the horrific beating
              in my head. How curious….

As he passed the tree, the thumps and bams grew more and more demanding. He followed the beat until his feet could feel a bit of the rhythm. He cleared the woods and found a large oval defined by a beautiful brown mix of old wooden benches and mature trees.

Sound rays were heading all over the place, bouncing here, spinning there.

Guy walked up to the drumming circle whose line was composed of four adults sitting on little foot stools. Each had congas, a darbuka, or bongos. The eldest person had a blue darbuka under his left arm and with the fingers of his right hand he created intricate rhythms with splashes of ferocity. He sometimes felt "bongo-happy," as he called it, and therefore never came to the circle without his bongos.

Guy would probably have sat on one of the chipped benches with the other three spectators had he not recognized HANS, a fellow architecture student who, like Guy, had Scandinavian ancestors. He was bent over, banging congas precisely; each hit was clean, distinct, and crisp. Guy had never heard congas played like that, but he expected nothing less spectacular from his friend.

Hans was the second-year Master's student that Guy would turn to whenever hours and hours of wrestling with the computer programs were lost in vain.

He saw a lot of himself in his shaved-bald brother figure who also practiced the great art of breakdancing. Hans was the only architecture student who could spin on his shoulder and do the flare for a good twenty seconds. Consequently, Hans was, by far, the coolest guy at the architecture school.

Not only were they both breakdancers, but each was also ambidextrous and honed a refreshing architecture style which fostered open spaces (the smallest trace of clutter would enrage them). Their buildings were simplistic, but never bare. Although Guy was three years younger, Hans often asked him for his opinion on his designs because, like Hans, Guy strove

Drumming Circle

to make every curve help the inhabitant feel just right. His buildings were all classy, but mainly *pure*.

Hans is playing with MELINDA, a vegan who sews her own clothes, NOMSO, a heavyset sculptor who is wearing bright colors, and JUAN, a chef with delicate features and very large hands.

A SPECTATOR: Go Baby! Go!

DARBUKA: Dip dadadadada dip dip Dip.
    Dip dadadadada dip dip Dip.

BONGOS 1: Badabladada BUM!
Badabladada BUM!

CONGA 1: Bli blu ble—BUM blu bli ble!
Bli blu ble—BUM blu bli ble!

CONGA 2: Bla blum blah bla blum bla.
Bla blum blah bla—BAH blum bla.

GUY: Hans!

HANS: Guy! Hey Nomso, could Guy—

NOMSO: *(nods at Guy)* Go for it!

Guy carefully picks up Nomso's bongos and sits on the grass with the bongos between his legs. He knew he was about to feel the worst pain in his already screeching fingertips. But the circle sounded great and he had to jump in, bloody or not.

BONGOS 2: BAM BUH BUM, BAM BUH BUM BLA BUH BAM!
BUH BUM, BAM BUH BUM BLA BUH!

The shade of his fingertips immediately ripened from purple to dark blue. He was certain that his fingers would break off.

Guy continues playing the bongos.

BONGOS 2: BAM BUH BUM, BAM BUH BUM BLA BUH BAM!
BUH BUM, BAM BUH BUM BLA BUH!

The more his fingers ached, the harder he banged them against the buffalo skin of the bongos. He didn't know how else to deal with the pain.

The music soon annexed his compliant body. He didn't see the friendly faces of his fellow band members, nor the ground he was looking at. He forgot himself completely and then suddenly, as the song's melody had transformed into a dark-goldenrod tune, he realized that his fingers were no longer burning. They were numb and felt weird, but "weird" was incredibly agreeable to the oft-suffering Guy; he played on until Hans was ready to go, one hour later.

Hans was finishing up his thesis work. Nonetheless, he made time to join the drumming circle every Thursday and he never wanted to leave. Fortunately for his silenced conscience, a lost storm unanticipatedly charged into Baltimore at full speed, threatening the fur, wood, and hide of the drummers' esteemed instruments.

Guy hands the bongos to Nomso. He could see the mellow man's face very clearly, despite the flush of rain.

GUY: Thanks for letting me borrow your bongos.

NOMSO: Anytime.

JUAN: Ah, Man! And we were just gettin' started!

NOMSO: Take care!

HANS: Been great, as always. Thanks guys!

GUY: Hey Hans, could I get a ride?

HANS: Sure, where to? Haha! Sorry I asked.

It was 6:50 p.m., another perfect time to be in the studio. The cool, refreshing water splashed viciously all over the now muddy terrain. Guy followed Hans through the woods, then finally to a nearby street where Guy was excited to see a big black pickup truck much like Ol' Suzie, his beloved truck.

GUY: I have the same truck!

HANS: No kiddin'?

Hans unlocks the truck doors and they hop in. Guy felt warm at seeing pieces of foam core wedged here and there and scrap wood haphazardly stored behind his seat, next to a big wrinkled plastic bag.

Hans starts the engine as Guy carefully picks up all the useful, precious scraps, placing them in the bag. A quick jungle drum and bass song starts playing.

He ties the bag tightly, making sure there are no holes in the plastic, and then places the large bundle behind his seat.

The truck was barely moving. Hans couldn't see anything but water and the general shape of the back of the SUV ahead.

GUY: Are you tired?

HANS: A little. *(Stupid windshield wipers! Whoever designed you didn't do a good job. I still can't see a thing!)*

GUY: Good.

Gauche cranks up the volume on Hans's radio while Derecha presses two buttons on his door, opening the front windows. The hurrying music made Guy feel like he and Hans were on a secret mission that was about to lose its anonymity.

HANS: What the—

GUY: We have to! *(He releases his numb fingers, gets out of his seat, and opens the back window.)*

GUY: It's the Big Black Pickup Truck Way!
        The harder it pours, the lower the windows go!
        (returns to his seat and buckles up, all the while bobbing his head to the song's fast beat)

RADIO: ChipoocheDee DuChi See? Nah! See? Nah! Chichichi Pubangbang!

Hans couldn't remove his throbbing hands from the steering wheel to close the windows. He was driving through downtown Baltimore and couldn't afford to be distracted.

Hans and Guy scream over the music.

HANS: **Guy! Put the—**

GUY: **But the view is so much nicer! Look out the window!**

Hans knew that Guy was a smart guy, so he heeded his feral friend's words.

HANS: *(genuinely amazed)* You're right! It's so clear!

The pickup truck slowly traversed a short stretch of the left lane.

Hans sticks his head out the window and is able to see where he needs to turn. The song's tune changes to a classical melody for seven seconds, then returns to the fast drum break beats.

HANS: Woohoo!

Hans felt like he was in a jungle in search of a nearby town, cutting through the thick, watery leaves that thrashed his face. The rain that splashed about his head was sent straight from the sky. Somehow, the window frame kept the water hugging the truck from touching him.

The truck stops for a red light.

RADIO: Badabada bam-BAM badabada bam-BAM!

Hans's left arm was completely soaked. He kept it inside, but Guy disapproved. He had his right arm out the window and drummed along to the synthesized bass line.

Mist seemed to emanate from random patches of grass next to a sleepy-looking white house with a yellow door frame. The house was on the edge of a residential peninsula bordered by watery roads. On its eyes could be seen the peering faces of young twins that giggled upon seeing Hans squinting as he drove with his head out the window.

Meanwhile, Guy was watching a tall tree swaying precariously in the wind. Its rhythm was remarkable; it looked as if its violent, manipulative movements controlled the music, for the radio seemed to absorb the branches' every push. Soon, the overcast sky lost its cool and decided to abuse the polarized troublemakers that didn't belong. The fed-up sky viciously manhandled a bright sphere of light, leaving a luminescent, piercing trail of burning remains for the little earth beings to contend with.

THUNDER: CrK KkunK CRNKuhhh!

GUY: Be extra slow here. You'll need to stop soon, almost there, nowww… **STOP!**

Guy turns down the volume.

Hans didn't know why he was stopping until he saw the amazing sight for himself. There, right in front of his truck, he saw two mature geese walking their eight tall, furry goslings across the interstate. They had miraculously passed all three lanes to the right of Hans and decided to gather in his lane.

Hans liked getting wet at first but soon became irritated at the stupid walking geese that should have been flying.

HANS: I can't believe this! I have to finish my work, Idiots! Get off the road!

GUY: Don't bother. They'll go when they're finished thinking. *(Guy gently whacks the rosary around Hans's rearview mirror, much like a cat enchanted by a necklace.)*

Happened to me every other day during Spring Break when I'd commute to the ARC from home. Strange, isn't it? My, how they've grown since the last time I saw them! Hi Fred!

The geese finally decided to move onto the median. Guy prayed silently for their safety.

Hans cranks up the volume this time and they drive on, nonstop, until they reach the ARC.

GUY: Thank you so much, Hans. And good luck with puttin' the final touches on your thesis work.

HANS: Thanks. Best of luck with your review tomorrow as well. I'll be in the Ramsey Building if you need me.

GUY: Sweet. Take care. *(He opens the door and drops out of the seat.)*

HANS: You too.

Guy closes the door firmly without slamming it. It felt much like his truck. As he waved to Hans on the glittery asphalt, he felt a bit stupid for always walking to the ARC. Earlier that week he found the perfect parking spot right behind his apartment building, so naturally he avoided using Ol' Suzie (finding another spot that close to his building would be impossible).

It was after hours again, so Guy used his key to open the front door of the Architecture Research Center. The liveliness of doomed architecture students loomed about the building and it was an ambience he had truly missed. He bonded with his studio mates. They were like family. He was glad to be standing back in the place where he belonged—at least until 8:30 a.m. when his final review would start. He couldn't wait to take a shower once that time had finally come.

Guy walks into the studio, unlocks his desk drawer, and grabs a shirt, cargo shorts, and his baseball cap. He leaves before his highly engrossed, stressed classmates notice him.

He changes clothes and puts on his cap in the bathroom. He quickly transfers the contents of his pants pockets and then uses the lavatory. Then, his left pocket decides to frustrate him.

CELL PHONE & TOILET WATER: Plop!

GUY: That's just great! I don't have time to wash you! I didn't even print my designs!

CELL PHONE: Riiiingg! Riiiingg!   Riiiingg! Riiiingg! Riiiingg! Riiiingg!

GUY: Of course. *(He sighs as he reaches into the toilet and picks up the phone with two fingers.)* As if you weren't wet enough already. Stupid phone.

Guy quickly places the phone on the tiled floor beside the trash can, throws his dirty pants on top of it, and then washes his arm. The ringing had caused the phone to absorb a lot of dirty water. He didn't care to see who called. He wouldn't care if someone were to steal it. For the phone, his pants, and any other nuisance no longer existed. All that mattered was his thirsty project.

Thoughts of his project made him salivate. He wondered whether or not he should buy the Drugless Studying Delight from his friend, CJ, who was in the studio next door. CJ's sister died last year in a car crash when she turned too quickly in front of a freight truck. The poor guy blamed himself for having lent her his car and had become more driven to succeed as an architect and a businessman, so that he could oversee the construction of a memorial for her. It was to be a life-size dollhouse, which she had always wanted. He decided he would donate it to the sister of one of the other girls killed in his car. He immediately started selling his roommate's energy-packed concoctions which were composed of 5% of this caffeinated beverage, 23% of that, mixed slowly with 12% of an edible polymer, and so on. It was an underground business, and they were very successful; the drinks were popular all night, every night, especially amongst architecture and computer engineering students.

GUY: No, I think I'll be safer drinking water.

He finds a water cooler and plucks the bottom grainy blue cup. He fills it to the brim and bends down to gulp the water. He felt much better. Only one thing was missing.

GUY: Twiiiix. I'm coming for you, Baby. You better be in this vending machine. *(walks a few steps away from the water cooler)*

It wasn't there. *He sees a redhead standing nearby.*

ELLIOT: Guy!

GUY: Hey! *(How do I know this guy again? Haha!... I can't keep from laughing! I wish I never heard that Elliot is half leprechaun.)*

ELLIOT: How's the left wing?

GUY: Broken. I hope you're a lot more productive over on the right side. *(Elliot does look magical.)*

ELLIOT: Nope. But it's not like we're procrastinating either. See, we start our projects ASAP, and we work nonstop. Yet, somehow, there's never enough time. I'm tired.

GUY: It'll all be over soon. Then we get to do this for money. Well, I'm off to find Twix. Toodles.

ELLIOT: Huhuh. See ya.

Guy walks downstairs to the opposite side of the building. He takes a special route which leads to two vending machines on the basement floor.

As he walked, he noticed a good seven Master's students pacing silently, looking possessed. He couldn't keep his eyes off NICOLE, the most attractive woman in the ARC. She was banging the side of her fist against the wall, which was quite amusing, yet nothing abnormal. He admired her for being a hard-core architect and felt inspired by her success (she was the youngest member of the team that designed the new grandiose theatre in Vienna).

Outside the ARC, the rain poured on and the sky was a bleak, unsupportive hue. It wasn't that late, but inside, it felt as if no one knew what time (or day) it was. Guy felt moved by the collective confusion and couldn't wait to finish his project.

The vending machine in the center of the basement had no Twix. He stared at where the Twix had been earlier that

Drumming Circle

week.

FRIEND?:   Guy! Man, you're getting taller and taller.

Guy doesn't recognize the voice. He turns around, slowly, meeting the friendly, tanned face of DIANE, who had been instrumental in helping him finish his final project during freshman year.

GUY: Oh, hey Diane! Wow. What's an alumna like you doing here?

She stares at one of his strong arms as she answers.

DIANE: Came to collaborate on the Wexler Brandt Prusse House in Vermont. It's going to be amazing! See— *(She notices the complete lack of emotion in Guy's long face and quickly finishes.)*

We'll talk about it more as soon as you finish your project. Good luck! And if you need help gluing hard-to-glue pieces again, let me know. Haha, good times. See ya, Shorty!

GUY: Thanks, see.

Guy felt dumb for not finishing his sentence properly as he walked towards the last vending machine, clear across the building. He looked through the student gathering by the black-framed vending machine. He felt like crying.

GUY: Twix!! *(looking upward)* I love you God! Thank you! Thank you.

(He does a heel click and then shakes the hand of each student around the vending machine.)

Heel Click

>It's going to be a great night, O, my lucky lady and gentlemany charmies. Teehee!

He opened up the smooth golden wrapper and after he bit the chocolate bar, he started singing. He then raced at full speed, curiously faster than usual, up the stairs, across the spooky hallways. He was making up for the tennis practices he had missed. (He only missed one, but his tired mind miscalculated the figure.)

Guy stops by the water cooler again and fills up seven plastic blue cups. He slowly carries them in his huge hands and places them on the right side of his table.

GUY: *(nods at the cups of water)*
Exhibit A.
A busy person's dinner and lunch. Huhuh!

He sat down in his seat and put the rest of the first crunchy chocolate bar in his mouth. As he chewed, he felt a rough cough coming up, but it was suppressed by a very pernicious yawn which threatened the completion of his project. He tucked away the second bar in his lower shorts pocket.

Guy quickly turns his head diagonally. His eyes meet NEEPA, a thoughtful, industrious fourth-year student from Jamaica who often visits the studio to help Veronica with her projects.

GUY: Neepa! It's time to awesome!!

NEEPA: How does one awesome?

GUY: I just gotsta print out my drawings and booyah!

A popular student named KRISTOPHER walks into the studio, carrying a small box underneath his left arm.

KRIS: Not gonna happen, Buddy.

Guy

> The plotter doesn't work.

ALEJANDRO, a talkative student who sits in the last row, is leaning over Jerry's desk, showing him a funny commercial that Ryoma posted on his website. He looks over at Guy.

GUY:　　You lie!

ALEJANDRO: It's true. Dude, where you been? It's been out of ink since after Environmental Systems class.

GUY:　　Oh, pooh!

JERRY:　　Haha! Guy said "pooh!"

Guy was in the same predicament two projects ago. Happily, it got repaired just in the nick of time. He had a strong conviction that this time he wouldn't be as lucky. Unable to formulate realistic methods of printing out his work, he reeled back to that time, when he had on repeat a rendition of Theme B from the Game Boy version of Tetris.

GUY:　　*My cousin! He filled my mind with hope, but how? O Chemical Engineer Ryan! Communicate to me! O... that you would! Then I'd be practically done! My foam core is naked! It needs my provocatively designed papers to clothe it!*

He presses the index and middle fingers of Derecha onto his forehead and tries to pick up a signal.

GUY:　　*Greg! Ryan's neighbor! Yes!*

Guy quickly signed onto his instant messenger account and sure enough, the future chemical engineering educator was online.

TennisGuy2242: **Greg! cuuld u PLEASE print meout the last drawngs of my final?**

xXxGREGGGG: Well, I'm not in the ChemE Bldg now...

TennisGuy2242: i'll design u a dream house! 4 FREE! PLEASE, Man, i need u!!

xXxGREGGGG: If I remember correctly, we had issues with the Rhino images...

TennisGuy2242: i'll find a way to converrt it2 whatevr form u need!

xXxGREGGGG: You're mighty lucky. Mary just came in. Hold on.

Mary was two years older than Guy. She was an Architecture and Visual Arts double major and graduated with honors before she decided to join her father's investment banking firm.

TennisGuy2242: SwEEET! Mary! i missu!

xXxGREGGGG: She said she'll help convert em. Send em BUT:

Guy's eyes were bulging with a red-orange slew of fatigue and bewilderment. His heart was pounding as he awaited Greg's answer.

xXxGREGGGG: We've been having issues with our printer as well. I'll do my best, but work as if it won't work.

TennisGuy2242: it hasnt ben wrkin?

xXxGREGGGG: Not for a week. But I haven't tried to repair it. Again, I'll see what I can do, but try doing your drawings by hand or something.

TennisGuy2242: tank u Greg! i'll be online allnight, so just lemme know... ASA the semester is dun, we gotta meet up and i'll do ur house, I PROMISE!

(Greg's screen:)
Messenger Service: Would you like to accept the file trans-
fer from TennisGuy2242?

xXxGREGGGG: Yes.

(Guy's screen once again)
xXxGREGGGG: Seriously Guy?!! 8 images!

TennisGuy2242: i luv u Greg, dont 4get that bro

xXxGREGGGG: Haha. Alright. Will message you once they're
printed. Peace.

TennisGuy2242: pax

Guy looked sadly at the images that might not get a
chance to be born. He put on his headphones and played his
Nu Metal Mix.

GUY: Why didn't I print them out earlier? They're—

Then he remembered. He recalled the frustration he threw
aside as he left for practice on Monday. He relived the times
he would beat around The Issue which he was "gonna hafta
fix later."

He had placed two women's bathrooms within nine feet
of each other. The men's bathroom was placed where he
had originally hoped to place the larger of the two women's
bathrooms. Guy looked up at the clock (although the time
was on the bottom right-hand corner of his screen) and
started fretting.

GUY: This is majorly, like, horrible? I so wish I could,
         like, punch my former, procrastinative self?
         Oh pooey!

He consciously became a fifteen-year-old snobbish girl

whose hip-hop dance was supposed to be fly for her birthday.

GUY: This just won't work? My dance is gonna be so lame! They'll hate me!

JAKE was right behind him. He was an annoying character who always exceeded expectations. During the day, he was histrionic as he feigned concern for his fellow classmates. At night, however, he was just plain arrogant.

Guy knew exactly why this insolent guy had strolled his way. He always asked classmates to see their designs in order to assure himself that they were all worse than his.

JAKE: What's wrong?

GUY: Nothing. Just frustrated that my project is so perfect that I can't truly commiserate with everyone else.

JAKE: Let me see!

Guy showed him the best picture he had, an electronic 3D perspective view that shows what a visitor would see when standing at the entrance of the Community Electronics Gallery. The attrition of Jake's teeth made the Behind In His Work Guy actually pity the Already Finished Jake.

JAKE: *(jerking his head)* That's good. Where is it?
          (He searches for Guy's display.)

GUY: It's not printed. I'm doomed. Say, where did you get yours printed?

The dismay on Jake's face instantly vanishes as he explains to Guy what he had done.

JAKE: *(chin raised)* I had foreseen this problem, so I

printed it on Monday. Well, I'm done, so if you need any help drawing...

GUY: You really think there's enough time to produce something decent? I mean, I did work on sketches earlier, but—

JAKE: No. Sorry. *(walks away)*

Guy decided that he wouldn't be mad, for he still felt bad for the man who was far from blessed physically. In addition, Jake probably couldn't even hold the tennis racket right, let alone play well. Guy was comforted in knowing that he could trounce anyone like Jake on the court.

He stares at the drawing of the extra bathroom on his computer for two minutes as his favorite song finishes. Then he skips over a song.

GUY: *(speaking softly)* Forget it. Ladies will just have to make more trips to the bathroom.

And now? Nothing is printed. Those magical two weeks spent manipulating editable meshes in 3ds Max—instead of going out with that new gorgeous girl on the tennis team. Yeah, those two weeks, and the other two weeks I spent mastering my 2D models. All to waste. That's just great! And that one grueling week of manual drafting (which was probably responsible for giving me Raynaud's Disease)— that week! *(He looks at his fingers and pauses.)*

I messed you up for no reason!
All in vain?
Maybe I should just stop torturing you.

But quit?
Guy, just polish your stupid hand sketches!

Guy feels as if the blood within each of his fingertips is condensing into little sharp thorns, scraping his skin. He violently shakes both hands.

GUY: *Wow. My fingers can't draw. What if I went to the hospital to get them checked? Nah, Andrew had a doctor's note for his injured hand last semester and still failed. Maybe I'll just go print it at the expensive—I refuse. Especially after last time. Greg will come through for me.*

Guy looked at the unfinished last wall of his model. It needed sanding.

TERRY, a Chinese man who sits in the back of the studio, starts running around, singing.

TERRY: It's *mid*night everyone!
          The *final* day!
          The *day* of our final revieeew! The—

CLARK: AWww, SHUT UP!

Guy felt good knowing that at least one other person was just as undeniably stressed as he was.

Suddenly, he realized that he hadn't changed the windows that Reuben had been adamant about mentioning. That was what he planned to do earlier that day. His professor never forgot any bit of criticism he had given. Reuben's every whim was magical and holy, so dismissing his suggestions would funnel all the sweat and nagging headaches into a big fat B... or a C, even. That is, if everything else were perfect.

Guy

Drafting

Guy sees a classmate approaching and turns down the volume on his headphones.

KENNY: Yo Guy, we're going to get some grub.
         Care to join us?

KENNY, who used to be captain of his high school's wrestling team, had just glued his model together and still saw visions of wood and glue. The large man needed a change of scenery.

Ordinarily, Guy would love to jump into Kenny's big van where he'd laugh with his infantrymen all the way to the 24-hour convenience store on North Running Road. However, he envisioned an evil, monstrous bird flying into the studio just to defecate all over his project. The evil bird smiled, unlike his ever-frowning relative, the Noble Eagle.

GUY: No thanks, but could you please buy me a tuna sandwich and some milk?

KENNY: I have no idea how much that costs.

GUY: Here. *(hands him $10)* Keep the change. *(slightly increases the volume of his metal music)*

KENNY: Awesome, Dude. Thanks. See ya soon.

Guy decided to use these last twelve hours wisely. He sprayed his drawing table with the disinfectant he kept in his drawer and wiped it with a paper towel, using the back of his hands. His fingers had regained their sense of touch and were cussing at him for having banged them so hard against the boorish bongos.

GAUCHE & DERECHA: *(in chorus)* Aaaaaaaaaaeh. Sleep, please.... Take painkillers, please....

We don't want to feel.

GUY: *(leans his head down to whisper to his hands)*
Listen guys, it's the home stretch!
You have to!

Guy banged his fingers against his drawing table. He forgot that his fingers felt as if they'd fall off before they finally became numb. Upon feeling that they were brittle, he let his fingers rest atop the firm surface. They felt useless. He shook his hands quickly, hoping to shake off the disgusting throbs that prevented him from working. With his knuckles, he turned up the volume of his music and let the metal distract him from the incapacity. He figured other architects died in the line of duty, so losing his fingers to polish up his basswood model wouldn't be so bad.

He reached into his pocket and took out his sandpaper, realizing how strange his people were for carrying such handy objects on them. The rough backing felt no softer than the grainy top.

He holds the sandpaper awkwardly in his knuckles and takes a deep breath.

GUY: Even if I have no drawings, this amazing model will speak for itself. *(looks at Gauche)* Where did I get these scratches?

Despite the shakiness of his badly scratched hand, he holds his model steadily with Derecha, enabling Gauche to polish the basswood.

THE REVIEW
XXVI

Guy walks five minutes early into the new conference room in the Ramsey Building. He is carrying a beautifully mounted display of eight images and an expertly crafted model.

Reuben wore the ugliest pants. It made Guy think of moldy rust. Next to him were equally strangely clad men and women. Three of them were wearing sandals. One man looked like an ostrich in a Polo shirt and jeans. The most distinguished of the lot, a sandals-wearer, was a very fit man whose skin matched the color of his khakis.

VERONICA: Oh my God, Guy! That looks great!

JAKE: So you paid a fortune to have it printed somewhere?

RYOMA: It's almost over!
I'm going to cook so much, Man....
I miss real food.
Party at my house Monday night!

KRISTEN: Sweet!

RYOMA: Provided I wake up by Monday....

MARAH: I can't believe we all made it here.

ABBIE: That's right, Baby! You're here! *(kisses Clark)*
Told you you'd make it!

Clark smiles although he has forgotten where he is.

CJ: *(to Clark:)* I can't believe you painted over the blood, Man.

MISHARI: It doesn't get more personal than that! It's got your DNA! *(Guy looks over at Mishari with whom he hadn't interacted since fall semester. Mishari is sitting in front of AARON, another familiar face that has recently become foreign to Guy.)*

Reuben stands up and addresses the class.

REUBEN: Ladies and gentlemen, thank you so much for being on time—I know how hard it must have been for you to get up after you slept *all night!*

CLASS: Hahahahaha!

GUY: Ha! *(coughs obtrusively)* Aaagh aaauh.

REUBEN: I'd like to introduce to you the selfless critics who agreed to personally assist you today in becoming successful architects. Heed the words of these men and women, for they are all most prominent in their respective fields.

GUY: *So that makes them automatically know what structures the future holds?*

REUBEN: Farthest to the left is Michelle, whose review column is read internationally, day to day—Thanks again for joining us Michelle.

CLASS: Clap Clap Clap Clap Clap clap clap!

AARON: *(pauses)* Clap!

IMRAN: Haha!

Reuben glares at Imran.

MICHELLE: It's a pleasure.

GUY: *Pleasure to rip us apart.*

REUBEN: To her right is the esteemed Skylar of East, the sole architect of the breathtaking Winifred Bojumps Building in Utah. We are honored to have you here, Skylar!

CLASS: Clap Clap Clap Clap Clap clap clap clap!

Skylar nods nonchalantly.

REUBEN: To his right is Priscilla, the president and founder of the world-renowned Jome Perilfor School of Design. Priscilla just came from a conference in Beijing this morning where she actually met an alumnus of our School of Architecture, Erik.

He has already designed two airports in use today, so it just goes to show you: if you do the necessary work here, and stop eating all day... *(pauses for laughs which he doesn't receive)* then you, too, will influence our everyday actions and our very perception of life.

Priscilla, thank you kindly for joining us today.

CLASS: Clap Clap Clap Clap Clap Clap Clap clap clap!

PRISCILLA: Don't mention it. I'm very inspired by this wonderful view. It's 8 a.m. and this hall is completely filled with brilliant, bright young faces! It's an honor.

GUY: *Bright faces? I'll bet everyone in the back row is asleep! Poor woman.... I suppose the critics got just as little sleep as we did—except they were probably doing more meaningful things. I can't wait to be in their place. I'll be a great critic.*

REUBEN: To her right is Lawrence. In addition to founding the Reflectionist Movement—

GUY: *No! I made that movement up!*

REUBEN: —and the Shadow Conception which he describes in his third bestseller, Lawrence has been the chief architect of such wondrous structures as the Porftly Essenger House, the Canver Mussington Theatre, the Pance Thomas Airport, and the Song Quescher Stadium; for...

GUY: *Wondrous? (He shakes his head, causing the world to spin a tad more.)* **No Guy, you have to keep practicing! Alright. "Hi, I'm Guy A—" No. How about "Thank you for coming to hear and help me with my design thoughts. I chose Linthicum because that's the place where—"** *No....*

REUBEN: ...to design a museum with an interactive gallery space and a library. The location was to be in Linthicum, Maryland, close to the BWI Airport. The building? The Historical Electronics Museum. I like to give my students the ability to think independently....

GUY: *Is this guy kidding?!*

REUBEN: ...As you can see, we have a diverse student body. Some more skilled with their hands, others digital wizards. In addition, they chose between remodeling the museum, tearing it down completely...

ASMA, a Canadian, pokes Guy who has fallen asleep.

GUY: Thanks.

Asma smiles.

REUBEN: ...to learn about the magical world of electronics. And now I'd like to introduce you to our first presenter, Guy!

CLASS: Clap Clap Clap Clap!

VERONICA: Go GUY!!

CLASS: Clap Clap Clap!

CJ: That's my boy!

CLASS: Clap Clap clap clap clap clap!

Guy walks up to the large white easel, carrying his poster under his left arm. He suddenly smiles, bends down, and picks up a small, smooth paperclip. He squeezes it in his right hand as he gets up. He then uses both hands to center his poster on the easel and drops his shiny good luck charm into his pocket.

GUY: Hello, I—augh-uh Auugh!—Oh no! Not today! Aughugh—Aaaghuh! *(Reuben doesn't at all look concerned as he glares at Guy coughing.)*

I'm Guy and this is my design of the museum. I've left each of the twelve galleries as is, and chose to design the interactive space as a virtual reality game center. *(He points to his 3D perspective image.)* Each heads—Aughugh! Augh!—Each headset has a game which describes each of the galleries.

Now, all the fun happens in your neighbor's basement game room. *(What am I saying?!)* I figure the farther down you go, the more exciting it is, which is why the stone walls resemble the limestone you'd see around Ruby Falls, the huge underground waterfall in Tennessee. The stone that separates the Historical Virtual Reality Game Room from the Science Fiction Game Room appears jagged and dangerous, but it is actually padded with thick, Aaaagh—Huh hugh!—sturdy foam.

PRISCILLA: Where is this room on your model?

Guy turns the model and points to a medium-sized room.

GUY: Right here.

PRISCILLA: I am assuming that room right next to it is a library?

GUY: Yes. Sorry. I... Auuugh Hagh hugh! Ughhuh!... got ahead of myself. My goal was to accentuate the actual galleries, while sheltering them as appropriately, but as discreetly as possible. If a visitor can easily navigate through the galleries, focusing on the displays and not at all noticing the room layout, or the wall structure, then my job was done to my satisfaction.

LAWRENCE: Son, architecture—

REUBEN: Your assignment was to design the building, not to glorify the interior accessories! Why not just have a big glass surround the building. You wouldn't need walls, for Pete's sake, if—

MICHELLE: Wait, such an interactive gallery room would be very expensive if the walls were to be completely built in padded stone—

GUY: *Lady, hold on! Okay, what architecture is, why I wouldn't do glass around building, then how I'd save costs....*

MICHELLE: —and the color would most definitely attract attention to the room.

Reuben stared at Guy, waiting for him to choke and cry in front of everyone. Guy felt his impersonal glare and decided to affront his professor's inherent desire.

GUY: I will address each comment in order. Architecture is a means of expression. I am by no means saying that our job as architects is to be submissive, subservient, and unappreciated.

Rather, I feel incredibly powerful and manipulative. I not only control the softness of the floor on which visitors walk, but also each section's climate which can send chills down their spines or warm their souls as they read about a scientist's struggles. I control the lighting which plays with their emotions, the styles of doors that they must go through— in order to go, I mean, to use the facilities *(what am I saying?)*, whether or not the ceiling makes them feel cozy or abandoned, and so on.

This is clearly inherent in every architect's job description. If I can explore these parameters enough to know what is most suitable for which type of ambience, then I can ultimately gain their comfort and compliance in feeling the way *I* want them to feel, to focus more on one pioneer's endeavors than another's and to vehemently encourage them to walk in these giants' shoulders.

(What the—It's "footsteps" or "stand on their shoulders"! O, to sleep!...

> *Haha, Mishari is sleeping on his desk!...*
> *Time for some more fake coughs!)*

Ahhhhugh huh!—Excuse me.

Lawrence nods his head very slowly, squinting his eyes in amazement at the exhausted, sick kid's passion. Guy decided that his nod was lauding his intelligent ideas.

GUY: If you'll notice, on the Interactive Gallery "cave" walls are spray-painted signs. They immediately draw attention to the big screen TVs which introduce the virtual reality room. For the bulk of the time, visitors are wearing headsets, and two of their senses are no longer under my guidance.

The pure shades of the rocks and their real shapes in the periphery subtly ingrain a strong desire to savagely explore the magic of electronics. You're absolutely right though; dark stones would definitely be so ostentatious that they'd wear out their energy. The limestone in the room, you'll find, has several different shades of brown. Most of the stones are pale goldenrod, and very small patches, maybe three in the whole room, reach saddle brown.

SKYLAR: That is the strangest-looking library! It's like a claw holding a trinket!

GUY: Since the electronics museum is very close to the airport, the "trinket" is actually modeled after an apron, where the airplanes are parked.

MICHELLE: How does the nearby airport relate to the museum's overall theme?

GUY: I—Augh! Au-augh-hUH!—Excuse me. I flew to South Carolina in February to visit a grad school and fell in love with the Charleston International Airport. Library-goers must feel how I felt.

The paintings upon the warm brown bricks give the small airport a personal, intimate atmosphere which any researcher should experience when exploring what captivates them.

(It has to have been five minutes already! Haha, the timekeeper is asleep! What a dumb face Abbie's making! Don't laugh…. Don't look at her! What is she doing, though?)

(He points to the layout.) The U-shaped atrium has two stores on the face containing the entrance. *(points to the bottom of the drawing)* The top of the bubble-shaped U has five glass walls and five white columns, underneath which is a wooden ledge. Researchers can eat a snack from the wood-framed bookstore in the east wing, or fiddle with a gadget from the shop in the west wing. On each flat end of the *U* is a grandiose painting of an established electronics aviator. Aaugh! Augh. The bookshelves—

REUBEN: Don't you think there are way too many lights in this runway library?

GUY: *(The runway is not part of the apron, O Intelligent Reuben. And if I did think there were too many, do you really think I'd have painstakingly positioned them in each of those places?)*

The library ceiling is glass so that the tarmac and the yellow stripes will seem as if they're truly on an apron outdoors.

MICHELLE: *Apron! Apron! Apron!*
Why doesn't he use another word?

GUY: The wall between the apron and the grassy field
         outside the museum is glass as well. The six
         bright lights are well above the visitors' heads,
         so they shouldn't be distracting or painful.
         Augh-huh! The lights will make the library
         exciting and vibrant at night. Augh AUGh!
         Hmph. Sorry.

LAWRENCE: This reminds me of the Ocean Pact Dome in
         Greater Michigan. Have you seen it?

GUY: No.

LAWRENCE: I'd recommend you check it out. I really like the
         way the atrium, which looks more to me like a
         V, seems almost as if it's a recuperation room
         where exhausted students can chill after re-
         search. But have you looked into the standards
         for bookstores? That one seems rather small.
         You don't want the cashier to be smashed up
         against a large customer.

GUY: *(What?!)*
         There is no cashier. It's self—

SKYLAR: You have two female bathrooms in your Com-
         munications Gallery. You tryin' to communicate
         something here?

MICHELLE: Wow! He does!

GUY: *(Nice to see he's listening to what I'm talking about.*
         Jerk.)

It's a mistake.

PRISCILLA: Why would you put the second one so close to the first? It'd be cheaper to combine them.

SKYLAR: The broad lines and minimal cusps make your building design nice and simplistic, but extra bathrooms... extra bathrooms clash entirely with the purpose of your style....

GUY: Again, it's a mistake.

MICHELLE: It's a really nice bathroom. Perhaps if you moved it to the—But no, it wouldn't make sense on the—Yeah! Why didn't you put it behind the Conference Room?

GUY: I didn't mean to—

SKYLAR: Why, you'll absolutely fry people in that library! God forbid they drop their ice cream on the dark floor. The milk will sizzle most distractingly before it evaporates onto the glass ceiling, preventing the poor, tired researchers from getting adequate light when the ridiculously large night lights are off, during the day. Their vision will end up getting way worse all because the architect decided to have so many glass walls.

GUY: *(Ice cream in my library? Is this man feeling okay?)* Actually, the windows will cut heating and air-conditioning costs by seventy percent in two years.

See, they use tungsten oxide technology, so when a potential is applied to the chemical, it either becomes dark or—

SKYLAR: Smart windows are quite expensive. What was the budget for this project?

PRISCILLA: The whole ceiling will have this technology, too? I mean, a little window I could understand, but...

LAWRENCE: I think you guys are missing the student's point. He is making everything else seemingly invisible so that he could spend a lot of money making sure that researchers don't get distracted. As a researcher, I commend you!

REUBEN: If I remember correctly, before you added these windows—which I don't believe have ever been used for a ceiling—before you added them, you were already—

MICHELLE: You're not going for a simplistic design at all! Why—

PRISCILLA: Yes he is! It's simpler to use the windows than to have to pay employees a lot less in order to pay for the expensive air-conditioning system. I'm sure such a ceiling will become the standard! Why, I never even thought about that! I like that; it's really the antithesis to Lawrence's Reflectionist Movement....

LAWRENCE: Not at all. It's very much in accordance with the principles. For the reflection is very much impressed into the glass and preserved within, only masked with the blackened chemicals. Once the chemical is reduced, the reflection shares its inherent mysticism which is the more enhanced.

SKYLAR: Stone room here, glass and bricks next door with

wood... where's the sense of connection?

GUY: Well, we're nearing five minutes *(we've probably passed fifteen minutes)*, so I'd like to quickly describe the other rooms, especially the—

MICHELLE: There is no connection?
            Lawrence, he has insulted your movement!

GUY: Not at all! I wanted the rooms to fit their purpose. When one is in an arcade, it wouldn't make sense for him to be in an environment conducive to reading. Now, the juxtaposition of these rooms actually enriches the flow, without necessarily thickening it. See, the light limestone—

REUBEN: Why on earth did you want that whole wall made of glass? It looks horrendous! It needs some stone in order to unify the building. Why, that wall looks completely out of place.

The exhausted architecture student glared at Reuben in disbelief. Guy's chest burned and his breaths burrowed through his nose vehemently.

GUY: *(He will make you look dumber if you remind him that this lovely glass wall was his doing. My goodness! He made my fingers burn so much in order to remove the "sickly hybrid" wall... That jerk. My poor fingers... and my time! And now he's trying to make me look dumb? What a hypocrite!)*

          If looked at from the inside, the glass windows make the small interior appear large. A refreshing—

MICHELLE: Pardon the interruption, but it seems you're holding back.

GUY: *You think?! Hmm... maybe I'm holding back my words because you people keep interrupting me and I can't finish explaining anything!*

MICHELLE: See, I feel so much character in your design. It's positively poetic and I love the vibes we get from each curve and window. I especially love how no two windows look alike.

GUY: *Score!! In your face! Stay silent, Reuben, please! She just made my day!*

MICHELLE: However, you shouldn't hold back. Be natural. Sink deep into your inner being and release the lever! Tell us the reasoning, and be real.

GUY: *(Boy, is **she** asking for it!)*
Why thank you, Michelle. I often feel suppressed. The strict requirements and the myriad standards make for a very tight straightjacket. The limited amount of time I feel is what hurts the design and the designer the most. But such is reality, full of budget constraints, finicky clients that don't know what's good for them, and—

REUBEN: *(glances at the clock)* Finish your sentence and that's it.

GUY: Augh augh Aagh-huh. Excuse me! And deadlines, which we need, to put a cap on our creativity, merely because we are mortal.

(Guy challenges Reuben with a glance and finds him looking at CJ who is wearing a most peculiar

face in the third row, by the wall.)

See, the clarity of the orifice manifests itself **to everyone**, yet ninety-seven percent of humans see a rusty, crumbling barrier riddled with poisonous, yellow thorns.

(Reuben's eyes quickly return to Guy.)

My arrow is to pierce the cobwebs of others' experience to let the occupants know for themselves what lies just beyond their misconceptions.

This cannot be done by daily strawberry picking or by painting over what was laced onto the rickety green bridge. No, and tattooing to their faces what needs accomplishing in order to truly live would only make them revolt.

So, by delicately squeezing the icing onto the mushroom, the bright pink rose will slowly but surely appear, much to the intoxicating mushroom's rescue. How does it save the toadstool from being devoured by the bored, lazy human spirit of prevention?

From above, the mushroom seems only an appendage. While grateful, the poor toadstool— Augh-huhue Aaghuh, excuse me— The toadstool has succumbed to the whims of the architecture's rose and is now the brighter and the safer for it.

CLASS: Clap Clap Clap Clap Clap Clap Clap Clap Clap Clap Clap Clap Clap clap clap!

REUBEN: Thank you, Guy.

LAWRENCE: Remarkable design, remarkable student. Please take one of my business cards.

Guy tilts his head and nods. He picks up both the model and his large poster.

GUY: *(I barely got to mention anything! All these renderings! So much for practicing. All those last-minute rehearsals.... And they didn't even mention the nice craftsmanship of this amazing model! Oh well, it's over, Baby!!!)*

Thank you all for your advice and criticism. I would shake your hands but, Augh-huh, Augh-Aahuh! I'm a bit sick at the mom**ENT**—AAAUGH-hUHAAAAuGH-HUh, Aaaghuh ahuh—Reuben, I need to—

REUBEN: Yes yes, you're excused. Good job, Guy. Get well.

CLASS: *Has Reuben become human?*

Guy picks up one of Lawrence's cards and nods at him, deferentially.

AARON: Clap! *(Maria looks quizzically at Aaron who answers her by looking right at her, extending his arms towards her face.)* Clap!

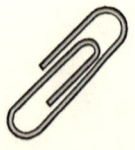

GOING HOME

XXVII

Guy walks across campus, annoyed that the conference room was in the building farthest from his apartment.

He felt neither relieved nor content about the review. He wished he could have presented longer to explain why he had made this move or that, and especially to go over the Fundamentals Gallery design. He felt angry, more at the critics than at himself, for having let down the Guy who worked painstakingly on the project.

GUY: Oh no!

He saw Kevin in a green shirt, and suddenly his stomach felt heavy. His friend had just robbed him of his dream. Instead of sleeping all day, he dismayingly recalled that he had practice that afternoon. He sighed as he overheard random lively bits of conversations.

PHIL*:   ...I know! I didn't get to bed til like eleven....

Guy frowns in disgust and is grateful that he is too tired to scream at him for such a stupid complaint.

ADRIANA: ...but would Copernicus have lived?

MOCKINGBIRD: Tee-uhr! Teee-uhr, Teeur!

MIKEY: ...scored forty-two points! It was amazing!

Guy smelled the soft scent of cherry blossoms and reminisced about those years when he could follow the Bulls. He hadn't watched a basketball game in two years.

OLIVIER: ...very unfair. I mean, he hadn't gone over half the...

STANLEY: ...probably eat at the Student Union. D-Hall is too far....

---

*I don't know these people so I gave them random names.

GOOSE: Gwawg.

Guy turns his head and sees the goose hanging out by the Biology Building.

MORGAN: ...around sixty copies, but the first two don't look nearly as real as the...

PIERCE: Hahahaha! HA!

CARLA: ...a ZERO! And I was on time! How can he start the class five minutes...

Guy was now by the pond which was etched in silver by the fluffy tummies of Mrs. Duck, Mr. Duck, and their six curious babies.

GUY: Gwawk! Gwawk!

None of the Ducks returns his call as they quickly paddle away.

GUY: Fine, stupid Ducks!
        Be unfriendly!

SPARROW: Tee-uhr!

GUY: Tee-uhr! Teeur!

Guy looks up at the library and finds the sparrow on a black wraparound light fixture.

GUY: Tee-ur!

The bird flies over him and perches atop a branch in a tree to his right.

SPARROW: Tee-ur!

GUY: *(looks up at the bird)* **Okay then!**

Guy's eyelids were being pulled down forcefully by Sleep Deprivation. He resisted and successfully squinted for some time before his eyes shut completely. He walked seven steps with his eyes closed before shaking his head. He took the small, muddy dirt path that students had worn into the grassy hill and finally made it home.

The door was unlocked. He dropped his project onto the sofa chair and went straight to the fridge. Upon seeing the task at hand, his fingers became inflamed, so Guy set down the water bottle on the counter and unscrewed the cap with his teeth. As he drew the one-gallon bottle to his dry mouth, a lot of water spilled onto his Polo shirt. He continued drinking until a fifth of the gallon was inside his weak body.

Guy wanted to prepare something to eat, but he couldn't help but envision his hand being fried with black pepper in olive oil. He laughed at the thought of eating his hands and then realized he was delirious.

GUY: But I to chew I should some food, so tired. But should eat so energy practice for!

His withering jaws finally convince him to sleep.

GUILTLESS HAZE
XXVIII

Guy went to the bathroom to wash his face. After drying it, he looked at the mirror, not registering whether or not his reflection was present. He was alone with his thoughts.

GUY'S HEAD: I live by the ninety-seven rule.

GUY: What?

GUY'S HEAD: *(silence)*

Guy always wrote down the random things his head would tell him. Once it said, "In this state and lousy community." Other times it would say made-up words or names of people who died in the 1800s. He always wrote down these "soundings," as he called them, on scraps of paper, and laid them on his desk to look up later.

Guy grabs the pen by the sink and writes on the index card he had left in the bathroom two weeks earlier.

PAPER: 97 RULE

He puts the piece of paper in his pocket and initiates a conversation with himself, still standing in front of the mirror.

GUY: I wrestled a bear. I went to unknown places.
         I pretty much wanted to not feel my pain,
         But willingly used it to keep me awake.
         I should have worked on my project more.
         I climbed that huge tree.
         I was naked around leeches.
         I made my fingers worse.

He raised his fingers and nonchalantly noticed the strange whitish green color his skin had become above each top knuckle. Then his eyes returned to the clear, opaque white glass that refused to show him his face.

GUY: I risked my life. Mom would have been horrified.
       I didn't call her. She's probably worried.

(looks left, at nothing)

       All these things and more I can't remember.
       Why don't I feel guilty? I actually am not tired.
       Strange. Right now, I am not even confused.
       I merely am, or am I? I should feel bad,
       But no, maybe I would do it again.
       But I don't care. I'm disinterested.
       I don't care to sleep. I don't care to feel.
       My fingers are ablaze in protest,
       But what did I do wrong? Was I wrong?

(looks back at the mirror)

       I should feel bad. But I don't. I don't feel guilty.
       I don't care. That's bad.

He leaves the bathroom feeling normal and undisturbed.

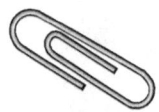

Guy had reached that stage where he was no longer capable of being tired. He only moved more slowly. He used to be alarmed when this state of inefficiency crept in, but this time, he merely stood in the middle of his room, looking up at the ceiling.

GUY: God, I probably sinned by putting my life in
          danger and by worrying Mom.
       I think.

I wasted a day that I needed to use writing and
   project doin'.
If I'm becoming bad, please help me,
But I feel more in control of my mental
   faculties than ever before,
For I'm not tired.
Really, I didn't care about whether or not You
   protected me.
You did, and I thank You,
But I don't feel bad at all.

I don't.

He looks down underneath his bed. He saw a bottle of a vitamin-rich drink that he had recently bought to make sure that his work wouldn't render him completely unhealthy.

The cap was blue with white drops of light flush with the firm plastic. The thin wrapper was shiny and the words written upon it in silver ink were so vivid that Guy could not help but stare.

He fell onto his knees, crying. He cried as he reached the bottle, cried as he felt the ridges of the container making hissing sounds as he slid his knuckle across the wrapper, and cried as he stared at the bottle even more.

An onlooker would not understand what life-changing phenomenon had just occurred. The astute spectator would most likely not be able to relate to the event either, for so few people have experienced what it feels like to feel his or her blood at every location of one's body. Even fewer have left a familiar world for one in which colors are finely textured, objects are experiences, and sounds splash playfully upon one's cognizance. And even then, nearly no one has truly been awakened to what it feels like to exist.

The second he saw his first object, he immediately felt the sharp tinge of being. His existence, although seemingly more confusing and exaggerated, rushed all around him, engulfing his body into a sparkling silver crate whose brilliance could never be ignored.

The feelings of a child taking a forbidden cookie haunted Guy throughout his life. His mind was merely a workstation whose activities were as innocuous to the worker as crawling on the soft, brown soil. Guy felt that his feelings, dreams, and infatuations (which comprised ninety percent of his mind's crystal clevises) were nothing more than old wind-blown dandelion seeds that had lost their feathery sails years ago. The seeds remained in his mind, disseminating all over though never producing any flowers. It was heretofore uncontrollable. The subtle discomfort remained padded as the emaciated seeds hit from all sides. But after feeling his presence, this overwhelming rush of incomprehensible moving feelings, his mind stopped.

ALARM: Ri—Riiing! Ri—Riiiiing!
             Ri—Riiing! Ri—Riiiiing!
             Ri—Riiing! Ri—Riiiiing!

DOOR: BUM BUM BUM!

ALARM: Ri—Riiing! Ri—Riiiiing!

SID: GUY! WAKE UP!

ALARM: Ri—Riiing! Ri—Riiiiing!
             Ri—*(Guy turns off the alarm.)*

GUY: Sorry.

Guy gets up, brushes his teeth, uses the restroom, then looks through his dresser.

He only finds socks and his last clean pair of shorts, so he walks up to the room of his thin suitemate, a Computer Science major who has been programming since yesterday.

GUY: Sid, could I please borrow a shirt?

Guy spots a shiny jumbo paperclip on Sid's dresser. Sid grabs a grey shirt from his closet, hands it to Guy while looking at his code, and then returns to his seat to program some more.

GUY: Thanks, Man.... *(points to Sid's paperclip)* **Hey, need this?** *(Sid looks up for less than a second.)*

SID: Nah, Man, you keep it. Happy birthday.

GUY: Thanks!

Guy smiles and immediately knocks one of the clip's knees outward with the middle knuckle of his index finger as he returns to his room.

He leaves the paperclip on his dresser and looks at it hopefully, looking forward to transforming it as soon as he has the time.

He quickly throws off what he had worn to the review and puts on his preferred attire.

His head still felt heavy, but he was incredibly awake. His eyes felt the same as they did when he was an energetic six-year-old walking to gym class at Bowie Mills Elementary.

He opens the white fridge. Guy appreciated the light radiating all over. He wondered how far the rays reached before becoming invisible. For clearly, every beam of light grew infinitely from the source. He stared at the fridge after pulling out bologna and felt honored to be able to free some light flashes whenever he opened the fridge.

His fingers hadn't improved, but he no longer acknowledged pain.

Guy grabs two slices of bread, tears open the bag of bologna, and makes his lunch.

GUY: This grayish buzzing taste. Why did I ever classify you as pain? This taste is not debilitating, but merely peculiar and intriguing.

He grabs his dark-green tennis bag and leaves, eating his sandwich as he walks.

Sadness, bitterness, despair—everything unreal had become very foreign to him.

In spite of his physical weakness, he walks upright towards the courts.

TREE TENNIS FANS
XXIX

It is time for tennis practice.

Guy's eyes were fixed on the green tennis courts as his black sneakers sped across the grass. The large leafy trees beside the eighteen-foot fence were splotched atop with yellow dew spread generously by the sun. The color difference was so sharp that Guy wondered if the yellow leaves were overhanging from another tree. He tightly held the strap of his tennis bag which graced his left shoulder, and quickened his gait.

Guy arrived and was welcomed by a strong, refreshing breeze which stifled his white shorts. His poor shorts were further assaulted by the aggressive shaking of his large tennis bag.

He sets down his tennis bag on the grass and starts running. With great speed, he dashed past the trees. The leaves waved and cheered like fans on the sideline, all in succession, as he dashed towards the locker room for halftime. He nodded at his tireless fans as they waved, blowing kisses of woodwind delight to his nasal passageways. As he stretched, some of his teammates started running. Guy glanced over at Coach Paul who was instructing EDDY, a junior, how to minimize arm movements without sacrificing force. Eddy is an incredibly agile Estonian whose amazing skills are a natural consequence of his ability to dynamically translate ideas into actions.

Two teammates approach Guy: ASHLEY JOE, a freshman recruit from Iowa; and SETH, a conceited half-Argentinian, half-German junior.

ASHLEY JOE: Guy! Where you been?

GUY: Hey Joe. I was sick, Man.

SETH: Paul is mad at you. Said you aren't playin' to-morrow regardless of how good you think you are. No big loss, though, cuz I'll still be there and our team will win without you. Don't worry.
(elbows Ashley Joe in the arm and smiles)

GUY: Thanks, Moron! I'm counting on you and your ugly face to scare away the other team. I know you won't let me down.

Guy felt warm and liberated at "moron." He smiled back at the ever-grinning Seth who expected a nonchalant "Well, I hope we win, but yeah, I'll be ready for the next match." Guy's polite, dignified comebacks always disgusted Seth, which is why Guy always made them. However, the hypocritical diplomacy of his words was never fully satisfying to Guy, regardless of how greatly it angered Seth. But now, Guy felt great as did the original taunter and there was no more genuine rancor between them.

Guy bent over to stretch his calves. He was grateful that his sweaty back could actually feel the warmth of the sun instead of knowing only joint pain and extreme weakness. He forced his back upright and was once again a six-foot-four man with remarkable posture.

COACH: Guy, I'm very disappointed in you. Two days be-fore a tournament and you go AWOL. Sad, because you're the most committed, reliable player we have.... Or *were* anyway. Work on your groundstrokes today with Jorge.

GUY: Yes, Sir. Won't happen again.

Guy just stands there, looking at Coach Paul as he starts to-wards the third court. Coach slowly stops and turns his head over his right shoulder.

COACH: And yeah, I know time is scarce for you Architecture majors, so see you Monday.

Guy's pang of guilt disintegrated, leaving in its wake a russet of hope for the following match, and an overwhelmingly warm blanket of comfort. He thought fondly of the studio last Saturday, when Veronica made a cardboard instrument, at the peak of her delusion, and Clark started dancing to the silent, visible music that their sleep deprivation allowed them to experience.

Then he realized that Studio II was somehow over. He nodded to himself, acknowledging the sense of brotherhood that was only going to become stronger as the years progressed and his studio-mates grew older with him during his senior and super-senior years. He then envisioned himself lying on his nice, cozy bed at home, within walking distance of his mother's tasty, fresh Mediterranean dishes. He was happy Coach wasn't going to make him go to the Saturday match to watch.

Guy turns around towards the other players. He walks up to Jorge who is by the water jug.

GUY: Want to do the Eight Drill?

JORGE: *(gulps the last portion of his water)* Sure.

On the way to their empty court, Guy couldn't help but watch Seth playing a practice doubles match on the middle court. He was faring decently, but he definitely didn't look as good on the court as Guy. The weirdo's comfort zone was just above his knee, so a goofy dance accompanied each slice and drive.

Guy and Jorge took their spots on the far court by the gym. Guy stood with his back facing the gym, looking on towards the Academic Services Building.

GUY: I'll go first.

Guy took his position behind the baseline, slightly towards the left. He released the ball and the court pushed it back up into his hand, forcing Guy to feel the coarse fiber of the bright ball's fur. He dribbled it once more and then it was time to serve.

He threw the ball high into the air and then felt his knees winding up for the spring's release. The ball was the only thing that existed for him at that moment. He didn't think about the thoughtfulness of the tennis court architect who knew exactly where the sun rises (and sets) and placed the court on the location that would protect Guy's eyes during this serve. He didn't think about yesterday's crazy adventures, or about how he needed to call his mother.

No. The ball was an extension of himself, connected to the rest of his body through his blue eyes' sinewy arms. And now, his mind was focused solely on his neon knuckle.

The tennis ball reached its point of zero velocity and sailed downward. Guy's strong left arm had been anxiously awaiting this moment. In less than a second, his springy legs bounced up and his biceps tensed as his hand carried the bottom portion of the white-gripped handle behind his torso. Becka's net found the bright green spider. Guy's entire sweaty arm glistened in the sun as his wrist turned behind his head, sending the tennis web spinning crosscourt.

Jorge's return was not what Guy had expected, which is why

Guy with his Instrument of Choice

Guy benefited from practicing with him. Jorge's right hand hit the ball down the line, causing Guy to quickly retreat. Guy's speed allowed him plenty of time to get in the perfect position for a deep topspin drive, since the ball remained suspended in the air longer than usual. Guy used both hands to give the ball the extra weight to drop onto the deuce court. Guy's drop shot beckoned Jorge to rush towards the net, which was exactly what Jorge needed. Jorge answered with a half volley down the line. In the spring break tournament in Virginia, his half volley cost him the match since he was naturally a defensive player. His discomfort at the net played out on the court.

The ensuing relay consisted of Guy constantly hitting crosscourt, with Jorge finishing up the figure eight by hitting down the line every time. Then they switched.

Guy thoroughly enjoyed this physical chess. Completely focused, he was able to learn about Jorge's techniques and reactions with each hit. He processed this information immediately and, although he had the information and the ability to destroy Jorge in a match, he used the opportunity, instead, to practice some of the harder shots and twist embellishments which made him a fun practice partner.

Jorge had a harder time reading the ambidextrous player's moves. However, the reason why had little to do with Guy's ability. Jorge had just broken up with his girlfriend, and although his mind was focused on practice, he was driven by a strong feeling of disgust and regret which tired him prematurely.

BLUE JAY: GAAAAaaaaa-auh! GAAAAaaaaa-auh!

Guy looks up and answers the bird's generic greeting while Jorge wipes his face on a white towel.

GUY: GAAaaaaa-aaaauh!

JORGE: You are crazy! Musta hit five twist serves!

Guy smiled. He looked out at the students on the sidewalk which formed a forty-five degree angle with the left side of the Academic Services Building. They were rushing to get to class, and he pitied them. While the same breeze caressed them also, there is no way it touched them in the same way. His body was more receptive to nature, to the scents, and to the sounds that enriched his life. This hard court was all his; he got to run all over it like he did when he was a kid playing tennis in the oasis, two streets behind his home, many trees away from the busy main road. The trees were not the same at his university, but the breeze's delicious aroma of nature easily erased thirteen years of his troubles so that he was once more an eight-year-old, running around, not thinking about all the homework that he was going to have to do in the fourth grade.

It was time to go lift. He felt exhilarated but could not bring himself to accept incarceration in the sweaty weight room.

EDDY: Hey Guy, what time is it?

Guy reaches into his pocket to find his phone.

GUY: Oh no! My phone's in the ARC!

He puts on his headphones and runs to the gym to put his tennis bag in his locker. He grabs his student ID and keys and then starts running. He makes it to the woods just outside the ARC in a record 4 minutes, 26.5 seconds.

THE 97 RULE

XXX

BIRDS:	Tweet! Tooouh! Toooouh! Titititi! Teeur Tooer Tahur!
GUY:	Teeur!
ROBIN:	Teeur Toour Teahr!
GUY:	Teeur! Teeur! Teeuhur Teeur teeur!
ROBIN:	Teeeur!
GUY:	Teeur!

The volume of his music was low expressly so that he could chat with his bird friends. The birds by the ARC never disappointed him. As he ran on, he noticed for the first time that the bushes outside the creek valley had berries. The green, purple, deep blue, and neon-blue berries caused Guy to stop and stare.

GUY: When did you guys grow? *(shakes his head)*

Guy does the limbo underneath a low branch which extends six feet horizontally from a light-brown tree trunk.

He then follows the worn out grass until he reaches the woods. To his left is a small mahogany pile of dog feces which seems to have glistening neon-green spots. As Guy walks past it, the flies buzz away, inadvertently leaving their brown malodorous prize vulnerable.

Guy looked at the beautiful shades of green and blue which colored the watery rocks in the creek. He felt a soft breeze which somehow sharpened his hearing as it delivered the creek's earthy green scent to Guy's nostrils.

CRICKETS: Kcreeeekuh Kcreeeekuh Kcreeeekuh...

Guy

The crickets' song blended beautifully with the song that Guy was currently playing. His mood turned slightly dour as he listened to the sixth song on his Mix playlist; the song reminded him of Project Two from earlier in the semester, and how his AutoCAD file could not be imported since his computer decided to delete it.

In the middle of the seventh song, which reminded him of one of the group trips in Kenny's car to the convenience store, he was at the door of the ARC. He put his music in his pocket and greeted LYNN, the sweet, petite, middle-aged secretary. He had often worked in the building during her entire shift, yet he rarely got a chance to see her.

Lynn is busy sorting files in the room across from her office.

GUY: Hi Lynn.

LYNN: Oh *hi* Guy!

He keeps running and swings open the steel door of the bathroom. He looks beside the trash can and sees his pants. He throws them to the side and sure enough, his phone is there, with its headset still connected.

He immediately picks it up and calls his mom.

PHONE: Beeeee-eep.   Beeeee-eep.

MOM: Hello?

GUY: Hey Mom!

MOM: Guy! I was so worried!
         You didn't answer your phone or email!

GUY: I'm sorry, Mom. Been so busy. I had my last review today, though.

MOM: That's great! So you'll come home tonight?

GUY: I'm in no shape to drive and I hope to sleep all night and day after I study... but I should be up by Sunday.... Maybe Saturday. I'll see you then, God-willing.

MOM: Alright. Oh yeah! About that strange bird: I think it's just a warning to stay inside when it's late. What a strange occurrence.

GUY: Huh? *(He then remembers emailing her on Wednesday night about the strange blackbird that followed him.)* Oh, right. I'll stay in my apartment by eleven thirty. Good idea. Thanks Mommy. Love you.

MOM: Love you too, Honey. Now go study!

GUY: Haha, I will. Bye.

MOM: Bye.

His mom hung up the phone less than half a second after saying goodbye. His eldest cousin was the same way; they always hung up quickly.

He shut his phone and then wondered why he had left it by the trash can earlier that day, or yesterday (he forgot when he last had his phone).

GUY: Oh yeah....

He turns it off, then runs it under warm water, using his green fingers to rub soap into the buttons and all over the headset. He figured the water might ruin the phone, but it was either clean it or throw it away without trying to rescue it.

Guy

He finishes rinsing it and lays it on the sink, to his left. He then washes his hands and ear.

METAL CRANK: Keeeee-eer.

He tears off just enough paper to dry off his hands, ear, phone, and headset. He then shuts the phone and puts it in his pocket.

Jake enters.

JAKE: Guy! Congratulations! It went great!

GUY: Thanks.

Guy dried his phone and headset, watching in awe as the clear water crept up the towel, sending little rays of darkness to alter the towel's texture when dried.

JAKE: The crits didn't always wait for you to explain, but I suppose my review was just *different*, which is also why they gave me extra time to *elucidate*.

Guy throws away the dampened paper towel.

GUY: Okay.

JAKE: And you know what else?
               [unintelligible braying]

Guy left, not feeling the least bit sad or jealous. He merely didn't feel like wasting his words or his precious time.

Guy, Cyril, and Kristen had already stuffed all their supplies in boxes and piled up in CJ's van shortly before the review. It was a fun ride to the apartments. Daftness, anxiety, and excitement filled the air-conditioned vehicle, for each was never to return to that studio again. As seniors, they'd most likely get into the new Rogers Building for Design Studio III.

Yet, there was Guy, looking at the chipped paint on the walls, the dark stairwells, and the blotchy tiled floor of his beloved ARC.

GUY: *I'm really gonna miss this place.*

Guy leaned over and poured himself some water in a blue paper cup. He filled it up, drank it all, and then filled it up again, looking up at the bulletin board by Lynn's office as he drank.

PAPER: Earn 67% more with Beads & Spiral Landscapers!

GUY: That reminds me!

He hurries to his old computer. Guy felt melancholy; it was strange seeing no one else in the studio. He felt as if the fan blowing inside his computer was singing of good memories that could never be relived.

He sets his cup by the monitor and turns the computer on to search online for the "97 Rule."

GUY: What is this rule by which my mind lives?

He found a dense site about the solar system and felt even more confused. He kept searching and finally, there it was.

WEBSITE: 97% of anything is trash.
          This includes 97% of what you do at work and
             at home.
          97% of what you say is trash,
          And 97% of the people to whom you speak,
          Will immediately forget what you say.

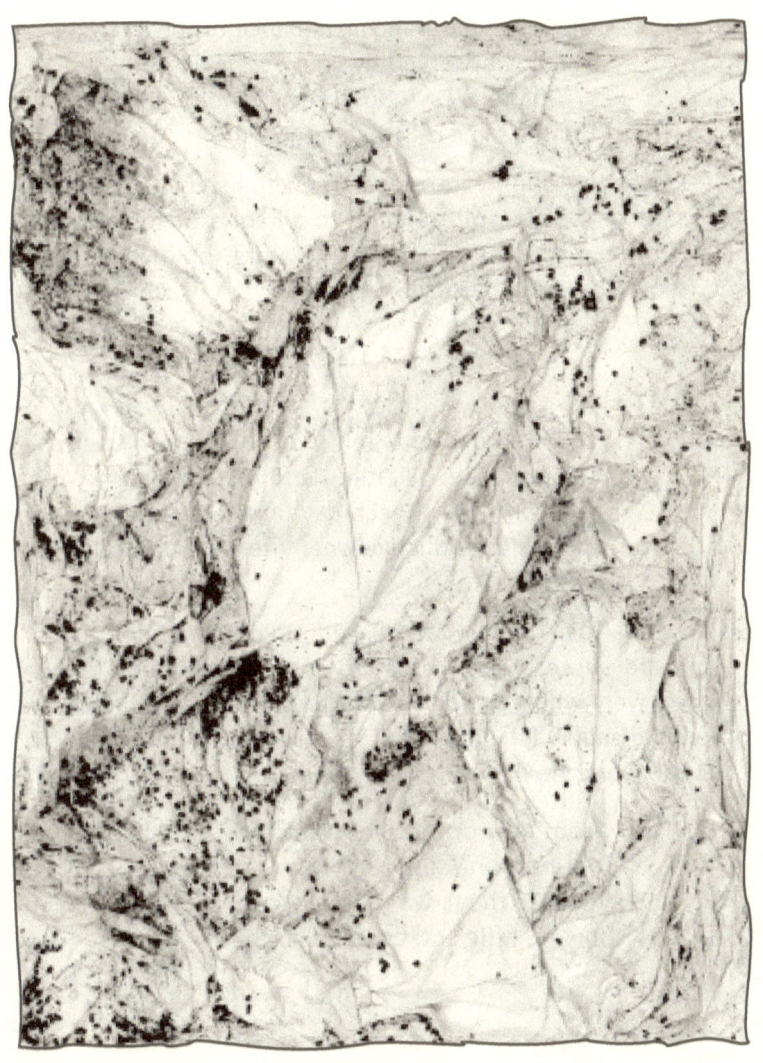

The 97 Rule

> These are natural consequence of the **97 Rule**,
> Which is observed by your very own body.
> 97% of your DNA does nothing for you,
> And the same is true about 97% of your brain cells.

Guy was thoroughly intrigued. The site listed 166 specific examples of a 97/3 split relating to all sorts of topics such as art forms, economics, history, literature, politics, health, entertainment, and pharmacology.

He rereads the definition and immediately formulates an extension of the rule.

GUY: 97% of emotions felt are completely useless, theoretical, debilitating, and unhelpful. Why, it's true! Only 3% of each day finds me clear-minded and truly productive when I feel that 3% of other emotions!

And so Guy knew what he had to do. In order to be happy and successful, in order to continue to enjoy tennis competitively while growing as an inspirational architect, in order to disallow Raynaud's Disease from dictating when he could do work, he had to reverse the rule.

GUY: From now on, 97% of what I feel will matter, 3% will not, until little by little, the 3 lends itself to the 97; then I will finally become 100% GUY: a loving, efficient, creative machine.

LEAVING THE ARC WITH PAPERCLIPS AND A BINDER CLIP ARM

XXXI

Guy had never heard of such a rule and wondered how the thought had come into his head. He searched online and found the script of the last movie he had watched.

In the Find box, he typed in all variations of the name (97, 97%, Rule, Partition, 3%, Split, etc.) but found nothing.

He rubbed his chin as he shut off his ARC computer, one last time.

Guy slowly rises from his chair, eyes wide open. He turns to face the empty studio and feels a sharp tinge of excitement as his eyes skim the floor, chancing upon five eclectic paperclips.

He smiled and jogged a victory lap towards each one as classical music played in his head. The first was a white medium-sized plastic paperclip with orange stripes. He winked at it as he picked it up and kept it in his right hand, Derecha. Five feet behind his desk lay the second, a large, dirt-speckled butterfly clip. He didn't like its unseemly appearance, but became fond of it nonetheless after bending it with ease. He smiled as he looked at his aching fingers which had deep grey lines where he had held the clip as he bent it.

The butterfly paperclip was about six feet in front of the third paperclip, the first serrated clip Guy had seen in a long time. He picked it up very slowly and ran the back of his thumbnail along its long leg, trying to glimpse the metallic sound that was felt by the blood beneath his nail.

He added the gregarious paperclip with the others in his right hand and quickly jogged to the last desk in the last row where he thought he saw a large, shiny silver paperclip. It was a broken arm of a binder clip. Although he only picked up paperclips that he could bend into shapes, Guy made an exception for the rigid arm whose shape and luster he couldn't help but admire. He then looked at the desk in front of him and reluctantly picked up a plastic green triangular clip which looked incredibly stupid to him. He remembered the 97 Rule and the brittle, modern paperclip started encouraging Guy, so he kissed it, laughed, and then put his new paperclip collection in his shorts pocket.

Guy walks back to his desk and picks up his blue paper cup with Gauche, his left hand. He then faces the empty room and waves.

GUY: Goodbye, my home. I never thought this day would come.

           Please—don't cry. I will certainly visit when a younger student needs my help.

           Take care.

He walks backwards, waving until he passes the doorway. He then does lunges all the way to Lynn's office. If anyone had witnessed his antics, they would surely have questioned his mental condition.

Lynn looks up, sees Guy, and smiles warmly.

LYNN: So you're finally finished with your studio class! Congratulations!

Lynn takes out his index card and hands it to him. He hands her the keys to the building, supply closet, and studio. By accepting the keys, he felt as if Lynn was relieving him of stress and suffering that Studio II still demanded. He knew it was over though, and that he no longer needed to work on his museum design. Instead of reassuring Guy that he could move on, Lynn's smile made him feel like he was forced to discard an epic chapter of his life. The discomfort quickly vanished, however, as he imagined how long he would have had to wait for Reuben to sign him out after everyone's presentation.

GUY: Yup, finally. *(He signs the card as she examines the numbers on his keys.)*

LYNN: You're all set then!

GUY: Thanks, have a great weekend.

LYNN: You too!

Guy returns to the water cooler, refills his cup, and gallops through the door, lifting his knees as high as he can.

GUY: Teeeur! Teeeeee-ur! Teeeur!

SPARROW: Teeeur!

GUY: Teeeur tee.

SPARROW: Teeeur.

The sparrow flies to another tree where he tells his wife that Ugly Bird said his class was over.

Guy racewalks while sipping his water. A gang of blackbirds looked down on him from a nearby tree. They wondered how Ugly Bird always had so much water. Did he have a hidden pond? Did he scrape the water off the windows of cars early in the morning and store it?

MR. HAY
XXXII

Guy looks to the right of the Architecture Research Center and sees the huge hill just beyond the woods. He had to climb it. He had always wanted to and there was no time like the present. He kept his music in his shorts pocket.

He jogs into the woods. He heard birds in the background and leaves being ruffled violently by some bigger animal. He ran on and followed the creek to a wide stream across from Mr. Hay, the big two-hump hill. There was no path worn by humans.

Guy looked back and realized he had already trekked pretty far. The corpulent hill was not as close as he thought. It was 4:30 p.m. There was plenty of light, but Guy somehow felt uneasy being in this wild area. He looked down and felt a bit comforted upon seeing a small pink plum which was half eaten.

GUY: Wonder which squirrel put you there.
           Wonder why he didn't finish you....

He reached a natural ridge separating the sides of the creek. He slowly crossed it, again quickly lifting his knees high, this time to avoid getting stuck in the mud (although the dirt was actually dry).

GUY: I wish I were wearing pants.
           This will be interesting....

He reached a patch of thorn bushes and was grateful for having looked down before walking through them.

SPARROW: Teeeur!

Five sparrows fly to a bush to Guy's right, away from Mr. Hay.

He follows them and whistles in gratitude.

GUY: Teeur! Teeur! Teeeur!

They had flown on top of a small, thornless path which Guy took, and now, diagonally in front of him stood Mr. Hay. No longer a huge, inaccessible celebrity, Mr. Hay presented its smaller hump to Guy.

After jogging to its base, he cautiously walked up the hump, expecting to sink into the mound of hay at any instant.

To Guy's surprise, Mr. Hay was a true hill in his own right. His stomach and limbs were made of the same earth as the grassy field around him.

Guy runs up the first hump and stops midway to look around. He looks over the woods, the ARC, and clear across campus.

GUY: Why hasn't anyone ever climbed this hill? What a view!

Guy looked straight across to Rhody Courtyard. He would always look at the distant hill of hay through the courtyard when he walked to the dining hall. It was nice to be on the other side for a change, seeing from the perspective of the friendly hill.

He runs to the top of the first hump and looks directly across the woods at the parking lot near the ARC.

SIREN: Oowwwaaaaaaaaaa'Aaaaaaaeeeeeeeeuu! Waow Waow Waow Waow Waow!

Guy sees a police car drive towards the satellite parking lot edge closest to Mr. Hay.

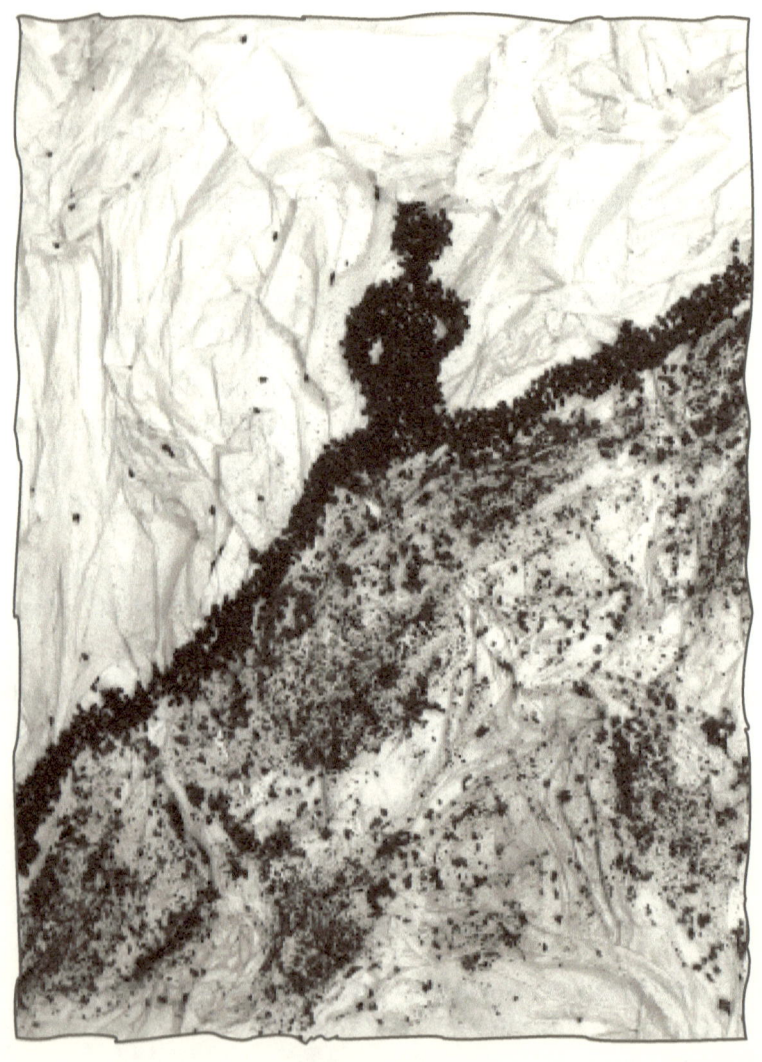

Guy & Mr. Hay

GUY: I've been seen!

He ran down the opposite side of Mr. Hay and wondered if the copper would know how to get to Mr. Hay without getting badly scratched. Guy ran past the straw hill and was frustrated at seeing tall spikes of straw sticking out from the ground. The scarce wooden spikes soon became smaller and more populous as he ran deeper into the field. He couldn't step on them, for the straw was wooden and could snap, apprising the cops of Guy's whereabouts. He carefully zigged through the small openings.

Guy could no longer walk directly towards campus. The sticks were so close that they formed a natural fence that only a small mammal could zag through.

He turned around and ran towards a section of the woods near the cops. He raced alongside the rocky catchment to get closer to the main campus. Awakened fear sparked his excitement which made him so adventurous that he jumped onto a rock, clear across most of the creek.

Twenty feet left of where he had jumped were rocks lined up nicely for him to cross. To his right stood a huge stone which would have been perfect to hold up his 195-lb frame while he pondered what move to make next.

But alas, he had jumped onto a tiny stone and was now balancing on Bruce, his left foot, about to send marine bacteria flying by falling into the water.

The moment he started falling forward, he quickly leaned backwards and grabbed a branch that happened to be the second largest in the woods. Luckily, it was secure and he was able to stay dry a bit longer.

He was far enough that he would not be able to return to his launch zone, but not too far not to hear the branches he left behind him. They cautioned him and soon, he knew why. The branch he was holding for support was cracking.

He could no longer gather information about his surroundings and possible escape routes. He leapt and searched in midair for the closest rock. His foot found a slightly smaller rock within stepping distance from the other side.

As soon as Santiago, his right foot, touched the rock, he jumped for land, sinking the unstable rock which splashed water onto his scratched legs.

Guy runs to his apartment.

The police car siren continued playing in his head like a dance song until he finally reached his apartment for a much needed shower.

BACK TO EVERYDAY
COLLEGE LIFE

XXXIII

Guy rubbed the olive drab towel all over his short damp hair and looked for his *Environmental Systems* book. He found the big paperweight in between other books which also served as weights that held together a torn book and its recently glued cover.

He felt his oft-burdened mind being cleansed when he moved aside the thick books about architecture theory, electronics, and design. (He was required to read them in the planning stages of his final Studio project.)

Guy lifts a short, thick book about electronic design.

GUY: Now that Studio's over, I will finally be able to read you.

Still holding the book, he glanced down at the blue *Environmental Systems* book which was patiently waiting for him. He felt guilty as he lifted the paperweight.

He turns his head, returning his eyes to the book with a dark-red cover. He pets it with the back of Derecha.

GUY: Well, finals will be over soon enough.

Guy stacks the electronics book with the others, picks up his Environmental Systems book, and places it in his backpack along with his notebook.

As he exits the apartment, he sees his suitemate, Bryan, walking up the sidewalk. He holds the door open for him.

BRYAN: Guy! You're alive!

GUY: Haha. How ya been?

BRYAN: Good. Tim treated the whole team to donuts after last night's win!

GUY: You won it. Congratulations!

BRYAN: Thanks, Man. Perhaps I'll see you again. Hah!

GUY: Huhuh—Possibly. Take care.

BRYAN: *(walks through the door)* See ya.

Guy walks down the steep incline perpendicular to the path leading to the library.

SPARROW: Tiht!

Guy looks up and spots the white sparrow who is responding to another bird.

A beautiful brown bird then flies right in front of Guy's eyes.

GUY: Tiht!

BROWNIE: Tiht!

Guy felt honored that the bird would respond to him while flying. Usually birds in flight would wait to disparage him from a safe distance up a tree.

GUY: Tiht!

Brownie flew away, still unconvinced that Guy was the bird talking to her.

Guy walks alongside Barberry Hall, vaguely recalling seeing Woman enter the main lobby of the residence hall some time ago. He looks up at the windows facing the apartment complex.

GUY: *I wonder which is hers.*

To his left, sitting outside the office of his apartment complex, he heard high-pitched tufts of laughter. The sounds were coming from two Humanities majors he met four weeks ago. He had forgotten their names, but waved anyway when he saw the younger one looking at him.

She waved back and poked her friend who pushed her in retaliation before she turned around, saw Guy, and waved. Her red face smiled in embarrassment.

Guy's eyes now turned to the sandy brown dunes that brilliant ant architects had deftly designed. He stepped around them and then noticed a green-and-yellow water hydrant that had a red *X* spray-painted across it. It was in the middle of the grass and Guy was surprised that he had never before spotted the old, gaudy hydrant. He then noticed two manholes.

MANHOLE 1: TELEPHONE

MANHOLE 2: ELECTRIC

He walked around them for fear of a Teenage Mutant Ninja Turtle suddenly bursting out. He smiled as he imagined MICHELANGELO, his favorite, popping out from beneath the first manhole cover. In his mind, Guy was as tall as "Mike," the orange-masked turtle that he used to imitate as a kid.

Michelangelo sticks his head out of the first manhole and speaks to Guy.

MIKE: Hey, Dude! Want a tour of the sewers?

Mike crawls out and walks down the hill with Guy, towards Rhody Courtyard.

GUY: Is there good food down there?

MIKE: I ordered pizza!

Guy thought that Woman might be watching from her dorm window. The thought made him pause an instant.

GUY: Sorry, Man. I have to study.
          Please tell Splinter hi for me, though.

MIKE: Alright, Dude! You'll ace the test, cuz you're Guy.

GUY: How'd you know my name?!

MIKE: Cuz I'm a figment of your imagination, Dummy!
          Haha!

Gauche holds his stomach and Derecha dances in the air as Guy laughs from his heart.

GUY: Hahaha! Good point. See you soon!

MIKE: Whenever. Later, Dude.

Guy had walked into Rhody Courtyard when Mike turned around for his manhole. He turned around and watched as Michelangelo disappeared. He then continued onward and saw two people barbecuing beef with Ethiopian seasoning; six more were sitting on the square picnic tables. A fluffy, reddish pup named Apollo was in one of the girls' arms.

Guy looked on and saw Mr. Hay, eight minutes away. He nodded at his secret friend and Mr. Hay winked back. Past the courtyard, he walked down a few steps, crossed Back Street, and skipped across the dirt field until his shoes felt the hard sidewalk leading to the dining hall.

GUY: Hi. *(He smiles as he hands the new cashier his card. The warm smile makes her feel like family.)*

MARION: Hi, Little Brother! Enjoy your dinner.

GUY: Huhuh! Thanks, Big Sister! Take it easy.

He walks past the lobby and grabs a red plastic tray, two plates, a fork, and a knife. He serves himself some chicken and sees the same woman he sees in the weight room every other day.

She felt his eyes nearby and quickly turned away, like a scared little girl. Guy thought she was sweet and always enjoyed scaring her.

She was first in line to serve herself some potatoes, and somehow, Guy managed to be second. He stood very close to her and reached over her arm to grab the black-handled serving spoon in the bowl of broccoli.

She smiled and quickly walked away, not quite sure if it was the tall tennis guy who was so excitingly close.

She walks to the grill in the center of the resident dining hall and spies from there, wondering if the tall guy in the white shirt is indeed the guy she always sees at the gym.

She saw another guy that fit that description and was mad at the random guy for having been so impatient and intrusive.

Guy saw the geeky, sweet gym rat return and pause as she saw him serve himself some milk.

GYM RAT: *So it **was** him!*

She bumps into an equally clumsy man.

GYM RAT: I'm sorry, Joe!

JOE: My bad.

Guy smiles, looking off to the side. The woman smiles, too, and watches him as he walks towards where the tennis team is sitting.

The woman had left her backpack with her group in the lab and set off to find help for a computer assembly project. She found herself in the dining hall instead and was now very grateful that she had come, for Pretty Man (she didn't know his name) was there. The gym rat then remembered that he ditched her earlier that day and decided not to think about him so much.

The sun was shining and everyone was happy to have finished their final project or their third test of the semester. The air was light inside the cozy D-Hall.

Guy joins the tennis team. He sits in a seat in the middle of the three adjoined tables.

KEVIN: ...when it comes out next Friday!

JORGE: It's gonna be sweet!

EDDY: The graphics are amazing and I heard each character has like seven new combos....

GUY: *I think I'll put an indoor court in Greg's house. What was it? Two coats of sealer and then the court paint, then the two coats of finish?... I'll definitely do the paint job. I can't wait. I mean, designing and managing is fun, but not as fun as physically making the wood become a court. I'll let him paint in his initials on the court, though. Yeah, he'd like that.*

ALDAIR: ...good times fo' sho'!

ASHLEY JOE: How long are you staying?

ERIC: Two weeks.

SETH: Hey Eddy!
           Isn't that where your girlfriend's from?

EDDY: That's *Phoenix,* not Fiji!

SETH: It's close though, right?

GUY: *There is no way I'm doing anything this weekend. Funny how foreign Mom sounded yesterday—or was that today? Wait, my review was today! That means it's Friday!*

ALDAIR: ...Hah! I can see him now, in a field of daisies, riding his pony.

ERIC: It's not mine, Idiot. It's my uncle's.

JORGE: You'd rather chill with a pony?

ERIC: Is it really that hard to understand? It's not a pony! It's an Andalusian, full-grown horse.

GUY: *Oh no! I have a test in Russian on Tuesday! Same day as the Environmental Systems test! I don't even re-member what chapters it's on.... Wow. I'll need to put in a good four hours of studying for that test. Twenty-five percent of the grade! I have to ace it. I'll do the Russian review Monday. God bless that teacher, the last test was taken verbatim from the review packet. I wish I made it to Thursday's class, though.*

Hopefully the review's online.

JORGE: ...Guy doesn't really care.

Guy follows Jorge's eyes and looks at Kevin with a neutral expression.

KEVIN: Whatever.

Guy spoons the last of his soup.

GUY: *I really need to go home. I'll finish all the studying I can tonight. There's no way I'm taking any books home this weekend.*

He stands up and puts on his backpack.

ASHLEY JOE: You going to the library?

GUY: Yep.

ERIC: Have fun!

JORGE: See ya later.

GUY: Later.

KEVIN: See ya.

Guy shoots a quick glance at the gym rat who quickly lifts her cup of milk and chugs it down, leaving shortly after him.

REFRIGERANT
XXXIV

The library was one apartment building away from where Guy lived. He used to spend a lot of his time there when he wasn't in Studio. When he walked down the pathway, he would often glance through the Barberry Hall Courtyard and ponder whether or not he should live in the dorms senior year. He barely stayed in his apartment; it didn't make much sense to have to pay a fourth of Sid, Bryan, and Uwem's bill.

As Guy walked, he watched the white saucer being thrown around by the Ultimate Frisbee team which practiced often on the Library Field. He vicariously enjoyed running for the frisbee without having to read three chapters of a certain *Environmental Systems* book.

The cherry blossoms smelled refreshingly sweet as the breeze rubbed at their petals. Guy took a deep breath and felt happy to be alive.

The trees were vivid, and the annoying mockingbird that used to cuss at him from the tree every day during sophomore year strangely left him alone just then (he was still there, peering at Guy who peered right back).

BIRD IN BACKGROUND: Bam ba$_{ba}$ba$_{ba}$ba$_{ba}$ ^{chii} dadadadadada!

Guy jerks his head up in amazement, searching for the bird whose song is so unique and difficult to imitate.

GUY: Bam ba$_{ba}$ba$_{ba}$ ^{chii} shiu sh$_{ih}$ do dadadadada!

BIRD: Badum bada bi ^{ba} daaaaaaa-aie.

GUY: Twee-eeur, tweeur tweeur!

He opens the right entrance door and notices a Korean woman smiling at him for being so carefree about whistling to the bird.

Guy returns her glance.

LADY: You whistle very well!

GUY: Thank you.

He opens the second set of glass-paneled doors and enters the library atrium which is full of empty chairs and clean tables. The coffee shop was closed and only two people were studying: one by the window, the other on the other side, by the entrance to the closed art gallery.

Guy walks past the atrium, to the stairs opposite the entrance. He climbs up to the second floor, looking straight ahead at all times, avoiding chatty acquaintances that might be typing on the computers on the first floor.

The library had eight floors, but Guy typically went to the second. It was significantly louder than the "Absolutely Quiet Floors" above, but generally had fewer annoying people than the first floor. It was perfect for Guy, an anemic man who—despite his incredible drive to succeed—fell asleep easily.

He grabs a seat in the first row, all the way against the stone balustrade that looks over the circulation desk on the first floor.

He heard someone on the floor below drop a thick book. He peeked in between the wide balusters and saw a girl with bright pink hair laughing at herself as she squatted to pick it up.

GUY: *Time to awesome.*

Guy turns on the computer. He then nods his head to his internal rhythm and scratches the beat into the black plastic strip lining the edge of the white table.

He found Professor Brooks's lecture slides online and proceeded to go through them, opening his book for reference when he didn't remember or understand what the slides said.

Guy clicks on the mouse with the side of Derecha's pinky.

LINK: Lecture 13: Green Building Design

The file opened. Irony was salient to Guy and he was constantly taunted. However, at that moment, he felt as if he had just quilted a few scraps of knowledge emblazoned with similar designs; the interior of each sustainable building he saw in the slides was instantly exposed by his imaginative mind. The pictures were photographs, yet he was able to draft mental blueprints of each one, drawing on his experience from past projects and research.

Guy felt the same sense of togetherness as he did in the middle of sophomore year when all his classes (including French) complemented each other. The curriculum gave him the opportunity to immediately apply what he learned, thereby making his craft more holistic and real.

SLIDE 1: Test 3: *Chapter 8 (50%) Sustainable Development, Building Components/Design, Construction, Water Conservation
*Chapter 9/10/11.2 (50%) Building Systems: Lighting, HVAC (both small and large buildings), How the systems influence human activities and welfare

Guy clicks on the right blue arrow.

SLIDE 2: Green Design: Making it Cost Effective

Guy goes back to the homepage and clicks on the eleventh set of slides.

SLIDE 1: Given constraints of the project, desired green building efforts may be minimally effective....

GUY: *What an optimistic way to start off a set of slides on green building strategies!*

SLIDE 1: ...Numerous parameters must be manipulated; ergo it is important to research construction systems, the environmental impact of new materials, new designs linking elements of separate buildings to save energy...

GUY: *My, how wordy. I might as well just read the book.*

He quickly clicks through the remaining slides in the set in order to see what topics the class went over. Then, he opens his book with his knuckles to a random page. The first of the two heating, ventilating, and air conditioning (HVAC) chapters stared up at him. He never felt comfortable with that chapter's material. Although he could feel his eyes becoming heavier, his undying enthusiasm easily won over his bodily fatigue.

BOOK: Condensing results from heat removal from a refrigerant.

GUY: Refrigerant.

BOOK: The condensing process, in the refrigerant cycle, involves extracting heat from the refrigerant, thereby cooling it, after having rejected heat generated in the evaporation process.

GUY: What's a refrigerant?

BOOK: The refrigerant is able to be evaporated and then condensed again once condensation is complete. Heat exchangers called condensers are used to condense the refrigerant.

GUY: Perhaps I should go back and review what this
         refrigerant is.

*Guy searches through his backpack and pulls out a sheet
of paper entitled "Definitions That You Forgot."* It was a list of
words he used to know that he compiled in his room using the
typewriter that was given to him five years ago by his uncle.
He hadn't used the typewriter ever since his fingers started
hurting, but he thought fondly of the huge thing which he
named Bertha. Bertha was probably the only typewriter on
campus.

The definitions were compiled from the heavy dictionary
which stayed on his desk. He grew very fond of the book,
titled *Dictionary of Architecture & Construction,* edited by Cyril
M. Harris. He always imagined that the Cyril in his class was
actually the editor, so he felt as if he were even more strongly
bonded to the book by knowing Cyril. He went to school
with sports stars, famous architects, renowned scientists,
singers... you name it. Life was more fun that way. In Russian,
for instance, a mixed classmate of his reminded him of a
rapper. Needless to say, Guy was constantly inspired in
Russian, thinking: *This celebrity is actually in my class! I'll work
just as hard and make it big one day, too!*

DEFINITIONS THAT YOU FORGOT:

         refrigerant– The medium of heat transfer
         in a refrigeration system which absorbs
         heat by evaporation at a low temperature
         and pressure and gives up heat on
         condensing at a higher temperature and
         pressure

GUY: Why, that's absolutely magical! It evaporates at
         low temperatures yet condenses at higher ones.

Guy then went back two chapters to read about sustain-ability measures, praising the discoverer of refrigerants as he flipped through the pages.

As a linguist, Guy greatly appreciated the beauty and pre-cision of architecture terminology. He always felt that conci-sion was the ultimate stroke of genius, and felt encouraged every day upon noticing how adept he was becoming at suc-cinctly describing this saddle tie, or that cant window. For that reason, he genuinely enjoyed studying for his classes. His Environmental Systems class was no exception. He loved learning about the mechanical and electrical topics, and also felt invigorated at being able to use his knowledge. He es-pecially valued gaining the ability to help his animal friends by designing eco-friendly houses. He eagerly envisioned the construction of the Guy Firm, which would implement all that he read into the glass building's design.

Guy read well into the night, looking up to his right each time someone walked by. Four hours later, he saw a short man dressed in a black shirt and dark-grey pants. He reminded him of the crazy blackbird that followed him a couple of nights ago.

GUY: Mom's pretty wise. If she thinks that the pos-sessed bird wants me to stay in, perhaps I should listen.

Guy looks at his cell phone.

CELL: 11:00 p.m.

GUY: Better go grab a snack for tonight then head home.

He dropped the thick blue book into his backpack, zipped it up, and helped its straps hop gently onto his shoulders.

Thoughts about chillers, pumps, boilers, actuators, dampers, and valves swirled in his head. He always wanted to be a mechanic, but never more so than after studying.

GUY:　　*I can't wait to have my own house. I'm definitely going to take apart the boiler room.*

He passed the bathroom on the way to the stairs and couldn't help but criticize its interior design.

GUY:　　*This is a library, so obviously people are going to bring their stuffed bags here when they have to go.* (He walks down the stairs.)

　　　　I can barely fit in the stall, let alone my backpack. And that hook for a jacket? So ridiculously small! It would hold up my green stencil, but that's about it.

Now on the first floor, Guy returns Uwem's wave in the computer area, waving back to Mellisa as well.

GUY:　　*Funny how I live with Uwem yet I rarely see him in the apartment. Anyway... yeah, and the doors opening in?! That sure gives us more space... if we're doin' our business outside the stall!*

Without mentally forming any words, he recalled the 97/3 inspiration and realized he was dwelling in everyone's 97% homestead.

GUY:　　*No. I won't think in vain; I've been living in vain up until yesterday. Wait, was that today? Yeah, up until I realized how much of a zombie I was, going through everyday motions* (opens the library's center glass door) *without even acknowledging the objects I moved, the handles I'd turn—Well, I did notice their design....*

Funny how doorknobs are becoming rarer and rarer. These push bars look mighty infantile to me. But yeah (walks through the Library Field, checking out a tall woman who is walking on the sidewalk), I never felt, I merely was. Didn't live, just played out the same routine I had memorized.

The goal was to design amazing buildings, get a lotta money, and then act out another script which would be written as I needed to write it.

This play! It's over.

He stops right in front of the two-lane street across Azalea Hall and sees a black Celica zip by. He stares at it until it disappears, admiring the way the black glistens with the streaks of streetlight gracing the vehicle's majestic, powerful roof. He then crosses the street.

GUY: *I still don't understand how my guiltless concern led me to see for the first time. To taste the oft-overlooked scent gleaming from my pain receptors' maroon ear.*

To feel the delicate implications that every sip has, as the subjugated chemical slides down my system to surrender itself completely to my body which rips it apart, sending that potassium atom here and this carbon over there....

Why, I don't even know which part of my body needs what! My cells never tell me how or what they're doing!

He takes the shortest route to the D-Hall store, through the grass, away from the well-lit sidewalk.

GUY: *Yet, I'm the captain. Subjecting all my poor blood to my every which whim.*

To his left he sees a tall figure crouching on the ground, completely still. Instead of greeting him, Guy decides to pretend he hadn't noticed him so that if this stranger was trying to hide from someone, Guy would not draw attention to his hiding place.

The untrusting Guy remained alert, ready for the strange guy to jump at him from behind. The young man did no such thing. He was indeed, merely hiding. Guy walked onward and saw the silhouettes of runners against the smoggy purple sky as they crept up a hill. They stopped and then ran the other way in pursuit of a daring runner who was trespassing.

SCOTT*: It's called improvising.

EFREN: Hey Blue Team! Get this guy!

JOSH: Did they jailbreak?

JACK: They freed us.

BEN: Hey, go back over there!... Go back over there!

GUY: *Are they playing Night Capture the Flag? They can't be! I don't see a flag... or glowsticks.... How could they know who's on their team? It's too dark.*

He walks on the sidewalk directly in front of the snack shop, looking at some dorm residents who are standing half a foot apart, glaring at each other. With some effort, Guy returns to the soliloquy, this time speaking out loud.

GUY: Yeah, so I wasn't born a tiny cell. I was born a strong, powerful person. An ungrateful imbecile I was. No longer. *(He opens the door and holds it back for a guy on the lacrosse team who is close behind him.)*

---

*I don't know these people so I gave them random names.

Guy walks into the store and sees Lili who is bagging her items.

LILI: Guy! You're still alive! Where've you been?

GUY: Studio, but it's over n—

RYOMA: *(turns his head)* Hey Guy! Too bad you had to leave so early today. *(He pays the cashier.)*

GUY: *(The review was today? Poor Ry's become senile.... Or I have....)*

 What happened?

Ryoma returns his eyes to the cashier.

RYOMA: Thanks. *(He walks towards the exit.)*
 Mishari started screaming at Michelle!

GUY: What?

RYOMA: Yeah, he said *(imitates Mishari's deep voice)*

 "I CAN'T TAKE IT ANYMORE! This design is SO MUCH cleaner and aesthetically pleasing than ANY of your LOUSY BUILDINGS!"

LILI: Poor guy. Did he end up failing?

RYOMA: I don't know whether to admire him or feel bad for him. Yeah, he got a zero.

GUY: Reuben should know that it was just his sleep deprivation that caused him to say that. Mish's design was nice; he should have gotten most of the points.

RYOMA: It was hilarious! Veronica gasped very loudly and so the whole class laughed! It was cuz of the way she gasped, but Reuben thought we were all laughing in agreement to what Mish said!

GUY: What'd he do?

RYOMA: He screamed at us for "unreasonable conduct."
Then he said he'd talk to us after the reviews
ended, but he forgot by that time.

LILI: Pity. Well, see ya later Guy! Come on Ry. *(to Guy:)*
We're going to see that new film about the tomato
mansion. As an architect, you MUST come!

GUY: Thanks, but I really need to catch up on some
sleep.

RYOMA: Haha, don't we all. Later Guy.

GUY: Take care.

Guy walked into the store and noticed for the first time
that there were exactly four brown shelves holding all the
nuts, cookies, and fruits. He grabbed a can of pistachios and
walked on, looking at the distorted image of himself upon
the metallic edge of the freezer. He stood there for some
time, behind a stout freshman in the narrow U-shaped line.
He rehashed what he had just read in the library until he was
at the front of the line.

*Guy grabs five chocolate bars and places them on the counter
with the pistachios.*

PETER: Meal or flex dollars?

*Guy hands his ID card to PETER, a thin brown-eyed man who
used to do commercials as a child.*

GUY: Hi. Meal and then whatever is left over on flex,
please.

Peter swipes the card.

GUY: Thanks, have a good evening.

PETER: **You too.** *(He looks past Guy at the cute woman beside him.)* **Hey there, how are you?**

Guy stands at the edge of the counter and has a tough time opening the plastic bag to put his candy and nuts in. His short nails aren't long enough to separate the plastic. He tries using his knuckles, but the obstinate bag still doesn't open.

He feels a nudge from SHAWNY, a friend with whom he had taken four years of Spanish at Marsh High School.

SHAWNY: I'm good. How are you?

PETER: I'm great now that your smile has brightened up my day.

Guy looks at Shawny who is indeed displaying a very beautiful smile.

PETER: Would you like to use a meal or flex?

SHAWNY: Meal please.

Guy finally gets the bag open, stuffs his items into it, and leaves.

GUY: *Now where was I? Minimization of erosion. In order to—Wait. What was I talking about before then?*

Right. I need to do something about this life of mine. Everything is so real now. If everyone felt what I feel, no one would ever be bored. How? Every little grain of soil is so intricate and mysterious.

The way that woman's mouth looked was provocatively uplifting.

Water rushes to the ground when it hails along-side small beads of ice that don't melt until they've felt the ground very well....

There's so much material to write about!

CAPTURE THE FLAG

XXXV

Guy walks close to the side of the snack shop, towards the two students who are still staring at each other. Upon closer examination, Guy notices that one is wearing a blue wristband on each wrist. He approaches the strangers.

GUY: Hey there.

Guy looks at the red fabric tied around the other student's right wrist.

RED: Hey.

GUY: Why are you staring at her and not moving?

BLUE: We're playing Capture the Flag. This is the cen-
         terline.

GUY: *(thinking while they speak)* How do you play
         Night Capture the Flag without glowsticks? I
         love them. Wonder what makes them look
         so awesome.... They'd look awesomer if I used
         them to breakdance.... I think I'll perform in
         the next charity concert like Hans did. We'll use
         a lot of glowsticks.

RED: The field beside Rhody Hall is their prison, and
         our flag is there. Their flag is in front of Pansy
         Hall, where our prison's at.

GUY: They're like half a mile from each other!

BLUE: Want to play?

Guy hadn't played Capture the Flag in ages. He noticed an
Architecture senior way out in the distance. He had to join in.

GUY: Sure. Where do I get the wristband?

BLUE: Right down there.... You see Cecilia?

The girl wearing red and blue wristbands?

GUY: Yep.

BLUE: She's the ref. She'll let you play. We're actually short a player.

GUY: Awesome. Thanks.

Guy runs down the hill diagonal from the dining hall entrance. CECILIA smiles and greets Guy, a handsome man she has never seen before, although she goes to practically every school event.

GUY: Hey, could I be Blue?

CECY: Sure. I'm Cecy. What's your name?

She ties two cotton strips of blue fabric around his wrists.

GUY: Guy.

CECY: Nice to meet you, Guy! Good luck! Go get their flag!

GUY   That's the plan....

He bends down to set his plastic bag on the ground beside her and then pauses, looking up at her.

GUY: Could I leave this here?

CECY: Sure.

He straightens his body.

GUY: Thanks. See ya.

CECY: Bye!

Guy had seen Cecy in the dining hall before and she never

struck him as attractive. But that night, her bright eyes comforted Guy and he would have been very happy just to be a referee next to her gorgeous self. Her curly brown hair reminded him of the hair on his sister's doll which he had cut off after his sister accidentally bent his baseball card, many years ago. They were nice curls and Guy felt like apologizing to Cecy for having cut similar hair.

GUY: *Perhaps I should ask if I could be a ref.*
         No. She needs me to bring back the flag.

Guy didn't have time to run around. He planned on surprising his mom by getting home early the next day and taking her and his sister out to a seafood restaurant for a Studio's Over celebration. He felt heavy and burdened upon thinking about how horrible it would be to go to prison. However, he couldn't just leave; Cecy would think he's a loser and a jerk that either wins or quits.

So Guy did what anyone in his position would do. He ran like a maniac to the opposite camp, zigging here, zagging there, and hopping over a little gymnast who slipped and tried to tag his feet. He started panicking, for he was in the thick of Rhody Field but could not see any flag.

RED: We need some defense! Defense over this way!
         They're all coming.

RED: I'm watching three of them.

BLUE: They're real geeks.

RED: Oh wait, you're Blue!

RED: Is Leif in jail?

RED: Tim, I'm gonna go.

RED: Steve, what are you doing?

STEVE: I'm tired.

RED: Where's Leif?

RED: We're gonna do this again, let's see if we can...

RED: Oh, boy! RUNNERS!

RED: Run! Run! Run!

RED: Alright, ready to go?

TIM: All of us at the same time.

Guy recognized Tim's voice. He and TIM, an acoustic guitar player, had many mutual friends and they happened to eat together at least once a week last year. Guy remembered Tim telling him about Leif, a cross-country runner who was very quick and obviously must have been stealing the flag very often.

Guy starts walking the other way, pretending to be Red for a bit.

GUY: Is Leif over there? I'll check if he's in jail!

BLUE: *(screams from the opposite field)* Cydnie, No!

RED: What just happened?

RED: Cydnie just got caught.

RED: *(telling a story to a teammate:)* **Here's the curb and here's his head.**

RED: RUNNERS! Blue! Incoming!!

Most of the Redmen race towards the centerline to catch the Blue intruders.

RED: I'm watching you, Son.

RED: They flanked the left side.

RED: There's no other way, trust me....

RED: Did you guys just jailbreak?

Soon, Guy's left wristband is spotted by a Red defender. His trail is soon revealed by the universal "I missed!" sound, "D'aaaaah!"

A Red defender reaches out to tag Guy, but misses.

RED: D'aaaaah!

Another Redman, closer to the flag, reaches out, but also misses the quick tennis player.

RED: D'aaaaah!

RED: *(in the background:)*
               Let's wait til they come back!

A soft breeze wafted across the purple sky. It seemed to swallow the moment completely; the players, the scent of Guy's cologne, the dining hall, the thumps of feet smashing against the resilient green grass, the screams, and even the excitement were all somehow trapped within the flowing air which Guy slowly inhaled. The sweet oxygen rose to his head and he closed his eyes briefly, realizing that this college memory was going to be a part of him for the rest of his life.

   (in the background:)
RED: He already tagged you.

RED: Oh, so close!

RED: Is he Blue?
RED: Don't tackle him.

RED: He was on defense.
RED: I think I ripped your shirt, John.

Guy runs on, past the Red defenders. He hears a guy rubbing his shoes against the gravel near the back parking lot of the dining hall.

He felt stealthy and that excited him. It was as if he were back in second-grade gym class, running with the flag, being cheered on by his teammates and derided by the opposite team.

It was dark and the playing field was spacious. No one knew him at Rhody Field. His allies were now far behind him. Few had the decency to feign an attack to help Guy succeed in their mission.

   (in the background:)
RED: Traitor!

RED: Maybe we should turn around instead of watching him.

RED: You guys need to spread out!... Okay!
           Three... Two... One... Go!

RED: Let's see how many of us can go at one time.

RED: Spread out!

RED: Did he make it?

RED: Man!

RED: Watch out for Jeff!

Guy runs on and then hears Red defenders screaming his name. This shakes him up a bit.

RED: Get that guy!

RED: That guy!

RED: The Blue guy's getting our flag!

GUY: *How do they know my name?*

BLUEMEN: Free us! Free us!

Guy was surprised to see practically all of his teammates in prison. He was right next to the flag that was spread across the blade of a hockey stick whose shaft was in a traffic cone. He had to choose quickly: either free his teammates or grab the flag. The Architecture senior was also incarcerated, so he felt it an academic responsibility to free his people. He strategized as he ran away from the flag and made sure that he tagged the hand of the Architecture major, thereby freeing the long chain of prisoners.

His plan worked; the prisoners ran about, blocking the Red defenders from seeing Guy, thereby preventing them from tagging him.

Guy was impressed that, despite the darkness, his Bluemen managed to leave him a clear view of the red flag.

The red flag was made of the same cotton fabric as the red wristbands his opponents wore. He zigged some more, realizing that a Red defender had been focusing on him ever since he entered her camp. She ran after Guy, but the Bluemen haphazardly blocked access to him. Some Bluemen ran back towards the prison so that Guy was not alone in walking in the northward direction, although most Bluemen returned to see their family in Pansy Field. Guy grabbed the flag, knocking over both the cone and the hockey stick. He then fled back to camp, all the while hearing cheers of support from his fellow Bluemen.

Guy returned to his country a hero. He felt great. Cecy blew her whistle and everyone crowded around the quick, nimble-footed tennis player.

BLUE: Congratulations!

BLUE: We won!!

BLUE: That's what I'm talking about!

BLUE: What's your name, Man?

CECY: *(answers for him:)* Guy!

Guy pondered what he had accomplished. He went to Rhody Field to grab the red flag. He didn't harm any of the Red people. They harmed themselves by trying to prevent him from bringing back what was meant to be his. He was indeed a hero, and all for Cecy. He walked up to the ref, who looked like a princess. She was showing off the biggest, most breathtaking smile Guy had ever seen.

GUY: Here you go.

He hands the flag to Princess and hears the slow, victorious music from the closing of one of his first Nintendo games, Super Mario Bros.

PRINCESS: THANK YOU GUY! YOUR QUEST IS OVER. WE PRESENT YOU A NEW QUEST. *(She hands him his bag from the D-Hall store.)* PUSH BUTTON B TO SELECT A WORLD.

GUY: *(Wait, that's not what she said! She's so beautiful. Wow. I'm not paying attention to her.)*

         Sorry, what?

CECY: I said you're ridiculously fast! We play every Friday night. You have to come next Friday.

GUY: I'll try to. *(He starts to untie the wristbands and looks at Cecy as if he is about to return them to her.)*

CECY: No, you can keep them!

GUY: Cool. Thanks. See you all later.

BLUE: Bye!

BLUE: See ya!

BLUE: You rock!

Guy goes off, happy to have made the right decision to free his brothers and sisters before going for the flag.

A BRIGHT MYSTERY IS SOLVED

XXXVI

Guy walks by Azalea Hall, enjoying the long way back from the D-Hall store to his apartment. He feels sweat dripping down his neck.

FRED: Teeer!

Guy smiles upon hearing his sparrow friend named Fred. He hadn't spoken to the bird that slept next to Azalea Hall for quite some time.

GUY: Teeeur!

Fred wasn't actually greeting Guy, nor did he ever consider Ugly Bird his friend. He had just been accidentally stepped on by another bird (Zoë) and was screaming at her. Upon hearing Guy's whistle, he looked at Ugly Bird and wondered if he was a special type of human.

Guy swung the plastic bag around his head and looked much like a helicopter to the confounded Fred. The sound of the bag pushing the air around was fascinating, so Fred and Zoë couldn't help but watch Ugly Bird until Ugly Bird was out of sight.

Guy suddenly hears what sounds like the flapping of wings overhead.

GUY: Teeer?

He looks up, expecting to see the white flash of light upon the back of the crazy blackbird from Wednesday night. Instead, he sees the clouds of light that had puzzled him before.

GUY: At last. I will find out whence you come!

Guy follows the stars which swirl around and then combine to form a brighter light before separating again into four

Guy

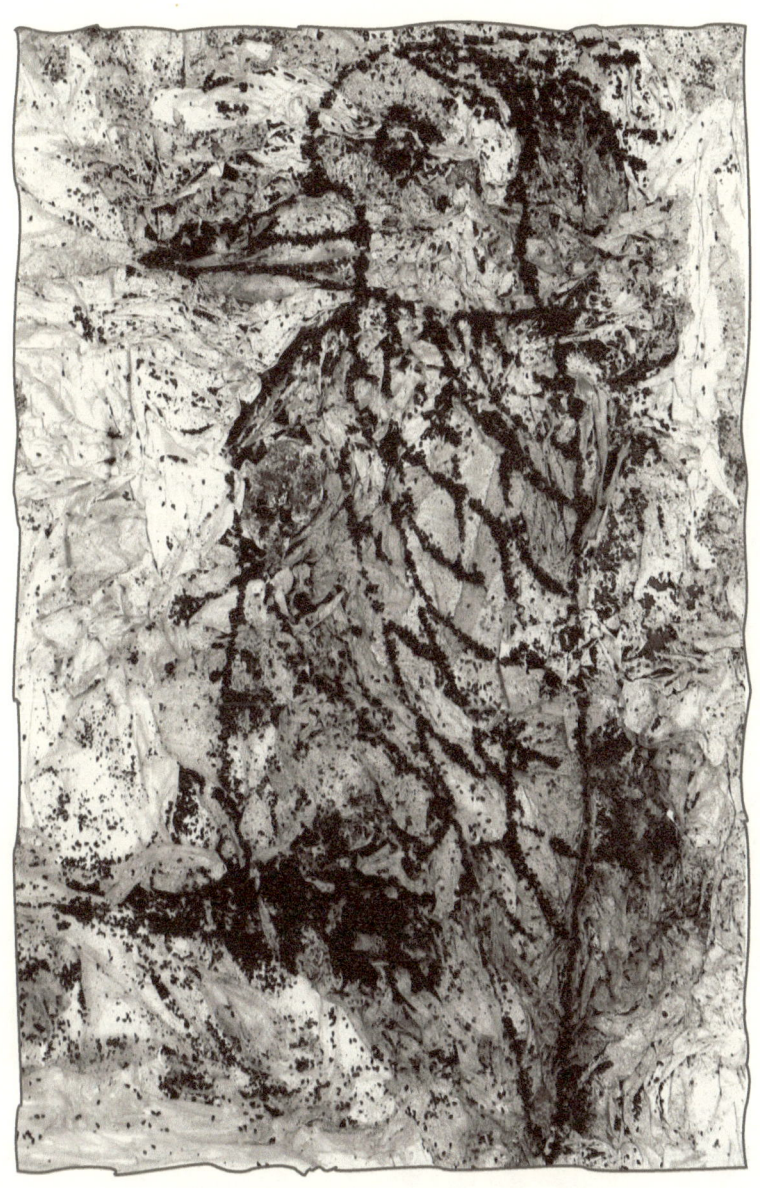

Fred the Bird

discrete clouds.

The silent bursts of light changed Guy's mindset completely. A strong hero, he became humbled and his body shook as he slowly walked towards them, looking up and following them to the garage by the tennis courts.

No one was around. Guy noticed some lights were on way back in Barberry Hall where Woman lived, so he didn't feel completely alone. He felt a bit safer. He continued on and lost them. He was right beside the barren garage and ran past it so that the trees surrounding the sidewalk wouldn't obstruct his view of the graceful lights.

Guy walked slowly again, unsure of what lay ahead. He felt like crying to God, thanking Him for the opportunity to bring closure to the mystery. He was following the truth and felt strongly that he would be protected. The chase encouraged him to create his own magnificent reality in order to do more to serve mankind than the world deemed possible. Although exhilarated about his future, he wasn't sure what the imminent truth would bring him.

He walked on, taking off his sweaty wristbands and placing them in his left pocket. His fingers ached (it would have been less painful if he had waited to use scissors to cut the wristbands off), but he decided that the pain was merely an annoyance. He didn't give it the right to debilitate him.

He didn't want to be seen, although it was too late. Someone was following closely behind him, unbeknownst to the bewildered Guy who failed to look back.

Guy was no longer moving of his own accord. His magnetized legs rushed to get as close to the clouds of light as they possibly could.

He crept into the street and traversed quite a distance in the middle of the sparkly black road. His ears were keen, as was his sense of smell. His blue eyes were wide open as they perceived the grey climate piercing far into the distance. He was reminded of his existence by his skillful hands which alerted him whenever the air made a movement across his ultra-sensitive fingertips. He was ready to taste the shining, almost blinding truth.

His alacrity was heightened when he saw one of the four clouds extend. It seemed more like a rod than a cloud.

Guy crossed over to the other side of the road and realized that his campus was on a hill. The depressed grass sunk deeply downward. He briefly looked down. The streetlights lit up the soothing green grass which was scratched into by sidewalks that cut the large field and climbed up the hill in steps. He slowly stepped down two of the thirty-six steps and sat, placing his plastic bag on the grassy hill to the right of the banister. He looked across the area of campus he had often heard when walking from the dining hall, but had never actually seen.

For the first time, he saw the grassy path that led to the soccer field which was far to his left, concealed by many trees. Huge bright lights illuminated the field, though there was no game being played.

He looked back up and smiled. The bird had indeed caused him to see the truth, for had the bird not haunted him, Guy would not have been there to follow the cloudy stars. He smiled from his heart, for what he saw disabused him of all the crazy notions he had about the lights and being "chosen."

Perhaps he was chosen. Perhaps he was special. But Guy felt that Smile was smiling at him from within for quite another reason.

The lights up above were neither mystical, nor mysterious. The smog of Baltimore helped darken their trail, making the spotlights appear as clouds. The four spotlights swirled and then joined together, separating and combining over and over again.

GUY: Probably for the grand opening of some big new hotel. Or just spotlights outside a club— Wow. Haha!

Guy did not feel disappointed about not being special. He was a normal man and did not see any abnormal things. He thought Smile would definitely take this opportunity to discuss Guy's position, but there was really nothing to discuss. Besides, the day Guy felt guiltless about his adventures was the day Smile became enmeshed in Guy's spirit. He could not come out. He was a part of Guy.

Guy leans his head against the round metal banister beside the steps. He puts his right arm around the post and then stretches out his legs across more steps. He then starts to stand up, holding the railing for support and continues to watch the spotlights until they flicker and stop.

Now standing straight, Guy smiles again and turns around.

WOMAN: **BOOooooo!**

GUY: **Aaaaah!**

WOMAN: Hahaha!
          Little Guyee Wuyee get scaredy waredy?

GUY: What are you doing here?

WOMAN: Followed you. *(Woman captivates Guy by un-bending a classic silver paperclip and sticking it into a tomato.)* You're quite a wacko, my friend.

She bites into the tomato-sicle.

GUY: If I weren't holding onto the railing, I woulda fallen down!

WOMAN: If you weren't holding onto the railing, I wouldn't have scared you.

GUY: Yeah, right!

WOMAN: Of course I'm right.

Guy walks up the steps without looking at the woman (although he feels happy that she is there). She walks beside him and skips ahead to an oak tree on the other side of the street.

Woman wipes the paperclip with a leaf and sets it behind the tree, returning with another tomato.

WOMAN: *(jumps up)* Tomatoes!! Yeah!! *(She offers him the tomato.)*

GUY: You're weird.
          (He takes it and holds it in Derecha.)

WOMAN: Thank you. Weird with Wacko on a Friday night. This is Bob, by the way.

She grabs two of Bob's branches and starts waltzing with her oak tree friend.

GUY: That's not Bob.

She lets go of the branches, curtsies to Bob, and then frowns at Guy.

WOMAN: Excuse me? You telling me I don't know my own friends?

GUY: Obviously you don't. That's Tricia.

Woman turns around, blushing.

WOMAN: Oops. In that case, you should dance with her. *(She jumps up to grab the end of a higher branch and hands it to Gauche. Derecha, still holding the tomato, reaches and grabs another branch. Then Guy just stands there.)*

Figures... you wouldn't know how to dance.
I shoulda known you've got no rhythm.

Guy lets go of the second branch and sets the tomato on the ground. He bows his head to the tree as he returns to an upright position, re-grabbing the branch. He then starts dancing salsa with the tree who shakes her leaves a lot more than when she was Bob, waltzing with Woman.

WOMAN: Hey Wacko! Why are you dancing with a tree? How pathetic are you?

Guy looks at Woman who suddenly looks a lot like Reuben.

WOMAN: I mean, you could be dancing with two trees!

She skips away and does a spin in midair, like a figure skater. Guy feels as if he has known this strange woman forever. She gradually slows down so that he can catch up.

In an instant they heard a soft clamor in the sky. It started pouring immediately. Woman ran past the garage, by the

Physics Building, and up the sidewalk towards the entrance of Barberry Hall.

She suddenly bent down towards a puddle. Guy ran around like a happy puppy enjoying the water. He stood by the strange woman, barely able to see what she was doing.

Woman hunches down. Three seconds later, two handfuls of water fly into Guy's eyes, unapologetically.

GUY: Why!—

He starts wiping his eyes and then looks for Woman who bends down again, returning upright with two more handfuls of dirty rainwater which she throws once more onto his big face.

Guy runs towards his apartment.

WOMAN: Wait! Aren't you gonna walk me home?

Guy stops and turns his head.

GUY: WALK *YOURSELF* HOME!

WOMAN: *(projecting with little effort)* Haha, Wacko! Thanks for standing there for me to throw water in your face! Haha!

GUY: I'd rather be wacko than weird. Goodnight, Weirdo!

WOMAN: Night night, Wacko!

Guy turns his head to make sure she isn't following him. He catches a fleeting glimpse of her walking towards her dorm.

Once Woman was out of sight, Guy stopped. He took a deep breath. As the air entered his amazingly calm system, he saw his life in a new light. The thick rain drastically subsided, but Guy did not notice. All he felt were the quickened, soft pulses of his heart and the raw air cleansing his lungs.

He soon sang praises in his heart for living. In a few days he would recall his dilemmas and start writing a play to help inspire others to feel the exact way he felt.

His mind and heart were loosely tied with heavenly silk cords sprinkled with the purest dew. His body shook ever so slightly, creating majestic, dignified vibrations.

And on his face, whose expression was so pure as to make one believe that he had been raised in the field of green flowers all his life...

On his face, whose warm wrinkles from stress were now creamy testaments of success...

On his very face lay the most beautiful picture, drawn by his lips that gently pushed his cheeks upward, speckling them with white circles from the sidewalk light.

He did not dare question his delight. Although he did not know why he was happy, he disregarded this fact and continued to smile.

From then on, each person who beheld Guy immediately acquired his powerful, positive attitude, for his semblance was not borne of blissful ignorance but of much reflection and a profound appreciation of life.

BACKWARD

I always hate reaching the end of a book that doesn't have an epilogue. What happened to the characters? I mean, yeah, many more stories could be told about what became of everyone, but I'm always curious as to what happened immediately after the last chapter, scene, or act.

First off, Theresa came up to Baltimore to visit her aunt two days after I solved the mystery of the cloudy lights. So although I didn't go back to Bakerstown to take her out, I still fulfilled my promise by treating her to dinner at an amazing Indian-Chinese restaurant near Baltimore. She asked what I was doing up in Bakerstown and I told her the truth. She thought I was just making up the story about the hayride. I'd love to see her reaction after reading this full account. (I changed her real name, of course, but "Theresa," you know who you are. Hope you enjoyed reading this!)

Well, one week after my dinner date with Theresa, I was off to Greensboro, North Carolina, where our tennis team ended up winning the Atlantic Coast Conference (ACC) Championship. I tell you, there is nothing like a nice long drive home with your teammates after a huge victory. Tennis is such a mental sport; having concentrated and having controlled our emotions throughout the tourney, there was nothing like letting it all go. I said some mighty poetic things—I remember. "You should write a book," they said. Haha! Kevin sang all the way back and Jorge decided he'd become an Architecture major, too. (He did just that and graduated magna cum laude.)

Speaking of graduation, we were all surprised when we heard that the Class of 2009 valedictorian was an Architecture major. I felt ambivalent knowing a jerk like Jake had been so successful. Others were downright angry. I congratulated Jake and he looked annoyed. He said, "Yes. I should have been valedictorian—Jerry's not nearly as smart as I am."

Jerry! The lazy guy with a Piglet watch! The Ultimate Frisbee player who failed all his classes! While Jerry never lied about failing, we all realized that he had failed projects and assignments early each semester. This "lazy" guy was never asked about how he did on the last projects and finals. He aced them. Each semester. I am happy he earned the distinction. Still surprised, but happy for him. Just goes to show you that even perpetual failures can come back in a big way, dispelling all biases by dominating the material. So, if you're doing very poorly (in anything), it's never too late to make your comeback!

Oh yeah! My editor kept asking me how I knew about Cyril's secret health problem. I'm happy to say that his health improved completely during our senior year. He still didn't talk much, but the Cyril we all disliked ended up being quite a hotshot architect. He beat me in getting a book published, that's for sure! His autobiography became a quick best seller nine years ago.

So what else happened after I finally started living? Exactly one week after my last final, I was off to Washington, DC to work at Studio Schiffleback. It was a pretty sweet arrangement. The company paid for lodging at a hotel with a nice business center (free printing!). It was three minutes away from a country club. Since I had pretty flexible hours at Schiffleback, I applied for a job as a tennis instructor there. Both jobs were fulfilling. I made great progress at the studio each morning and then helped inexperienced little kids gain self-confidence as they mastered the fundamentals of our sport.

I still vividly remember the first day. There was this tall six-year-old named Logan who stood out. He was very serious and passionate. He reminded me of the little Guy I used to be. We kept in touch and I mentored him over the years before he moved to California where he trained on to qualify for numerous national and international competitions. He's currently training for the Olympics! Is that amazing or what? I sat with his family at several events and I must say, it is unbelievable.

Happily, come summertime, my health had improved tremendously. I had this huge burst of energy. So after the internship (a week before I finished giving tennis lessons, on July 15), I joined Hans in performing at a benefit concert for flood victims in Southeast Asia.

What an experience! All my friends and family came and I was able to do the flare! Haha... I was probably putting more effort into practicing that move than into my summer jobs, but everything got done. The flare is really unlike anything else in the world. It's as much a physical feat as it is mental. You have to use your abs (balance!), lift your legs (keep them straight!), support your body on one arm (don't collapse!), swing your legs underneath your arm (don't be sloppy!), all the while swinging your hips and rotating your body. Once I performed the flare for the concert, I knew I could do anything.

We ended up raising $7,520, which encouraged us to make it an annual event. The following year we raised more than twice that amount. This year we raised $176,543! Haha, as you can see, I never lost my love of breakdancing.

Now about writing *Guy,* I wrote a lot of the dialogue in 2007. Yes, I wrote the dialogue, and therefore I wouldn't at all be surprised if I greatly misquoted people. Sorry, I'm not a guy with an amazing memory and no, I wasn't wired. However, I did my best to capture the essence of what each character said while preserving the jargon. I hope that I haven't offended any of the people quoted in this book.

It was this year that I finally put the scenes in order. I was so unorganized in college, though—scenes were all over the place: in scraps of paper here and a few notebooks there. (I dreaded going through all the papers laden with barely legible handwriting, which is why I postponed assembling this monster.) Since my life was so crazy back then, if I had indeed messed up the order it wouldn't have had much of an effect on the style anyway.

Editing is so dangerous, and that's why I kept a close watch on the changes that the editor implemented. Her job was to make sure the stage directions were written in the present tense and the novelistic parts mostly in the past tense. I explained to her what was a real word in my world and what was not. The result is this, a book I wrote fourteen years ago, in its purest form.

Wait, not exactly. I had my crush's real name everywhere where it says "WOMAN," but my lovely editor objected to that and insisted on keeping her anonymous. She suggested referring to her as "Woman" because she didn't feel comfortable letting the world know who she is (plus, she didn't want to put a fake name). Of course, her words were: "It adds mystery." She's also responsible for all the "remarkable posture," "handsome," and "strong" words that were used to describe me. I didn't describe myself that way. I tried to change such inaccurate descriptions, but the pushy editor put her foot down. Thanks, Woman, for making me sound narcissistic. (Just kidding.... Love you!)

That reminds me... nowhere in the book do I mention my father. He's an English professor and an amazing photographer. It was his advice that helped me bring this book to life. When I got a chance to go home to visit during the weekends, he'd repeatedly remind me to "appeal to all the senses. Not just one or two!" Dad, sorry I didn't talk about you in any of the scenes; I love you and greatly appreciate all your help! You're a wonderful dad.

Now on to an update from the recent past: two years ago, Greg (now very wealthy) finally built his new house in Minneapolis. He called me up and asked me to alter the design I had made. (I pretty much made him a new one—his style had changed so much.) Still, it was wonderful to see such a spectacular design, full of history and remembrances of past dreams, to its final realization. I wouldn't accept a dime, of course, for if it weren't for him, I wouldn't have passed Studio II!

One more major thing: I actually wrote much of Scene XXII around the time I was redesigning Greg's house. See, I had remembered Arena, Smile, and the drumming circle.... Somehow, I remembered the elevator scene as well. But for some reason, I had no scene written about Roger. It's quite fascinating how it slowly came back to me. See, I was driving and saw a huge billboard about a "Roger's Baltimore Tennis League." I've always loved watching random people play and analyzing their styles, so I thought I'd attend a game. The schedule was on the billboard and I made a mental note to attend the June 10, 2017 game. I got there early and sat towards the front, near Roger who was staring at me. (I had no idea who he was at the time, so it was pretty creepy.) He finally approached me, said I wasn't Drew's son and then thanked me.

ME: Drew who?

ROGER: You've forgotten your famous father?

I thought nothing of the strange man until the following week when I found out where Roger worked. I wanted to call him and tell him how awesome his escalators were. (I'm not even kidding. I'm a big fan of escalators, especially transformable ones.) So I called and he sounded excited when I said my name. I asked about who Drew was and then he told me about what had happened the day the lillies made me considerably miserable. He invited me over. "You should visit Cat, she remembers you fondly," he said. I still thought he was a nut, but I humored him. As soon as I got to the nineteenth floor, I heard Pachelbel's song and started shivering. I slowly started to believe Roger's words. He was very helpful in describing what happened. And so, Roger, Catherine, and I worked together to construct the dialogue.

He offered me a position as head coach in the Roger's League, but I refused. (He didn't even know if I was good or not!) But anyway, Scene XXII is one of my favorite scenes, and it just makes you wonder.... What other unwritten events occurred? Such is life. I wish there were some button we could push that would make us forget awkward events and a lever we could pull to put our memory on vivid mode.

My biggest accomplishment, I'd say, is finally earning enough so Mom could retire early. She did so five years ago. (Finally!) I love you, Mom, and am grateful to finally be able to provide for you—at least, until you remarry. That's right, Men (65 and older)! My amazing, funny, selfless gourmet cook polyglot mother is on the market! (Sorry to embarrass you, Mom! But you never know!)

So this is the very end of the book. There's nothing harder than finally closing a scene of your life. I suppose we are never quite able to do that, as long as our memory is still strong. Man, in high school and college I was so much better able to express myself! Mind you, my heart isn't nearly as restless and rebellious, and my belittling facial expressions that so defined my youth have become less caustic. Why look grumpy? Life is so magical. It may sound trite, but it's true.

Now, here's what I have to say to my younger readers: wake up and find the courage to follow your dreams. When your mind is full of questions, never put off researching answers. If you wait until after you're done with this or that, your creativity and livelihood will likely wane. As for my older readers: please visit your younger selves often and remember that it is never too late to make that kid's cherished dream come true.

ABOUT THE ARTIST

Hey there! My name is JR Rockwell and I was born in Lafayette, Indiana on June 22. I grew up in neighboring West Lafayette, but moved to Baltimore for college. I immediately fell in love with the beautiful metropolis and got to know it intimitely as I rowed all across the harbor with my school's crew team and volunteered all over the city. I drive and walk around all the time, sometimes for hours. The architecture, people, and history inspire me. There are so many places to discover and adventures to unlatch.

I currently work as a consultant for an engineering firm. This is the first roman à clef play that I have illustrated. Guy, of course, would like to be featured in an "About the Writer" section, but he had the whole body of the book to describe himself.

Alas! I decided not to talk about myself in the third person in this section, but I have failed—for the soul of me is the mind of Guy.

https://www.jrrockwell.com

www.ingramcontent.com/pod-product-compliance
Lightning Source LLC
Chambersburg PA
CBHW020841020726
47497CB00005B/1207